I070013

also by fae

SPOOKY BOYS SERIES

Bite Me! (You Know I Like It)

Possess Me! (I Want You To)

FREEBIES

There's a Monster in the Woods

Cloudy with a Chance of Dildos

Let your hearts be light

FAE QUIN

Cover Art and Interior Artwork by Fae Loves Art

WWW.FAELOVESART.COM

Typography and Interior Formatting by We Got You Covered Book Design

WWW.WEGOTYOUCOVEREDBOOKDESIGN.COM

A full list of content warnings and tropes

is available on my website:

WWW.FAELOVESART.COM

Dedicated to my husband,
the grumpy to my sunshine.

For anyone who needs a little
extra holiday magic.

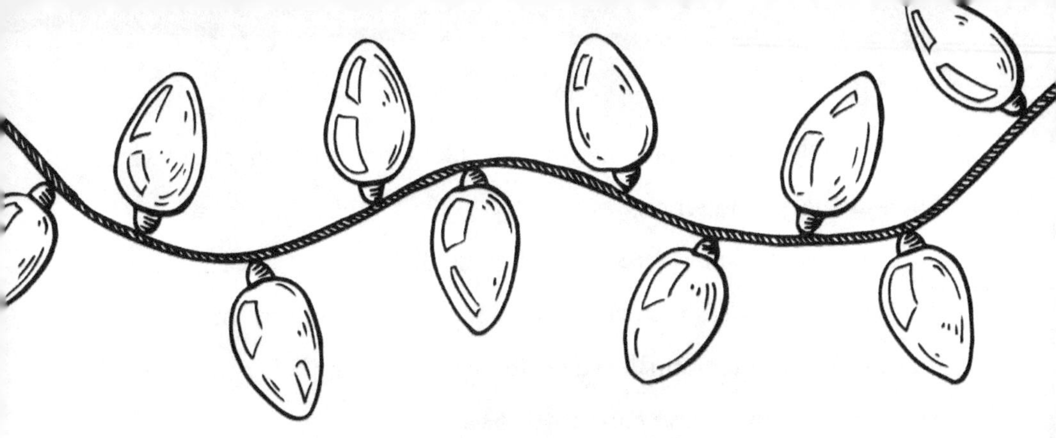

one

BAXTER

THE FACT I WAS A forty-two-year-old single father with a broken bakery, limited funds, and a prickly teenage daughter wasn't going to dissuade me from having a fantastic Christmas. I'd do it. I'd force Becca to love it, and everything would be fine. Totally, completely, *toootally* fine.

Maybe buying her a dog wasn't my best idea.

Because buying Pogo hadn't stopped Becca from deciding that I was apparently completely useless and needed a sixteen-year-old's help making friends. I loved my daughter, truly I did, but she didn't seem to understand that part of my charm was being friends with everyone—even if that also kind of meant I was friends with no one simultaneously.

A blessing and a curse.

That was the downside of being popular.

"Dad." Becca blinked at me, her green eyes narrowed, her blonde hair piled artfully in a little bun that wobbled like a soufflé atop her head when she was angry. "I'm serious."

"Yeah, yeah! I know, Becca-boo, I really do." I waved her off, turning back to the ball of Christmas cookie dough I was currently kneading on the kitchen island. Normally I'd be doing this from my bakery but…as I'd mentioned earlier. It was currently broken.

So Baxter the baker was now baking from home just like I had when I was just out of culinary school at twenty-four.

It would humble me, so surely it was a good thing, right?

"Dad." Becca whined, stomping her foot. She was wearing socks so the effect wasn't as dramatic as she'd probably been going for, but…the result was the same. I stiffened up with a sigh, turned back around, and held my flour-coated fingers in the air in surrender.

"I'm listening."

"My school is doing this thing this year that's called the Christmas Buddies program. Single parents are connected with other single parents in the effort to experience fun holiday activities between meshed families." She blinked. "What that really means though, is that they're trying to help old—"

"I'm not *old*."

"*Old*! Boring, adorable little daddies make new friends."

"Like I said—"

"Dad!" Becca stomped again, I stared at her wobbly bun, and her tiny little hand zoomed up to hold the hair still as she huffed.

"Alrighty, jiggly puff."

"It's *Jigglypuff*. I can hear the pause when you say it—ugh. You're…just! Ugh, Dad."

"You really care about this?" I sobered. Usually she got upset at me like this but it was all games. Becca and I were close. Less so now that she was 'too cool for school' and her little cheerleader friends were more important than dear old dad. She'd been spending more and more time with them since the beginning of the school year and I couldn't help but miss her.

I was desperate.

Hence the dog.

"Yes." She nodded definitively and I sighed, resisting the urge to scrub my hands over my face.

"Why?"

She didn't answer me. Instead she just handed over a pamphlet with a horrible green and red graphic on it. I was basically the king of Christmas, which was why I had every right to judge the design. Half the words weren't even legible, but I ignored that fact as I began flipping through it, my lip caught between my teeth.

Anxiety fluttered in the pit of my stomach but I did my best to shake it off.

This was fine.

It would be fine.

I was a people person, so why was I so worried?

"The first activity is next week. They'll draw names out of a bowl and pick your buddy."

"And you don't care that we're going to be stuck with strangers for the season?" I clarified.

"Please." Becca flashed me a grin, "I'm like, the queen of socializing."

That was her. Queen bee Becca.

Cheer captain and student council president.

Blonde as a bumble bee and twice as buzzy.

Was she…really doing this for *me*? Why did she think I needed help in the first place? I was…confused, but ultimately flattered. It was sweet she cared. And obviously, in her adorable little cheer-brain she'd decided I needed some extra holiday pep this season. She could probably tell how much it frustrated me that the bakery was closed.

Hell, since I'd closed the doors in July I'd been off my rocker, hopped up on caffeine, and practically hallucinating from exhaustion.

I couldn't fault her for that.

I could see the way she looked at me sometimes, and as much as I appreciated the worry, it also made me feel like a shitty dad. She shouldn't have to worry about me at all, so I just pasted on another smile and flipped back to the front of the pamphlet.

"Fine." I handed her back the flier. "Sign me up. But only if you know it's not going to affect my ability to throw our Holiday Hullabaloo."

"You can still bake and make friends, Dad." Another eye roll. Oh joy.

Pogo wandered into the kitchen, his little claws *tick-ticking* on the tile as he flounced across my bare feet, his hairy body warming my toes.

"Pogo is my friend," I teased, just to watch her roll her eyes again. Eye roll, eye roll, eye roll. I wondered if she rolled them any harder if they might fall out of her head. I didn't ask though. The last time I'd asked that she'd given me the silent treatment for an entire week.

Christmas Buddies.

Hmm.

Maybe it wouldn't be such a bad thing?

Besides…if it made Becca happy, it would be worth it.

And maybe I could get her to stop looking at me like that—like I was two seconds away from a mental breakdown.

The next week passed by in a blur. I solidified my Christmas cookie designs. I fulfilled my pumpkin bread orders. I plotted out how much I'd need to sell to be able to afford the new phone Becca wanted for Christmas, as well as the repairs on the bakery, and the supplies I'd need to cater my annual Baxter's Bakery Christmas Hullabaloo.

I held it at the bakery every year.

The whole town attended, flocking in droves for free apple cider, peppermint hot cocoa, and pastries of all kinds.

It was my way of giving back after they supported me year round. It was something I'd done every year since I'd opened up the Bakery at thirty, right after I'd graduated from gay uncle to gay dad.

Becca had been the love of my life since the moment she'd blinked open her adorable green eyes, and scrunched up her sweet little freckled nose, her first *uuuuuugh* screeching through the world as my sister had cradled her close to her chest.

Rebecca and Charles, her husband, had passed away when Becca was only four. She barely remembered them now and I wasn't sure if that was a good or bad thing. Sometimes it felt like I was the only person left in the world that remembered Rebecca's smile or Charles's horrible meatloaf.

I hadn't gotten in a car for six months after I'd heard the news.

That was behind me now though.

I had a sixteen-year-old to support and a business to keep alive despite the fact that everything, no matter what I did, seemed to go wrong at every turn.

Good thing I was positive!

I'd just finished wrapping up my last loaf of bread to deliver when Becca burst through the front door in a flurry of fall chill, her cardigan flung wide over the crisp white button-up of her school uniform.

"You're going to be late!" She yelled, far too loudly, considering the fact she was only ten feet away.

"I'm not going to be late," I laughed and shook my head. "The meeting isn't till six."

"Um. You're not dressed?" Becca crossed her arms, her whole face scrunching up with her ire.

It wasn't nearly as cute now that she wasn't a newborn, but she was still adorable. Even when she was annoyed.

I looked down at my flour-covered yellow sweater and chocolate-stained jeans with a thoughtful hum. "Could've sworn I was wearing clothes," I told her, tapping my lip. "Weird."

"Get changed!" Becca herded me up the stairs, careful not to brush against the still fresh chocolate on my pants as she pushed at my back with huffed little angry mutters under her breath. Apparently I was both '*the worst*' and the '*most embarrassing*'.

I should probably get an award for that.

Pogo tripped me halfway up the stairs and Becca apologized to him for me, like I truly was the worst asshole in the world.

The corgi just blinked at her, unfazed.

Fifteen minutes later, I was dressed in what Becca deemed 'acceptable' attire and quite literally forced into the driver's seat of our shared minivan.

The drive to the school was as beautiful as it always was, the white wicker fences framing the sidewalk on either side of the road, the fall leaves glistening gold and red in the setting sun. I'd have to deliver the bread after the meeting rather than before it, but I didn't complain. Instead I just turned the radio to an oldies station and blasted the music loud enough Becca pinched my thigh in retaliation.

I grinned at her, turned it down, and rolled down the windows to let the scent of autumn fill the car.

Today was going to be a good day.

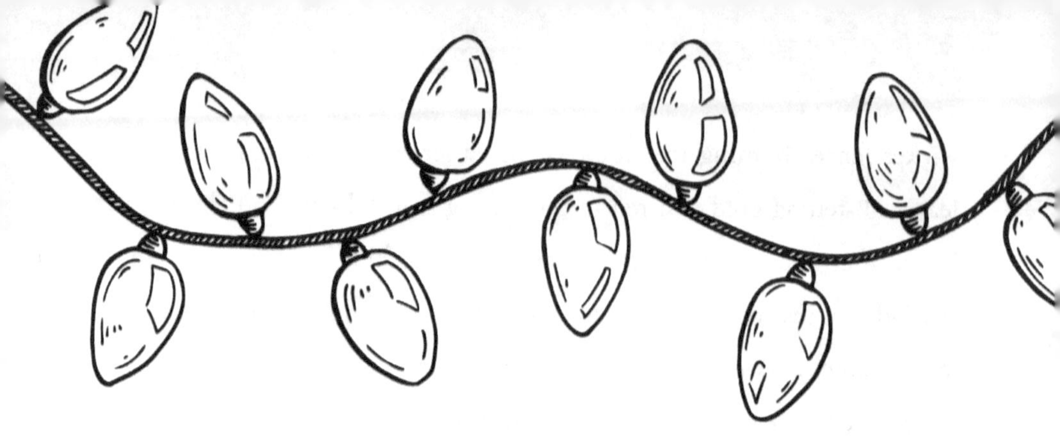

two

PAXTON

TODAY WAS GOING TO BE a horrible day.

I didn't say that lightly. When my son had come home from school, sheepish, his dark hair hanging limp around his ears I'd known something was wrong. Normally he was excited to see me—always enthusiastic. I was one of the only people he really opened up to, but today he was surly, embarrassed, and guilty.

"What did you do?" I folded my arms across my chest, arched an eyebrow and exuded as much *'I am your father'* vibes as I could.

It worked, because he folded.

His gangly teenage body wilted like a flower on a cold day as he collapsed on the couch I kept by my work bench and threw his hands in the air.

"So…I did something. And you're not going to like it."

That was the understatement of the century.

Half an hour later I was standing awkwardly on the sidelines of the high school gymnasium, my hair full of wood dust, and my son drooping beside me.

"I can't believe this," I muttered, though really, there was nothing we could do at this point.

I wasn't about to give up. I'd driven all the way here after all.

I'd just quit the program if it didn't work out the way that Nathan so clearly thought it would. He claimed he'd rigged it. Whatever that meant.

"You're sure this girl…*Becca*…even wants to talk to you?"

"Um." Nathan shrunk. For a massive kid he was incredibly small at that moment. "Maybe? I don't…even know if she knows I exist, really."

"I thought you said she liked you."

"Well, yeah, I mean. Maybe when we were in seventh grade? But…this is senior year, Dad. Things change." He sounded so wise and world worn I didn't know what to say. "She might not like my hair anymore."

"Did she ever like it?" I teased, leaning over to pluck at his too-long bangs. Nathan just snorted and shrugged helplessly.

"I dunno. We…um." He shook his head. "I just like her dad, okay?"

"Okay." I grunted, surveying the crowd thoughtfully. I didn't like it here. But then again, I didn't like it anywhere, really. This town was too small. Too crowded. Too…cheerful. Everyone here was friends with everyone else. They shared laughter like they were all privy to the same fucking joke that I didn't know the punchline to.

And the worst of them all was Baxter Baker.

The father of Nathan's crush.

The man—if Nathan was right—I was about to be stuck with for the next two months. Oh joy.

Baxter was…sunshine.

I hated sunshine.

He bounced off the fucking walls, laughed at every joke spoken, harpooned around like a jester on crack. He was friends with everything that had a pulse and more giving than a charity on Christmas.

I hated him on principle.

But…there was nothing I wouldn't do for my son, even apparently this.

When the crowd quieted and the principal made his way to the long white table that was wedged along the back wall, I knew my fate was about to be sealed. I could feel Nathan vibrating beside me and across the room I spotted both Bakers and their blond heads, bobbing along as they whispered furiously back and forth.

Like father, like daughter.

They were dressed spotlessly. Not a crumb, fleck of dust, or hair out of place. I watched the way their tall figures bent toward each other as Principal Adams finished his speech and began working his way through the bowl full of names.

I knew how this would go.

Nathan had briefed me.

I had no idea how he'd managed to rig something as simple as a name draw but I didn't really want to know so I didn't ask. The muscles in my arms tensed as I glared at the Bakers and their giggling.

Why was I doing this again?

I looked at Nathan and noted the way his big brown eyes were wide with anticipation. He had the beginning of stubble creeping along his jawline and I was more than proud of the way he was growing. Maybe this was all part of the aging process. I needed to support him. Whatever that meant.

Even if it meant going on holiday 'excursions' with the man who probably annoyed me most in the world.

It turned out Nathan hadn't needed to worry. One by one, parents were connected with other parents, their families converging as they whispered and gossiped and the Bakers remained silent on the sidelines. By the time Adams got to the last two names everything fell into place.

"Baker and Montgomery?" he called, waving the two little pieces of paper around with a triumphant grin.

Nathan fist pumped surreptitiously beside me, then smoothed his hands down his unironed button-up to wipe away the sweat as he peeked up at me through his lashes. Soon enough we'd be the same height. "It worked!"

"Sure did," I grunted, grimacing as I watched Baxter and his daughter turn toward us. They whispered the whole time they walked over and I tried not to let my annoyance show too much. Nathan's fingers brushed my wrist and I glanced down at him one last time to meet his imploring gaze.

"Please, please, *please* don't mess this up for me?"

God, the kid had so much faith.

"I'm perfectly fucking friendly," I grouched right back, though I did make an effort to smooth the furrow between my brow as the Bakers finally reached us. I knew I could be intimidating. It came with the size, the muscle mass, and the multitude of tattoos I had etched across my body. I'd also been told I had a "resting bitch face" by my brother Trent on multiple occasions. Whatever that meant.

I tried to look less bitchy as Baxter's huge green eyes blinked up at my own and his lips twisted into his usual friendly little grin.

"Paxton! My favorite *x-tra* cool magic man."

"I prefer handyman, or general contractor."

"Sure, sure!" He blinked at me, clearly waiting for me to get his joke. I didn't laugh. I was well aware that we were the only two men in town that had the letter X in our name. I didn't, however, feel like it was something worth celebrating.

He cleared his throat, fidgeting a little as he glanced down at his daughter. They shared a look and he turned back to me. Awkward looks all around. I narrowed my eyes at them both, noting their similarities. Matching button noses. Matching freckles. Matching eyes. Though Baxter's were big and soft as a doe's, with spiky brown lashes that were far too heavy as they fluttered after each blink.

He had dark circles under his eyes, the skin fragile and bruised, a pale violet that only served to make his green eyes look…greener.

"Looks like we're buddies now," Baxter tried again, smiling. Always fucking smiling. Just like he had been every time I'd gone to his bakery when it was open. Just like he had been every time I'd seen him buy groceries, or trim his lawn, or pick up his dog's shit at the park.

It meant nothing.

Empty.

"Sure," I grunted, searching for patience.

Nathan, I reminded myself. *Think of Nathan.*

Nathan cleared his throat, turning toward Becca, his cheeks flushed. "Um. Hey." He said, playing it cool, giving her a half-wave because a full one would clearly be too much commitment.

"Hey," she waved back.

I waited.

But neither of them said anything else.

Becca nudged her dad surreptitiously enough she probably thought I wouldn't notice. But I did. Baxter launched into speech again, his freckled cheeks a little flushed. "So…Aside from the mandatory ski trip at the end of the season, what else did you want to do?" he asked, some of his earlier bluster gone.

Good. Let him squirm.

I shrugged.

"Dad loves cookies," Becca piped up, clearly taking control of the situation. "We could bake them. Decorate them. All that! Very Christmassy."

"Oh yeah. *Way* Christmassy," Nathan agreed. *Jesus Christ.*

"Fine. Cookies."

It took twenty entire minutes for the three of them to decide on the other three mandatory holiday activities. *Mandatory.* Fuck. This was ridiculous. Didn't it defeat the purpose of 'holiday cheer' to plan it like this?

Cookie decorating.

Holiday movies.

Tree cutting.

And a goddamn trip to a ski lodge.

Kill me now.

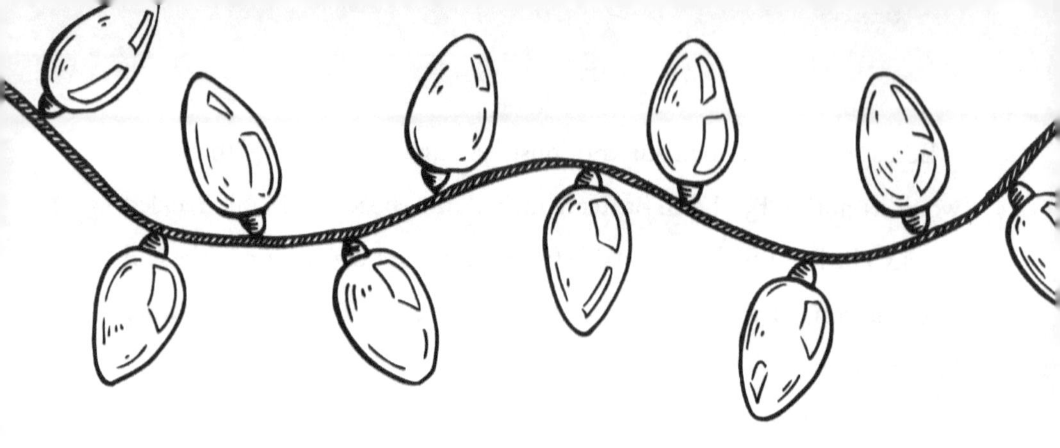

three

BAXTER

MAYBE I SHOULD HAVE BEEN more alarmed that my assigned Christmas Buddy was the only man in town that genuinely hated me, but I was optimistic. I figured I'd accept it as a Christmas challenge. Something to get my mind off my bakery–and my constant exhaustion. I was a likable man; I smiled often, I laughed at jokes—even if they weren't clever—and I prided myself on being generous to a fault.

In fact, if I couldn't get Paxton Montgomery to like me through my million-watt grin I could certainly do so with a few well-chosen batches of cookies, or my world famous pumpkin chocolate chip bread.

Despite the fact that Becca had been the one to coerce me into this friendship business in the first place, I was feeling pretty excited about the whole thing. A new friend would be nice! Useful even. We could spend time together, share holiday stories, drink cocoa, and sing carols.

Though, admittedly the idea of Paxton Montgomery singing a carol was laughable at best.

The man was…for lack of a better word. Well…

Grumpy.

Big. Thick. Intimidating. With tattoos galore and more salt than pepper in his beard and wavy, sandy-brown hair. I was maybe only a little ashamed to admit he looked like he'd stepped straight off the webpage of the *Nice Wood* lumberjack porn website that I paid a monthly subscription to.

I had my secrets, so sue me.

In comparison to his bulk, I was lanky and compact with a softness to my belly that came from the years catching up to me and all the delicious food I enjoyed on the daily. My morning runs—that had always been solitary but now were accompanied by Pogo—helped keep me lean but there was nothing I could do about the fact that I was aging.

Honestly, I was at peace with it.

Aging meant I was still alive and that was a blessing.

My hands were shaking as I stepped out of my car and onto the pavement outside the front of the Montgomery household. It was across town from my house, pretty much as far as you could get, actually. I didn't want to take that as the omen it probably was.

I had three of my famous pumpkin loaves packed in tins, my arms laden with goodies and good will as I traversed the perfectly trimmed walkway and hopped my way up the surprisingly sturdy front porch.

The Montgomerys' home was one of the older buildings in town. Cozy. Small. Homey. With an addition on the back that I was sure Paxton used for all of his…talented shenanigans. He said he preferred 'handyman' but I couldn't help but privately think of him as a house-magician. In fact, maybe it wasn't very Christmassy of me, but part of me was hoping when I managed to save up enough money I might be able to convince him to let me hire him to fix up the bakery.

Not all of it.

Just.

Some.

I raised my hand to knock and before my knuckles rapped on the wood, the door swung open and I was met with the suspicious but adorable face of Nathan Montgomery.

"Hello!" I said cheerfully, wagging my shoulder at him because my hands were currently occupied. The scent of pumpkin and spice filled the air between us and I watched Nathan's eyes begin to bug out as he stared at the loaves of bread with a childlike wonder—then distrust.

"Hi, Mr. Baker." He peeked behind me, and it didn't escape my notice how crestfallen he looked when he realized I was alone.

Maybe he'd thought Becca would be here?

Or! Maybe he'd heard about my new dog.

"Becca's at school," I hummed with a smile and an eyebrow waggle. "Doing very important things. Her words, not mine."

"Ah." Nathan nodded, trying to look cool as he bobbed his shaggy head and I watched his shoulders slump.

Interesting.

Hm.

"I'm excited for our first activity!" I tried to cheer him up as I waited on the porch, the crisp autumn chill making my cheeks flush. Or maybe that was the fact that I hadn't been invited in yet, and I wasn't sure I would be.

I hadn't been lying when I said that Paxton didn't like me.

I didn't understand why, but I figured it was his own choice and if I couldn't get him to like me by the end of the holiday season, well…that friendship was a lost cause.

"I brought you bread," I offered. Nathan stared at the loaves again, cheering up considerably.

His stomach growled and I held back a laugh.

"Is your dad home?" I asked, trying to peek over his head. He was tall. Taller than most kids his age. He'd hit puberty early and shot up like a bean pole. Though honestly, that wasn't a surprise considering how absolutely mammoth his father was. The man could carry an entire tree trunk on each shoulder should he decide he wanted to.

Paul Bunyan. But sexy. And mean.

Ugh, he was just my type.

"Dad's in the shop," Nathan told me, eyeing my bread. I offered them to him, figuring this was a lost cause. My olive branch—or in this case, chocolate chip laden bread—would be left unacknowledged for now. That was alright. All he had to do was taste it to realize what the secret ingredient was.

Cinnamon.

Nutmeg.

And just a dash of friendship.

"I'll head out," I told Nathan so he didn't have to squirm any longer. He was admiring the tins with big brown eyes and it made my heart soar. I loved sharing what I made with people—seeing the way they smiled, seeing the way their faces warmed and their eyes grew soft. There was nothing quite as heartwarming as a freshly baked present straight from the oven.

It felt like love, even when it wasn't.

My grandma had taught me that.

"Tell your dad I said hi." I gave Nathan one more parting grin before I hopped down the steps and headed back to the car.

Mission accomplished.

Kinda.

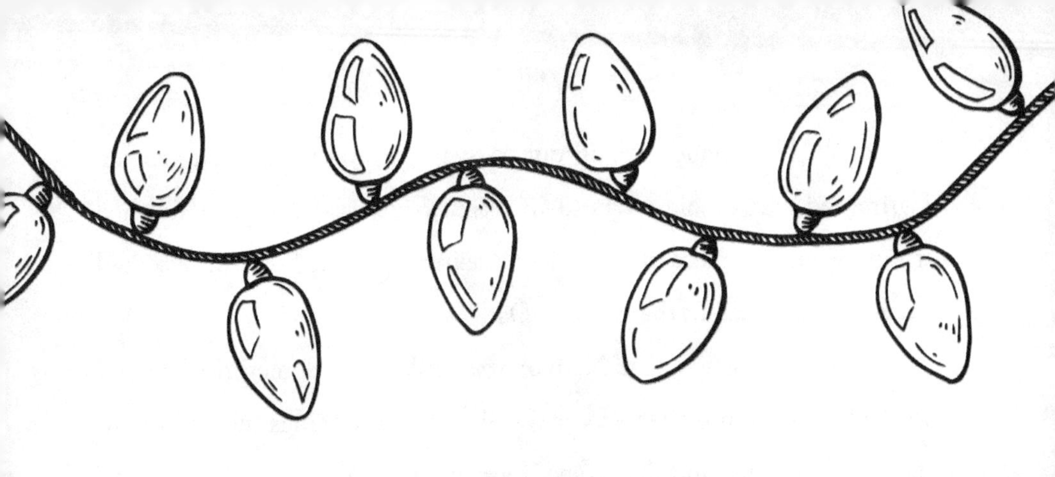

four

PAXTON

"WHAT WAS BAXTER DOING OVER here?" I asked the second Nathan popped into my shop with chocolate smudged across his pleased grin.

"Dropped off goodies."

I rolled my eyes.

Of course he did.

He was probably trying to sweeten me up, the bastard. As if that would work. I didn't like suck-ups. I never had. He more than likely had an ulterior motive. Actually, scratch that. If he did have one, I would probably like him more. The man was a saint and it made my skin crawl just thinking about it.

"Did you get to see Becca?" I asked, because that was the only relevant thing I cared about.

"No. School stuff." Nathan shrugged forlornly and flopped down on the couch, his tongue flicking out to swipe away the chocolate smear. I grimaced and shook my head in disgust. He was silent as I finished trimming up the piece of wood I was sizing to fix the hole a mouse had chewed at the back of the garage. "Dad?"

I startled, surprised that Nathan was still there. Sometimes when I worked I got so into the zone, it was like the only things that existed in the world were me and the project I was working on.

I liked my job.

I liked…fixing things.

Building things.

Creating.

Despite being large, I had a delicate hand when needed. I was good with my hands. Real fucking good.

"What is it kiddo?" I turned around when I made sure the saw was off, my arm hair coated in sawdust as I lifted my safety goggles and gave Nathan my whole attention. That particular *dad* had said far more than my name.

"Why are you such a dick to Mr. Baker?"

Wow. Straight to the point.

"I don't like him."

"Is it because he's…you know?" He waved a hand, his brow quirked as he chewed on the word gay like he was worried he'd offend me by saying it.

Which was ridiculous.

But I didn't blame him for not knowing that about me.

I was a bi-sexual man who had married a woman and sworn off dating the second we divorced and I realized I didn't know shit about the kind of person I wanted around my kid. So yeah. He wouldn't know that about me.

I wasn't particularly forthcoming with that sort of thing. Figured it was private. Most kids, in fact, probably didn't *want* to know their father's sexual preferences. Keeping it quiet had always just made sense to me. Though…this did pose a problem I hadn't realized would come up. Did my own kid think I was…No.

No, right?

Oh hell no.

"My dislike of Baker has everything to do with his absolutely smarmy, shitty little smile and absolutely nothing to do with the fact he's gay."

"Oh, thank god." Nathan relaxed. "Because I love you but like…if that was the reason you didn't like him, I don't know I…"

"Yeah. No." I shook my head. This seemed like a great opportunity to come out to him but for some reason, my mouth remained stubbornly shut.

Maybe it was the years of silence clogging my throat.

Maybe it was the fact that deep down I figured it didn't matter. I wasn't going to date anyone, marry anyone, be with anyone. As far as he needed to know, I was a monk.

"I don't like the way he's nice to everyone."

"Why?" Nathan cocked his head at me and I was struck with how annoying and adorable he was at the same time. I rolled my eyes and rubbed my hands over my beard in frustration, realizing belatedly I was now covered in even more sawdust. Great.

"Usually the ones that smile a lot like that are liars. Manipulators. That sorta thing. I don't like people who aren't genuine, and I don't trust a man that doesn't know how to frown."

"I don't think Mr. Baker is like that, Dad."

"Why?"

"I mean…" Nathan chewed on his lip. "Don't you think he's…"

"What?"

"Don't you think he's kinda sad?"

"Sad?" I scoffed and shook my head.

"Seriously." Nathan wiggled, scrubbing his hands over the knees of his jeans as he got serious. His brow furrowed, his hazel eyes sincere. Man. Seeing him like that, all grown up, made my heart hurt. It felt like just yesterday he'd come home from first grade with a picture of himself decorated in foam Santas for Christmas, and now here he was…telling me he thought I wasn't being fair to a man he barely knew. "You don't…" Nathan shook his head. He tried again. "Sometimes when he picks Becca up from school he has to wait a long time."

"Okay? And that makes him sad?"

"No." Nathan laughed, his lips twitching, though the smile fell away as quickly as it had come. "When he's sitting there in the parking lot, I pass by him on my skateboard, and he's always just…sitting there."

"He's sitting there when he's sitting there, got it."

"No—" Nathan shook his head again. "I mean…he's like…*Sitting there*, Dad. All empty. Like he shut down. He just looks…so sad? You know?"

It was hard to picture Baxter Baker being anything other than his bubbly champagne self. But I supposed it wasn't impossible. Besides, Nathan was a good judge of character, even if he was a bit naive and determined to believe the best in everyone.

He hadn't gotten that from me.

"When Becca comes out it's like he comes alive again. Like…magic, or something."

"Okay." I didn't know what else to say.

That night the thought of Baker sitting alone in his car staring off into space followed me like a specter as I went through my nighttime routine. His green eyes haunted me as I brushed my teeth. His freckles, a poltergeist where their memory hung overtop my bed frame as I lay naked beneath the covers.

Baker.

Sad?

Impossible.

When we arrived at our first designated Christmas Buddies meet-up I was more than a little apprehensive. Nathan had forced me to shower after work and even put on cologne. He'd insisted that my image reflected on him, and I figured he wasn't entirely wrong.

I didn't want to fuck things up for him and the bobblehead so I did as I was told. Even went as far as to trim up my beard and put some pine-scented beard oil in it. I hadn't done that in ages. At least since the last time Nathan had spent a week with his mom in the summer three years ago and I'd gone to the gay bar an hour out of town and fucked a cute twink in a bathroom stall.

It felt weird to dress up for this.

It felt weird to dress up at all.

"Play it cool," Nathan warned me under his breath as if he hadn't already fucking told me that eighty times while we rode over in my truck. He was bursting at the seams, dressed in a flannel that screamed 'trying too hard' but looked nice on him all the same.

His jeans were too tight but I didn't comment.

Kids these days liked to squash their legs like sausages and it was none of my business how the hell they managed to walk around.

The Bakers' house was on the nice side of town. Picket fences. Security cameras. New builds. No problems aside from the occasional pothole that was remedied by the city far quicker on this side of town than it was in other areas.

The two-story home glared at me atop the manicured lawn.

They had a fucking HOA so it wasn't like Baxter took care of it himself, but still.

I did notice however that his mailbox had been dinged and I wondered who had been the culprit. It wasn't my business though.

The house was yellow—*figured*—with white trim and jolly Christmas lights strung up year round. Nathan stared at the whole picture with his jaw dropped like this tiny but nice home at the other end of Belleville was somehow the Second Coming of Christ.

"Which room do you think is Becca's?" he asked, like an absolute fucking creep. But he was my creep, so I loved him anyway.

"Weird question, bud."

"Right, right." Nathan shook his head, smoothing his hands on his jeans again to clean them of sweat. "I didn't mean like…for creepy purposes. I was just curious. You know."

"I know."

I noticed a pile of dog shit at the base of the porch and for some reason that little imperfection made me smile as we made our way up the rest of the steps and Nathan whacked his fist against the door. When no one answered, I rolled my eyes heavenward and raised my own to knock.

"Gotta use your knuckles."

"I didn't want to be too loud—"

"You kinda gotta be loud, dude."

The door swung open after the first rap of my fist and I was met with the absolutely harried expression of Baxter Baker. It was a new look on him. His cheeks were flushed, his hair a wild mess. He had flour smudged across his temple and he was wearing an apron that had chocolate smeared across it like candy stripes.

"Oh my god," he said, clearly alarmed. He shoved the door open wide and I stepped inside, trying not to stare at how…nice it all was. "I am so sorry." Baxter continued to talk but I ignored him for the moment as I stepped on the heel of my work boots and shucked them off.

Nathan hurried to follow after I nudged him, but I couldn't help the way my eyes kept snapping back to Baxter and his…very human panic.

"I know we were supposed to start at six but the power went out and everything just…went to complete and utter shit."

Shit?

He knew the word shit?

Of course he did. What the fuck kind of thought was that?

"Shit, sorry! Probably shouldn't swear." Baxter flapped around and I stared at him, more than a little shocked. This wasn't at all the man I usually saw walking around town, conversing with all the who's whos and selling his glorified candy. "I just…I may have to postpone."

"Dad!" Becca came pounding down the stairs. For such a tiny thing she sure was fucking loud. She skidded to a stop when she reached the bottom, her hair wobbling. She was dressed in shorts and a Baker's

Bakery T-shirt that was just as coated in chocolate as her father's. "You didn't call them?"

"He didn't." Nathan was…star-struck apparently.

He was staring at Becca like she hung the sun and I had no idea what the fuck to do.

"We'll have to go to the movies another time. I truly am so sorry—" Baxter was about ready to push us out of the door but Nathan stopped him.

"Wait! Wait." He held up both his hands, his voice wobbling a little, his cheeks flushed. "Can we help?"

Baxter froze.

I watched the way his entire face did a ballet before he settled on apprehensive acceptance.

"Yes. Um." He glanced over at me, grimacing a little, his eyes flashing down to his own flour-stained outfit as his cheeks grew a deep, ruddy pink. "Yeah. I…"

"We would love the help," Becca piped up. Before I knew it we were being herded into the frankly massive kitchen, and Baxter was doling out orders like a drill sergeant. I hadn't realized baking could be so… complicated.

He was behind.

Half his dough was going bad and he had to bake it all and sell it before he wasted what little he had apparently.

By the time we finished it was nearly midnight. I was just as coated in chocolate as he was, and I was pretty sure my nicest shirt would need a trip to the trash can because there was no way in hell I'd be able to get out all of the stains.

Baxter sent us home with armloads of thank-you bread. His words, not mine. And I drove the entire fifteen minutes in silence, contemplating what I'd seen.

Maybe it had been a fluke but…Baxter had been almost an entirely different person. He smiled yes, but there was something else there, just as Nathan had said. He was more complex than I'd given him credit for.

Or maybe he was just really fucking good at lying.

Who knew.

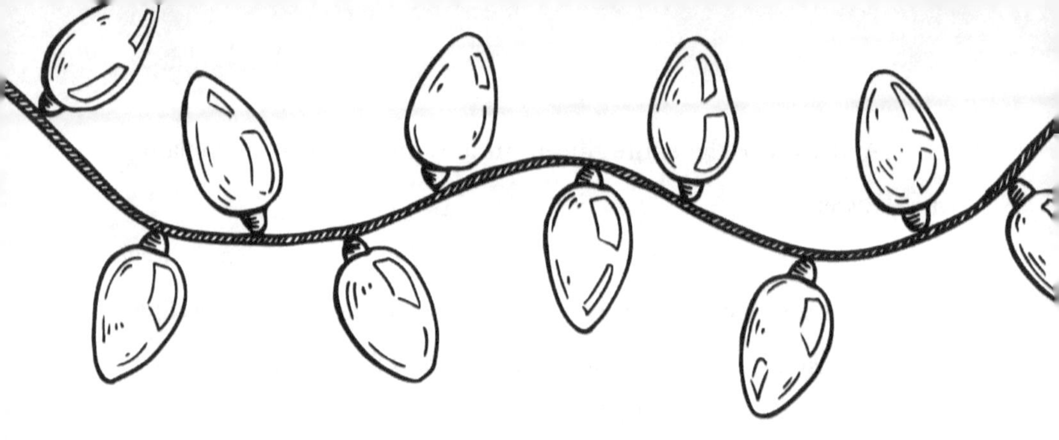

BAXTER

"ALRIGHT, THIS CANNOT GO LIKE last time." I patted my cheeks, watching the way the skin flushed from the pressure as I released a soft sigh and gave my sore back a well needed pop. When the pressure at my spine released, I groaned in relief, glaring at my own reflection as I waited for the steam in the mirror to fade away.

Movie night.

Round two.

I'd royally fucked up the last one. Been a complete fucking mess actually. It was lucky that the Montgomerys had agreed to a do-over in the first place. I wasn't sure what was in this for them. Somehow I doubted that Paxton was over eager to become my friend.

I'd felt his eyes on me for years.

Dark, brooding, judging.

There was something about me that bothered him and I could never for the life of me figure out what it was. So I just smiled harder when I saw him walk by and hoped for the best. Without fail, despite giving his family a personal invitation to the Baker's Bakery Hullabaloo, he never showed up.

Ever.

And now…Becca had forced me to spend some quality time with him. Maybe we wouldn't end up friends like I hoped but at the very least I could break through enough of Paxton's icy exterior that he'd stop snubbing the best party of the year.

Dressed in my nicest Christmas sweater—green with trees around the collar—and a pair of khaki slacks, I made my way down to the living room to be subjected to Becca's judgment.

"Hmm," she hummed, tapping her lip. "Acceptable."

I rolled my eyes, but didn't complain when she made me switch my New Balance tennis shoes for a pair of leather loafers that had been stuck in the dark recesses of the back of my closet for close to a decade.

"I'm glad we decided to meet them there," Becca mused as she plopped into the front seat of the car and I slid into the passenger side. I let her drive us whenever possible. She was in the process of getting her license—a fact that gave me literal nightmares—and I wanted to help her, even though admittedly, watching her get behind the wheel was the most terrifying thing I'd ever seen.

Becca wasn't a bad driver.

She wasn't a *good* driver.

But.

Yeah.

She just wasn't a good driver.

"Why?" I asked, fumbling with the radio and flipping it to the Christmas station. Becca rolled her eyes at me, the whites flashing as she reached over and deliberately, slowly flipped the station back to the pop channel she favored.

"No Christmas till December, Dad, remember? We had an agreement."

"*You* had an agreement. I don't remember signing anything." I grinned at her but I didn't push as I buckled up and settled myself in for a rollercoaster of emotion.

God, I hated cars.

Hate.

By the time we arrived at the movie theater I'd sweated through my sweater (Ha!). Becca had consoled me at the stop lights but there was only so much I could do about my frayed nerves. I tried to hide it, I truly did. But she saw through me. She always had.

Maybe it was because she was my kid.

Or maybe it was the bits of her that were her mother just peeking out like the sun through storm clouds.

Every year, the Belleville theater held seasonal movie showings on Saturdays starting the first week of November. Each week it was something new, something exciting, something…Santa oriented.

I fucking loved it.

When Becca was little it had been our weekly outing. We'd pop to the theaters, binge ourselves on the seasonal white-chocolate, peppermint popcorn the theater only sold during the winter, and we'd leave with our heads held high and Christmas spirit buzzing bright in our chests.

As she'd gotten older she'd gotten busier.

Friends, activities, commitments she hadn't had when she was little.

Maybe in a way this Christmas Buddies thing wasn't so bad after all. This was the first year we'd gone back to the movies since Becca had started junior high and I couldn't help but be grateful to the program and my so-called 'lack of friends' if it meant having this with my daughter again.

It wasn't that I didn't reach out.

She did too.

Sometimes growing up meant growing apart and that was the hardest pill to swallow as a father who didn't know how to be anything but…Dad.

Paxton's truck was already parked at the front of the theater. His parking job was immaculate, and I couldn't help but glance back at the crooked swerve of our minivan with a grimace. Becca wasn't the best at driving. She was even worse at parking.

"It's not that bad," Becca whined at me. I just pursed my lips and let my eyebrows do the talking for me. "Ughhhh."

Ugh, indeed.

I was weirdly nervous. Butterflies in my belly. Tingles in my fingertips. The entrance to the movie theater was lit up gold and red, gorgeous in its timeless simplicity. It felt like stepping onto a vintage movie set, and I couldn't help but feel my spirits lift as I pushed through the front door and the woosh of heated air met my sweaty skin.

I wished there was time to rinse off before we saw the Montgomerys. But alas, God was not on my side.

Paxton's massive figure was waiting right at the entrance, his arms crossed, his dark eyes assessing. I tried to ignore the way my throat became dry and my cock gave a helpless little twitch as I watched his tattoos flex and the overhead light caught the silver at his temples.

Jesus, fuck me.

Not literally.

Oh hell.

I was going to hell.

"Hi, Nathan!" Becca called. I realized I hadn't even looked at the younger boy and I grimaced in apology, shuffling behind my daughter like a dejected child. I watched her head bobble about, amusement and affection bubbling up inside me as I noticed the fact that she'd missed a piece of hair in the back when she'd been putting her hair up in her signature bun.

She had holly decorating her artfully styled do and it was more than a little adorable to me how much work she'd clearly put into her cream sweater dress and overlong leather boots. I could just picture her in her room deciding for hours what constituted the 'best holiday movie outfit for setting up your lonely dad with a friend'.

"Hi, Becca." Nathan's whole face grew bright red and I paused, my head tilting curiously as I glanced between the two of them.

Were they...

No.

Right?

No.

Becca would've said something.

"You're late." Paxton said. No greeting for me. Nooope. No 'hi, Baxter.' No 'how are you Baxter?' No 'sorry about the hot mess you landed yourself in last week Baxter.' Just...'you're late.' As if I wasn't already completely aware.

"Sorry about that." I smiled at him, though it felt a little brittle.

"We took the scenic route." Becca beamed at them both and I watched in fascination as some of Paxton's walls seemed to melt away. It seemed his ire was reserved for me and me only. Not bubbly little bumblebees. Alas.

"Oh!" Nathan perked right up. "The one by the apple orchards?" He was trying. Cute guy. His voice was a little stutter-y and lower than it usually was, almost like he was faking it. But he was trying.

"Oh, yeah! Totally. Dad and I love the leaves this time of year."

"We also love the fact that Officer Judy doesn't park at the end just waiting to give out tickets like she does at the intersection by Elm and Wood," I tacked on, hoping for a laugh.

"That sounds like a personal story," Nathan replied sagely.

"Yeah." Becca laughed. "Dad's gotten like three tickets this year alone."

"I don't even speed." I huffed grumpily, more than a little embarrassed. "I'm just—"

"Unlucky." Paxton finished for me, arching one of his dark brows in my direction. Underneath his gaze I felt about two inches tall and I shuddered, crossing my arms over my chest to protect myself, like maybe if I held tightly enough my heart would stop pounding and I could think straight.

Ha, think straight.

Impossible.

"Dad always gets tickets there too," Nathan piped up helpfully. My gaze snapped to him, then back to his father as I waited to see his response. Would he be angry to be lumped in the same boat with me?

Or would he not care?

God.

Why did I care?

There had to be something wrong with me. I mean, clearly I wanted to be friends but…why did I care so much about his opinion of me? Why did I care that he hated me?

He wasn't the first person to think I was too much.

Paxton just shrugged and I was forced to flounder for something to say. Except, as I glanced at him again, I noticed his lips were curled into an amused little smile and heat washed through my body at the sight. My toes curled, my fingers tingled, and my heart gave an unsteady *thump, thump.*

Paxton's chest flexed as he moved and I had to close my mouth for fear of drooling. He was all muscles. Dark curls. Honey eyes. With chest hair curling at the collar of his shirt.

"Movie!" Becca clapped her hands together, then pointed toward the concession stand with a flourish. We all followed her direction. I was in a daze as I handed over my credit card and tried not to cringe over the fact the popcorn had gone from ten dollars a bin to fifteen dollars in just five short years.

Inflation apparently didn't have the Christmas spirit.

Feeling chipper however–because I had snacks now–I popped a handful of popcorn in my mouth and waggled the box at Becca until she grudgingly accepted. I could feel the heavy caress of Paxton's gaze on the back of my neck and I did my best to ignore it, trying to play it cool. Why did he make me feel like a grade schooler? Suddenly all fumble-footed and out of my depth.

I hadn't felt this way since I was a kid.

We took our seats and I was both apprehensive and excited when it became obvious that Becca had forced us to sit together. Nathan sat on her other side and I watched the way his cheeks reddened as she offered him some of our popcorn with a polite waggle of the box.

It was weird seeing my mannerisms reflected in her.

Like looking at a tiny almost-adult clone.

I cleared my throat, shifting a little to get comfortable before I decided to just bite the bullet and talk to Paxton. Get the fear out of the way. How bad could it really be? The man hadn't been completely awful after all. He'd even helped out last week, no complaints, nothing but a solid little chocolate-pumpkin soldier.

God.

The man's biceps looked like they could command a troupe all on their own.

"So," I started, only for my words to be interrupted by the blaring of the speakers. The lights dimmed, the room falling into darkness as I twisted enough I got to catch the twitch to Paxton's dark eyebrows.

He didn't respond, just held up a finger to shush me.

So.

There was that.

When the movie let out, despite my earlier unease, I was bouncing off the walls with excitement. I fucking loved *Elf.* He was my favorite movie character in probably years and without fail, he never ceased to get a laugh out of me. Becca always rolled her eyes but she was in a surprisingly charitable mood as she bumped up against my side and cocked her head toward where the Montgomerys were traipsing ahead of us.

Couple of giants.

I shook my head, mouthing 'no.'

I'd had enough of Paxton's rejection for one day, thank you.

I didn't want my Buddy-the-Elf high to be completely ruined by his judgmental (but sexy) eyebrows.

Bad dick, I admonished internally as my cock gave a little twitch at the memory.

Ugh.

I wasn't a teenager anymore. I didn't do dating. I didn't do sex. Why was I thirsting after a six-foot-five boulder with a fabulously groomed beard?

The Montgomerys surprised me when instead of stopping at their truck without saying goodbye they followed us all the way to our car. Nathan was fidgeting like a cute little puppy, all long legs, coltish as he chewed on his bitten-raw lip. I glanced at Becca and noted the way she was watching him, all big, curious green eyes.

Were they…? I caught myself wondering for the second time that day.

I glanced around, searching for something I could say that would give me an excuse to let them be alone together. *Ah!*

"I want hot cocoa." Paxton and I both blurted at the same time. I glanced over at him, surprised, a smile flickering across my lips. It was chilly out and the coffee shop just across the street was famous for its peppermint hot cocoa. My favorite. He clearly didn't know that. In fact, I was certain he had his own agenda but that didn't mean I wasn't excited that we might, after all these years, have something in common.

"I don't." Becca told me with an arched brow.

"Oh—" Did that mean we should go home? Was that code for her not wanting to spend time with Nathan? I'd thought I was being covert about giving them time alone together but apparently not.

"But I was thinking…" Becca chewed on her lip, glancing between

Paxton and I. "Why don't you two drive together and Nathan can drive me?" She blinked, turning her doe eyes on the tall gangly boy with a flutter of her lashes. "You have your license, right?"

"Yeah," he squeaked, cleared his throat, and then repeated in a much lower register. "Yeah, totally."

"Cool!" Becca clapped her hands together and turned back to me with a sly smile. "Bye, Dad!" And with that she utterly fucking abandoned me.

The stars flickered up above and I tried to see the beauty in them like I normally did but instead all I felt was their laughter. It had gotten dark while we'd been inside the movies even though it wasn't late yet. That was the winter curse.

God, what had I gotten myself into? Alternatively, wasn't this exactly what I'd wanted?

Alone time with Paxton.

To clear the air.

Time for Becca to spend with Nathan?

My head was such a mess. I got exactly what I wanted and here I was complaining about it. God, what was wrong with me?

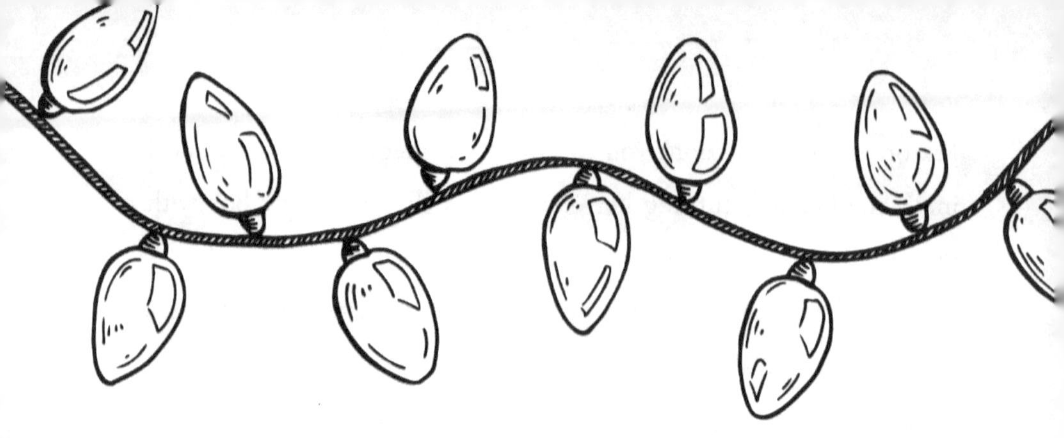

six

PAXTON

BAXTER WAS SILENT FOR THE first two or so minutes of the drive. For a moment, I was convinced he wasn't even the same man I'd coexisted with for the past fifteen years. But he proved me wrong, speaking up the second we took a left toward his side of town and the autumn breeze blew in a flurry of early snowflakes.

I watched the way he eyed them distrustfully before he shook himself and turned back to me, those massive green eyes glimmering with starlight almost like he'd caught the stars themselves within them.

The freckles on his nose scrunched as he spoke and I forced myself to look away for fear of crashing.

"So." Baxter fidgeted, his fingers bunching up around the seatbelt. I could hear the way he scratched at the fabric. *Scratch, scratch, scratch.* Fuck. Why was he so nervous? He was making *me* nervous.

"So," I repeated, waiting for him to continue.

He didn't.

For a long.

Long.

Time.

Eventually when he did speak we were only a few minutes away from his house.

"Can you loop back around? I want to give them a chance to chat before we show up."

"Aren't you afraid they're going to start making out?"

Baxter laughed, the noise loud and squawking.

"Ah. *No.*"

"Why not?" I bristled. What the fuck was that supposed to mean? His little bobblehead would be lucky to date a kid as good as mine. Maybe Nathan was a bit awkward but he was kind. Sweet. Soft. Unlike half the assholes I encountered on a daily basis.

"Oh. Oh, shit." Baxter waved his hands, that same anxious flurry of fingers I was starting to recognize he only did when he was truly uncomfortable. "I didn't mean it like that. It's not Nathan."

"Then what is it?"

"Becca." Baxter shook his head with a wry grin as I flipped a U-turn and headed back the way we'd come. Figured he might not be too off about the idea of giving them a bit more time together. I waited for him to speak and eventually he did, his voice quiet, contemplative.

"Becca and I have a rule. She's supposed to tell me when she does any of that stuff."

"And you really think she's going to follow through with that when the time comes? If she finds someone she likes?" I asked, curious.

Baxter nodded. "I trust her."

I trust her.

As if it was that simple.

Well…maybe for him it was. Maybe in his perfect world things were built with picket fences made of trust and responsibility. Maybe he'd never seen the dark side of trusting people the way that I had.

Good for him.

Lucky fucker.

"Nathan's not forward like that anyway," I admitted after a moment. "I taught him to be a gentleman. He'd ask her out first."

"Good." Baxter was quiet, then *scratch, scratch,* he began playing with his seatbelt again.

I reached over without thinking, snatching at his fingers to still the anxious movement. He paused, his skin warm and solid beneath mine, his hands frozen as he let me manhandle them neatly into his lap.

"Does Nathan like Becca?" Baxter asked curiously. I ignored him. It wasn't my secret to tell and like hell was I going to betray my son's confidence to a man that I didn't trust not to turn around and spill the beans to his daughter. Somehow Baxter didn't strike me as the kind of guy that knew how to keep a secret.

Baxter didn't push, even though he could've. Instead, he just curled his fingers against his knees, digging them into the meat of his thigh as I pulled over on the side of the road and parked the car. Driving around was proving confusing and more than a little distracting.

Maybe it was best I clear the air now?

Let him know I wasn't interested in the friendship side of this.

That I was only here to help my son.

That the last fucking thing I wanted for my holiday season was to spend it with him.

But…something stopped me.

Maybe it was the way he glanced over at me, his plump pink lips chewed raw, a scared sort of flicker in his eyes I'd never noticed before. He visibly relaxed the moment I flipped the ignition off and I twisted to look at him, inspecting him with a frown. He wilted beneath my gaze, like it was hot enough to burn.

What did he want from me?

Was he really in this for the *friendship*?

Or was it for something else?

God.

Confusing as fuck.

"Did you like the bread?" He asked after a quiet, tense moment, his freckles twitching as he scrunched his nose again. I wanted to… I wanted…Fuck.

No.

Don't think about that.

No.

"It was fine."

Fine was an understatement, but the last thing Baxter needed was another person to toot his motherfucking horn. The man was a fucking locomotive of ego already. Except he kinda…did this little wilting thing again, like my words were…*hell.*

Like he cared what I thought.

Like I'd hurt him, but he didn't want me to see.

I swallowed, my throat suddenly dry.

Was I reading this all wrong?

Had I read *him* all wrong?

"So…when you're not 'fixing things' what do you like to do?" Baxter asked, clearly trying to salvage the conversation.

"I'm a dad and I fix things. That's it."

He wilted again.

What the fuck.

I glanced at the clock, relieved when I realized enough time had passed that we could head back to his house without interrupting what would hopefully be a pivotal moment in my son's pursuit of his blonde-haired muse.

We didn't speak again the entire drive over.

Baxter didn't try, and I didn't either.

When I watched him walk up the front steps, something inside my chest gave a weird little lurch. Heartburn probably. From the popcorn.

Nathan hopped into the truck, a grin on his face that chased away the cobwebs of my last encounter and I headed home, resolutely not thinking of sad green eyes and rejection.

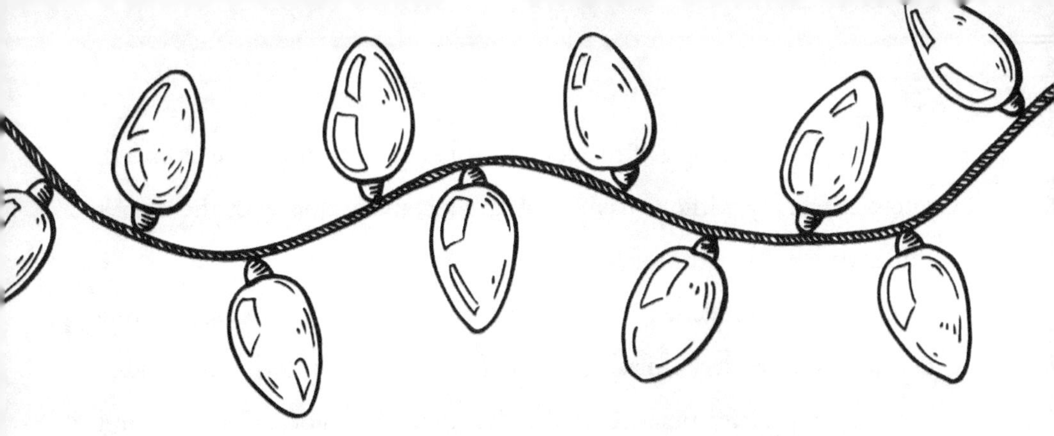

seven

BAXTER

IT WAS TIME FOR ROUND two. Three? No, two. The first one didn't count. We'd invited the Montgomerys over again, this time for some Christmas cookie-decorating shenanigans. It had been Becca's idea. She didn't like the way things were progressing between Paxton and I, and honestly, I couldn't blame her.

Clearly, things weren't looking up.

Our time alone together last Saturday had only further solidified the chasm that lay between us. Deep and cavernous. I didn't know how to cross it. I didn't know if I even wanted to. Truly when I thought about it, Paxton had been nothing but a total dick to me the entire time I'd known him.

He was, however, super hot.

Unfortunately being hot didn't excuse dickery though.

Luckily I could ogle him from a distance and enjoy the muscled, tattooed scenery without having to have a conversation with the man if things truly went south.

"Look," Becca coached me, her hands on her hips. She was wearing one of her Baker's Bakery shirts again and had her hair up in her high pony leftover from cheer practice earlier that day. She'd gotten out late and hitched a ride home with one of the other kids. Her ponytail swung as she spoke and I tried not to stare at it because I knew how much she hated that. "Things aren't working."

"I know, Becca-boo. But what am I supposed to do? The guy doesn't want a friend."

"Um. Dad." Becca bobbed. "Clearly he does. He signed up for the Christmas Buddies program just like you did."

"You're the one that signed me up," I reminded her.

"Same diff."

"Not really." I turned back to the cookie sheet, checked the pan, and deemed it cooled down enough I could pop the cookies onto the cooling rack. Ornaments, Christmas trees, and snowmen. I wasn't sure how well this was going to go. Somehow Paxton didn't strike me as the kinda man who enjoyed sitting down and decorating for hours.

But then again, he was kinda artsy in his own way.

So honestly I had no idea what was about to happen.

"Does Nathan like art?" I asked curiously and Becca shrugged.

"Um, I dunno? We barely take classes together." She was pink though, so my smile returned as I nudged her shoulder.

"You think he's cute though," I hummed, nudging, nudging, *nudging*.

"*Stooooop.*"

The doorbell rang and I banished Becca to answer it, my heart thudding unsteadily as I waited with baited breath for our guests to arrive. It had been so long since I'd invited someone over like this. Becca knew this. I knew this. This was probably why she'd been so adamant about me joining the program in the first place.

You have no friends, Dad, she'd said.

And I'd scoffed.

But she was actually right. When was the last time I'd spent time with someone that wasn't business related? The fact I couldn't even remember was answer enough. God, I was just as pitiful as she thought I was.

When Paxton Montgomery walked into the kitchen, it was like my heart stuttered to life again. His massive figure filled the entire doorway and he paused, assessing me, dark hazel eyes glimmering nearly gold in the overhead light. He smelled like pine trees and something earthy that made my mouth water.

"Is Nathan still out front?" I asked, breaking the silence.

"Becca asked him to take her to get icing for the cookies."

"But we already—" I blinked, frowning down at the bowls of icing I had premixed on the table. "Oh."

Paxton clearly had the same thought I had, because he glanced at the table and then cocked his head, smoothing one of his hands over his beard with a thoughtful expression.

"Your daughter likes to force us to be alone together."

"Yeah, she does," I agreed with a sigh. "She…" I shook my head, turned back to the cookies and continued to scrape them up off the tray and onto the rack. One cookie at a time. *Plop, plop, plop.*

"What? She what?"

I paused, glancing back up at him again, my cheeks flushing.

I didn't want to admit this, but…

Man.

What was the worst thing that could happen?

"She thinks I need help making friends," I admitted, more than a little embarrassed.

Paxton looked…surprised. It was a new expression for him, and I watched the way it unfolded across his face like a present. My heart did that unsteady *thump, thump* again.

"*You*…need help making friends?" He sounded disbelieving.

"Well," I shrugged. "She seems to think so anyway."

"You're friends with the entire fucking town," Paxton pointed out.

I supposed he wasn't wrong. From an outside perspective, what I shared with most members of Belleville could be seen as friendship. What it was however was…good will? The desire to chase off my demons. Chasing light instead of shadows. Drops of sunlight in puddles of darkened memory.

They'd opened their arms to me, accepted me as family, but they weren't…friends.

"I don't know if I'd call it that." I disagreed, though I didn't push. Instead, I just turned back to the cookies, way too aware of the back of my neck where I could feel Paxton's eyes trailing across my skin. My hair prickled and I shuddered.

"So is that why you're doing this?" Paxton suddenly asked, his voice nothing but gravel and stone. It rumbled through the air like thunder and my toes curled in my Rudolph-themed fuzzy Christmas socks.

"Doing what?"

"This. The program. The cookies. The—whatever the fuck."

I blinked, turning back to him, spatula in hand. "Yes? I mean, why else would I have signed up?"

Nevermind the fact I'd literally just told Becca she'd been the one to sign me up. He didn't need to know that. God. *What was his problem?* Why did everything I do cause him to react so negatively?

"Why do you hate me?" I blurted, my heart racing a mile a minute as my words caught up to my brain. Fuck. I hadn't meant to say that out loud.

Paxton stared at me, his eyes widening, mouth dropping open in surprise for the second time that night.

"What?" He croaked, voice deep and sweet as honey.

"Why do you hate me?" I asked again, sticking to my guns. "You're…" I waved a hand at him, encompassing all of his muscled, flannel-covered glory. "You're always glaring at me. Like I did something to you. And I don't understand. I'm just…" I shook my head. "I'm just wondering what I've ever done to you to make you look at me like I'm…"

"Like you're what?" he asked.

"Like I'm a piece of shit."

There was silence in the air. The clock on the wall clicked, the oven dinged, and I moved to flip the switch that would turn it off. Paxton was quiet for a long time, and I tried to ignore the way sweat beaded at my temple, and my heart rebelled against my ribcage.

"You smile too much," Paxton finally said.

The words were so ridiculous I couldn't help but laugh.

He continued.

"You're nice to everyone. You do…things for people. You laugh at fucking everything. You're always happy. Even *now* you're fucking smiling at me."

"You hate me because I'm always happy?"

What a…ridiculous thought.

"Yes."

Wow.

Wow.

I laughed.

Once I started laughing I couldn't seem to stop. The sound burst from my chest like bullets, tearing through my defenses, through the walls I built around myself, through the shield I had protecting everyone around me from the shrapnel of the broken emotions tearing apart my heart.

"I'm not happy." I stared at him, suddenly unafraid, despite the way his brows lowered and his eyes only grew darker. "If you hate me because I'm happy, then you're just…" I shook my head. "You're just completely fucking stupid."

"What?"

"I'm not happy, Paxton." I pointed my spatula at him, my voice wobbling as the words that I'd kept barricaded inside of me since the day my sister died barreled to the front. "I'm absolutely fucking miserable."

My hands were shaking, shaking, *shaking.*

"Now, go wash your fucking hands."

Paxton did as he was told.

The rest of the cookie decorating went without a hitch. Becca arrived with sprinkles, and not icing, as well as the meanest little shit-eating grin I had ever seen in my entire life. I couldn't be mad at her. Not when her dimples were out like that.

Didn't mean she wasn't on my shit list though.

Nathan was adorably attentive, and also incredibly slow. It took him about four times longer than anyone else at the table to decorate a single snowman cookie. And when he did, he held it up with a triumphant grin to reveal possibly the most horrible decorating job I'd ever seen.

It instantly became my favorite cookie and I made the mental note to bargain with him at the end of the night for three of mine in exchange.

Paxton though…

Paxton was surprisingly good at decorating. He had an attention to detail that rivaled even my own. He was wicked fast, skilled, and more than a little creative. Watching him work was truly an experience and I couldn't help but forgive him a little for his earlier rudeness when I saw the pink tip of his tongue poke out in concentration as he plopped a carrot nose artfully on one of his snowmen.

By the end of the night everything had ended up absolutely adorable. Becca's cookies were all decorated with pink hats, ornaments, and scarves depending on the cookie. Nathan managed to decorate a whopping three cookies. And Paxton had an entire tray of his own.

"You think Uncle Trent will eat them all?" Nathan asked, glancing at their tray with barely concealed possessiveness. Apparently cookie sharing was not part of the Montgomery Christmas spirit.

"He better fucking not." Paxton grunted.

The entire time we'd worked he'd kept glancing at me through his lashes, his dark honeyed eyes more than a little conflicted. I…regretted opening up to him. Not because what I'd said wasn't true but because it was information I hadn't shared before with, well, anyone.

It was my most private secret.

I wasn't sure what it was about his questioning that had so easily broken through all my fortresses, but it had.

Maybe it was because I liked him.

Maybe it was because…he was supposed to be my friend, and he so clearly wasn't.

Either way, I ended the night feeling more than a little unsettled as I watched the two massive men make their way out to their truck. When Paxton flipped the headlights on they lit up a flurry of snowflakes that had begun to flutter their way to the ground.

I'd heard the weather forecast that morning, but in light of my anxiety about the Christmas event that night I'd forgotten.

Snow.

I hated snow.

Which was hilarious considering the fact I lived in fucking Vermont.

Luckily it was Sunday so there was no reason to leave the house the next day. I made a mental note to warn Becca off driving. In our house we had very few rules. Tell me if you start dating. Always fold your own laundry. Honesty is the best policy. And don't drive in the fucking snow.

That last rule had only recently been implemented.

Technically speaking, Becca wasn't supposed to drive alone with her learners permit but…no one in Belleville cared. Half the high school drove themselves to school. I didn't let her do it often but I also was guilty of sending her on milk runs when I was feeling particularly stressed at work.

Becca was an asset.

My sanity.

My heart.

My everything.

That was why the idea of her driving in the snow made me want to explode.

I watched them peel out of the driveway, my heart in my throat, my palms sweaty where I scrubbed them on my jeans.

"Why'd you want one of Nathan's cookies so bad?" Becca asked curiously beside me. I turned to face her, choosing to ignore the flicker of snowflakes in my peripheral vision.

"It's cute." I shrugged

She accepted my answer with a flash of her cute little pearly whites and I leaned heavily against her, sagging against her pointy little bones as I let myself soak up her sunshine.

"How did it go with Mr. Montgomery?" Becca asked, patting my head consolingly.

I sighed.

"That bad, huh?"

"Worse."

"Maybe this was…" She trailed off. I could hear the words where they hung suspended in the air between us. *Maybe this was a bad idea.*

Maybe it was.

Maybe not.

I was too tired to tell.

eight

PAXTON

I THOUGHT ABOUT BAXTER THE entire drive home. Actually I'd been thinking about him a lot lately, but our most recent conversation was fresh on my mind as I navigated the quiet roads and listened to Nathan snore in the passenger seat.

He'd passed out about two minutes into the ride, and I couldn't blame him.

Sometimes growing up was a lot of work, for many reasons.

His rest, however, meant I was stuck alone with my thoughts.

Was what Baxter had said true? He was *miserable*? He didn't look miserable. I was…more than a little confused. Wrong-footed. Guilty. I hadn't been exactly fair to him. From the moment I met him, I'd judged him. Just like everyone else, I'd looked only at his shiny exterior and didn't realize the cracks beneath it.

Everyone had their cracks.

But Baxter's were empty and gaping and it seemed that no one in his life had noticed.

Well, maybe Becca had.

The fact that she'd signed him up for the Christmas Buddies program was proof enough of that. Could she see that her dad was slipping? And if that was the case, why did I care so much? Why did my heart hurt?

Why did remembering the painful, angry bite to his words, the quiver of his lips, the flutter of his wet lashes—why did *that* make me want to fucking punch something?

I parked the truck and got out, gently rapping on Nathan's window until he stumbled his way out of the car and we plodded through the few inches of powdered snow that had fallen during our short trek across town.

I couldn't help but compare my home to Baxter's as we stepped inside.

Our house was…homier than his was. I thought so at least. Dirtier too. Our coats hung on their hooks over the staircase bannister, and across the back of the large lumpy sofa we called home most nights while we devoured TV dinners.

It was home with its blue paint, newly repaired trim, and handmade door frames.

Using the pencil marks I'd painstakingly etched of Nathan's height and ages as he'd been growing, I'd permanently carved into the wood of the open kitchen archway in a place of honor.

I liked to look at them and remember just how quickly time had gone by.

"You should head to bed," I said softly, my voice a quiet rumble in the dark. Nathan nodded, yawning again as he paraded his plate of cookies into the kitchen and plopped them on the table. All the loaves of bread from the Bakers' last meeting with us were gone. We'd chowed through them that first day and once again, I was struck with an immense feeling of guilt.

How did you like the bread, Baxter had said.

I'd said it was *fine*.

The way he'd…

The look on his face.

God.

When had I become such a fucking asshole?

Nathan pushed his way past me, turned back, and gave me the most awkward—kinda smelly—bear hug I had ever received.

"Thanks for everything, Dad," he said, his face pressed into my neck. I gave him a squeeze back, genuinely unsure what I'd done to warrant this level of affection.

"Why…?"

"You were really nice to Mr. Baker today," he explained, giving me another squeeze. "I think it made Becca really happy. So." He released me, gave me a big sunny smile and then thudded his way up the stairs as loudly as possible.

I watched him go, feeling somehow more lost than I had before.

If what I'd done today at the Bakers' was considered being nice…well. I was going to fucking hell.

I couldn't help but think about him again.

His dark circles.

The exhaustion written in his every pore.

It was no secret that Baxter's bakery was down for repairs. Everyone in town had heard of it the day it had happened. Suddenly it went from "don't forget to pick up your everyday bagels from Baker's Bakery" to "poor Baxter, I wonder what he's going to do now that he's out of work."

Clearly, he'd made it work though.

His massive kitchen had been full of all the appliances that had somehow survived the death of his bakery. It hadn't been a tragedy that had ruined the rest of them, but the curse of time. When Baxter had bought it from old man McMillan the place had already been old as fuck.

Ten years in and well, things were bound to break. There was only so much duct tape and determination could hold together.

Maybe…

Maybe.

Maybe I could help.

I penned down my thoughts on my notebook in the shop, flopping down on the couch as I mulled over what I could do to make right what I'd done.

How do you say sorry to a person who you've wronged for no reason for years?

You don't.

Or…

Fuck.

I stared out the window, watching the snowfall with my heart in my throat, my pen leaking ink onto the pads of my fingers. That was when the idea occurred to me.

I could fix up the bakery.

I had the skill set. I had the time. What I didn't have were resources. However, we just so happened to live in a town that thought that Baxter hung the moon. It wouldn't be that hard to find people willing to either help or donate to the cause. Everyone was still hoping for a Baker's Bakery Hullabaloo this year. Maybe I could use that as an incentive?

I ran through a few quick calculations as well as jotted down my ideas for where the bakery could use some improvements.

Technically speaking, the entire interior could use some work.

It was old as fuck. The tile was chipped and yellowed with age. The counters were older than I was.

I'd need donations for sure if I was going to do something about that.

I'd call around tomorrow morning and see what I could do.

With a goal in sight, I melted into the project. Page after page of notes littered my lap and my work table as I constructed blueprints for improvements, calculations, and a plan of action for how to proceed. Next came names. Phone numbers. Lists of those I thought would be willing to donate in the name of Christmas spirit.

By the time I finished it was nearly four a.m. When I glanced out the window again it was to see a blanket of white coating the world around me. It felt a bit like rebirth, the red and gold autumn leaves having fallen to earth, covered in a blanket of snowflakes and purity.

As I rose I groaned, popping my sore back, my knees creaking as I was forced to perform a few feeble stretches before I headed up the stairs to my own bedroom.

As I lay in bed and stared out my window, loneliness crept up on me for the first time in a long time. I watched fat snowflakes fall from the heavens and my heart tapped an unsteady staccato against my breastbone.

Somewhere halfway across Belleville, Baxter was at home, sleeping in his empty bed too.

If he looked out the window maybe he'd see the same flakes I was seeing.

Mirrored anyway. We weren't so different after all.

Maybe fixing up his bakery would help him financially but…

It wouldn't fix the mess I'd made of his feelings.

Maybe I shouldn't care as much as I did.

Maybe I was growing soft in my old age.

A new idea occurred to me, one on a much smaller scale, and with a small smile I set my alarm, tipped onto my belly, and let sleep consume me. Tomorrow was a new day and I knew exactly what I needed to do to make this right.

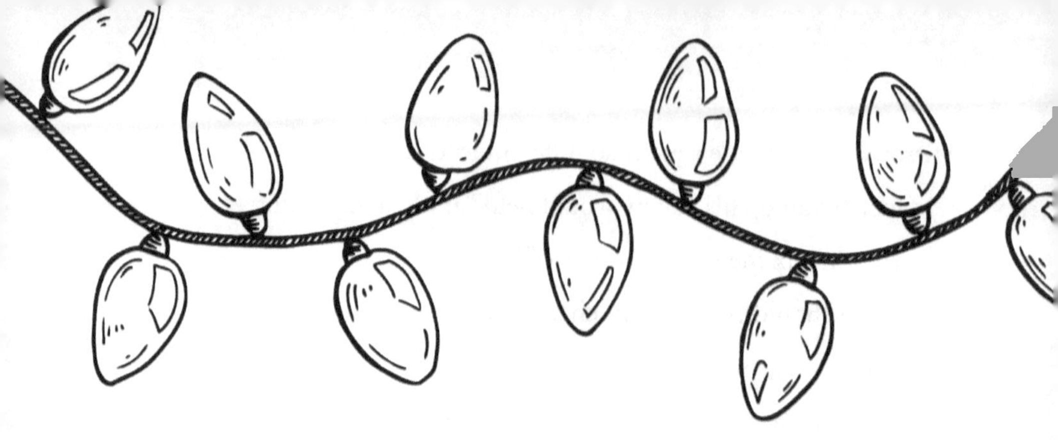

nine

BAXTER

IF YOU HAD TOLD ME three weeks ago that I would be waking up on a Sunday morning to a snowstorm and a very sexy lumberjack at my front door demanding entrance I would've laughed in your face.

Apparently this wasn't a dream though, because Paxton Montgomery glared down at me from my doorstep, the winter air blowing in and making my nipples perk up against my silk pajamas.

"Um. Hi?" I blinked up at him, scrubbing the sleep from my eyes, not entirely sure I wasn't seeing things.

Except when I moved my hands he was still there.

And he was…dressed in snow pants?

"We're going sledding," Paxton said, his voice a firm growl that had my knees growing weak and my nipples hardening even more. My cock gave a feeble twitch. It didn't like the cold either.

"We're *what?*"

"Get dressed. I'll wait." Paxton pushed inside my house without so much as a greeting. He shucked his frankly massive boots off politely, then plodded his socked way into my kitchen, the rustling of his snow pants filling the silence. After him came Nathan, who saluted at me with a jovial grin and two massive sleds strapped to his back.

It was a wonder they even fit through the door.

"There's a hill in your backyard." Paxton's voice echoed through the kitchen and I turned, starstruck and more than a little confused as I shut the front door and shook my head in disbelief. I followed after both men, scrubbing at my arms to warm myself, self-conscious of my silk Santa Claus pajamas.

I wasn't feeling particularly festive after our conversation last night, but…they'd been comfortable. A comfort. Both.

Paxton was rustling around in my cupboards and I couldn't help but admire the way his massive back tensed and flexed as he pulled down four mugs and a pot that he thunked onto my stove gingerly. The man could swallow three of me in one bite, and I wasn't even particularly a small man.

"What is…?"

"Surprise!" Nathan cheered, flashing jazz hands my way as I did my best to stop ogling his dad in snow pants. Wow. His…*wow*. His everything was just—

I needed some quality time with my right hand and an incognito tab if I was going to survive this.

"I am very surprised." I wasn't even lying either.

What were they doing?

I glanced at the clock, more than a little disgruntled, to realize it was only seven thirty in the morning. I was a baker. I woke up at ass o'clock hours, so that was why Sunday was my designated sleep-in day.

Apparently not today though.

Nathan popped outside, deposited the sleds, then returned, his cheeks pink.

"You like milk?" Paxton grunted, and I found myself nodding in a daze, unsure why the hell he needed that information until he headed out to his truck and then came back with his arms laden with plastic grocery bags.

It took me an embarrassing amount of time to realize he was cooking hot chocolate.

From scratch.

In my kitchen.

Wearing snow pants.

Becca came down about twenty minutes into the bizarre show, her hair a mess of curls around her face, her own set of silk Santa pajamas creased from sleep. She flopped down at the kitchen table, somehow not at all concerned that we had two actual giants invading our kitchen.

"Surprise!" I said, waggling my fingers in a mimicry of Nathan's earlier performance. He peeked over his shoulder at me, beamed so hard it blinded me, then turned back to help his dad.

Watching the Montgomerys work was like watching a circus.

They never spoke, but they moved in sync. Back and forth, this and that. Swing, swing, pass, stir, pour, stir, swing.

It was clear they did this often, and I wasn't sure why the thought of massive, grumpy Paxton Montgomery making hot chocolate with his little boy so often they had the routine memorized had my heart lurching in my chest.

When they finished, both Becca and I were passed steaming mugs and I watched in amazement as Paxton tore open a ginormous bag of marshmallows and came over to personally dump them in both our cups.

I wanted to ask what the hell was happening, but…

I was kinda content to ride it through.

I'd regret that decision later, when I was standing at the top of the hill in our back yard with snowflakes in my eyelashes and Becca's screech in my ears. She'd just made her way down the hill and I watched in horror as she spun around at the bottom, a massive 'whoop-whoop' echoing through the snowflake-filled air.

"Dad!" She yelled, scrambling up from her spot on the sled, her arms held out in triumph. "Your turn!"

Nathan had gone down first, and he was watching her with these big adorable heart eyes I could see even from thirty feet away. My heart, however, was in my throat as I turned around to stare at Paxton where he stood sentinel behind me.

He was coated in snowflakes, his bare muscular forearms flexing as he passed the sled from hand to hand. I watched his tattoos dance and wondered distantly why the hell he didn't have a coat on. Or a scarf? He needed a scarf.

"You go first." I said, because there was no way in hell I was going at all.

If I could get him down to the bottom, I seriously doubted anyone would force me to follow. Well. Maybe after they'd come to the top, but by that point I could run back inside and fake death. So.

"You're going with me." Paxton said. His honeyed eyes were twinkling beneath his dark brow, his beanie pulled down low, just wisps of his chestnut-brown hair sneaking out from the edges. They curled around his ears, the flicker of silver catching the foggy light as I glared at him with a resigned huff.

"Saw through that, did you?"

"Course." He flashed me a smile.

I was so completely derailed by the way my heart leapt out of my chest, my stomach twisted, and butterflies erupted throughout my entire body that I didn't even notice him sit down atop the sled. Thick fingers wrapped around my wrist and for a moment I was suspended through the air before I plummeted to the sled with an uncomfortable thump—right into Paxton's fucking lap.

"Breathe." He murmured, his own breath warm where it caressed the shell of my ear.

I breathed.

And then we were off.

The wind whipped my cheeks, howling in my ears as snow burst in splashes of icy delight on either side of us and the world blurred white. When we hit the bottom the sled spun, once, twice, three times before stopping.

I didn't even recognize my own voice for a moment as I let out the loudest 'whoop-whoop' I ever had in my entire fucking life. Becca howled in response, as did Nathan and Paxton—to my surprise—our voices echoing through the quiet morning air.

I was lucky my neighbors were at the top of the hill, otherwise I'd be hearing about this for weeks.

I just climbed to the top of the hill again, sat down on Paxton's sled and took him for another ride.

By the time we headed inside, my cheeks were burning from the cold, and my ears were numb. My hat had slipped at some point despite the fact that Paxton had generously pulled it down for me at least six different times.

He was…different today.

Kinder.

His eyes were softer as he herded us all inside, a growl to his voice I was coming to realize wasn't exactly mean—though it wasn't exactly nice either.

"Hot cocoa," he threatened, and we all piled at the kitchen table and let him do the work.

It was my second cup of cocoa but I wasn't complaining. I couldn't remember the last time someone had made something like this for me.

Maybe it had been grandma before she passed?

Or Rebecca, for my birthday the month before she'd left the earth and joined the other angels.

Either way, it felt…good, to be cared for.

Made me realize that maybe in the midst of all this madness it was possible that I could be just Baxter again—and Dad—at the same time.

Becca was cackling beside me. She hadn't put her hair up and it was wet where it stuck to her cold cheeks, her eyes bright, her smile brighter. She grinned at me, leaned over, and gave me a happy nudge.

"Never knew you liked that so much!" She cheered, nodding toward the back door where we could still clearly see the silhouettes of the sleds laid out on the now no longer pristine coat of snow.

"What can I say?" I hummed, watching as horror dawned on her face.

"I'm a sled for it."

She blinked.

Nathan cocked his head at me in confusion across the table.

I glanced between the two of them, waiting for them to get the joke.

Nothing.

"You know because I'm a—"

Paxton's laughter broke the silence, interrupting me as the quiet rumbling chuckle filled the room like an avalanche.

"Sled for it." He shook his head and I turned to stare at him, my jaw dropping.

"Like slut?" I offered, in case for some reason he was laughing at something else—something that wasn't my amazing (horrible) pun. That apparently no one else got.

"I got it." He reassured me, continuing to chuckle and shake his head as he poured his own cup of cocoa before making his way over to the table. He sat beside me, our knees bumping, and I was—for the first time— grateful that I'd opted to buy the more sturdy dining set. I doubted a paltry IKEA version would've held up beneath all that bulk. Jesus Christ the man was built like a brick house.

His thigh burned where it touched mine and I shivered, sipping at my cocoa to hide my smile.

"Dad jokes." Becca shook her head in disgust, and Nathan joined in commiseration.

"Dad jokes," I agreed, flashing Paxton a secretive smile that he—to my surprise—returned.

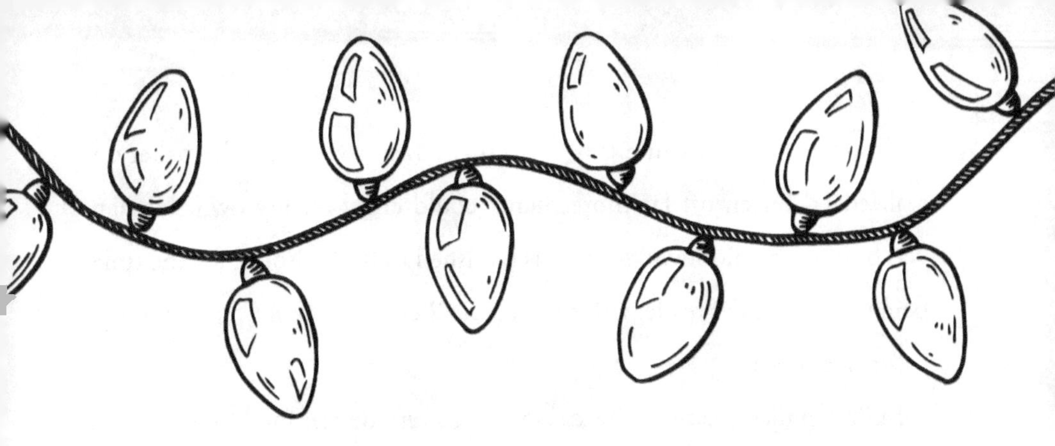

ten

PAXTON

BEGINNING CONSTRUCTION ON BAXTER'S BAKERY was easier than I thought it would be. After I'd called over to Charlie, the locksmith, and told him what I was up to he'd eagerly agreed to break the law for me. Getting into the building was easy with his help; having an excuse to keep Baxter away was even easier.

All it took was one phone call from Ernie, the local pest control company, and suddenly Baxter was banned.

Maybe he was a little more stressed out than before, but I hoped my efforts would make it worth it.

Bob supplied tile.

Jillian supplied wood.

Wiring came from my own collection, as did the custom bread counter I spent the first week building in my shop.

However, when it came time to actually begin work on the bakery, I realized I'd bitten off far more than I could chew on my own. Nathan was busy with schoolwork—he was banished to his bedroom for the time being so he could wrestle with the Algebra 2 class he was currently failing.

We had a deal.

Failing grades meant no Becca, so he was very determined to rectify the situation.

Unfortunately for me, that meant I was out a helper. Since fixing up the bakery was something we were all keeping under wraps, I had to rely on word-of-mouth and Jason at the local—and only—grocery store for help.

My *help wanted* ad maybe wasn't the prettiest but it got the job done.

Fifteen dollars an hour, under the table.
Required: responsible nature, timeliness, and silence.

I'd barely finished rewiring the kitchen when I heard a rap on the back door. The sound echoed through the empty space; I'd had to gut it to prep for the new floor I was putting in hopefully the next week. Though, at this point it was clear to me that there was no way I was going to finish in time for Baxter's Christmas Hullabaloo. God, what a mouth full.

Hullabaloo.

The man was clearly sadistic.

I wiped my hands off, shifted my goggles up and headed toward the door. I figured maybe Jason had found someone who could help me. An older gentleman perhaps? Someone retired looking for something to fill their holiday season.

What I didn't expect when I opened the door was to be faced with none other than Becca Baker herself.

I almost shut the door in her face on instinct.

But I didn't.

Instead I opened it wider and arched a brow, waiting for her to tell me what she was doing there. Would she spill the beans? Had she heard through the grapevine what I was doing?

Only time would tell.

Becca blinked up at me, tipping her chin up with defiance, her lips wobbling. Green eyes flashed and I watched as she gathered herself together, bun bobbing, a piece of paper tucked tightly to her sweater clad chest.

She shoved the paper toward me and I latched onto it in response, glancing down at it, my eyes widening in surprise. The scent of roses wafted up from it and I shook my head to clear it as I took in what it was.

"I know how to keep secrets," Becca told me, shuffling in the doorway as I stared down at her…pink? Resume?

"You want to work with me?" I was…confused.

"Yes."

Clearly she wasn't.

"You understand that this job requires physical labor?" It wasn't that I thought she wasn't capable. I just knew kids her age usually didn't understand the full extent of what I did. There was heavy lifting. There were nails. There was the possibility of injury. I was as careful as I could be—safety goggles and helmet required—but even then there were always risks.

"I'm a hard worker, Mr. Montgomery." Becca told me, straightening up to her full height. She was tall for a little girl, taller than most her age,

Nathan excluded. "I need the money. I'm responsible, like your ad said, and I'm really, really good at being quiet."

"Do you know how to use power tools?"

"No." Becca shook her head, and for some reason the fact she was being honest kind of…charmed me. She wasn't the same girl I saw when she was with her father. Her smiles, like his, seemed mostly for show.

Why did that make me sad?

"But I have a PhD in Googling." Becca held up her phone, her lips tipping up into a smile. "I'm student council president, and last year I was captain of the cheer team."

I didn't bother asking why she had specified she was captain last year, and not this year. But I figured it was none of my business.

I squinted at her for a moment, watched the way she stared at me, all defiant and confident, though vulnerability quivered like a hummingbird's wings behind her eyes.

Then I looked at her resume.

I hired her.

We had to drive half an hour to get to the indoor Christmas market. If this had been at the beginning of November I would've complained. But as it was I was starting to warm up to the Bakers so I stayed silent, only piping up when Becca took control of the radio and the *bleep, bleep* of her pop music became far too unbearable to listen to.

I switched the channel to the Christmas station and when I glanced at Baxter where he sat in the passenger seat beside me, I saw the way his eyes lit up.

"Daaaad," Nathan complained from the back. I flipped him off, and turned the music up louder.

Baxter was smiling now, though he hid it against his shoulder as we continued our trek through the switchbacks and down the mountain. Luckily, the roads had cleared up since last week. Though we'd had flurries here and there, the heaviest of the snow wouldn't hit till January. Hell, last year we'd even had a storm all the way in April.

It was like every year winter's true arrival was pushed further and further back.

Baxter's jacket didn't look nearly warm enough, but I didn't bother him about it. Figured the guy could freeze to death if he wanted to. We were in fucking Vermont; he should know better. However, when we got out of the car in the horrifically crowded parking lot at the market he just waggled his eyebrows at me, opened his coat like a drug dealer, and pointed to the little button inside that signified it was heated.

A heated coat.

What the fuck.

I was impressed, and I couldn't help myself.

A heated coat?

Why had I never thought of that?

Jesus.

It was forty degrees in November and it was only bound to get cooler, and here I was like a total schmuck with my fucking wool flannel Carhartt combo. I shook my head in disbelief.

Nathan wandered ahead of me, gesturing us through the crowd like he was Moses parting the Red Sea. I hoped to fuck we wouldn't run into anyone in my family here but I was doubtful. Every year the Montgomerys bought booths in every local fair and market to advertise their tree farm just outside of Belleville.

I'd grown up on that farm.

Grown up peddling pamphlets and coupons like a tree-wielding jester at markets just like this one.

For some reason I wasn't ready for Baxter to meet my family yet. Maybe it was because they were embarrassing. Maybe it was because they all knew shit about me I didn't want him to know. Maybe it was because... well. Maybe it was because he was fucking pretty, and all they'd need to do is look at me to see right through the mask I'd had to throw up around him since that night he put me in my place.

I deserved what he'd said to me.

I'd been a dick.

Judged him for his coping mechanism of choice, like it was his fault I was fucking miserable too. Man, what a joke. Ever since he'd been honest with me though, it felt like the wall between us was slowly crumbling. I was letting myself feel again and it was...terrifying.

We made it to the front door with Nathan's badass crowd-splitting skills and I watched as he directed a winning smile Becca's way.

She was red and green today, wearing gloves that covered up the blisters on her palms I'd bandaged the day before.

Becca was...a surprisingly hard worker. She didn't complain. She didn't ask stupid questions. She always Googled shit before bothering me. And most importantly, she seemed to genuinely enjoy what we were doing.

Because I didn't trust her I'd made her sign a document that stated she wouldn't tell her dad about the bakery and its current renovations.

Instead of rolling her eyes, like I'd expected, she'd just nodded seriously and signed the fucking paper.

The more time I spent with her the more I was beginning to enjoy her presence. Cute kid. I'd thought that more than once—which was shocking because the only kid I'd ever liked in my entire life was my own.

The crowd at the market was worse than usual. It was the last week of November and we'd caught the early shoppers. Since the market was only open on the weekends, people had a limited amount of time to spend browsing.

The after-Thanksgiving rush was the absolute fucking worst.

We'd skipped our weekly meetup in favor of spending time with family but I couldn't help but wonder what the Bakers had done for Thanksgiving. Mine had been just as loud, just as hectic as it always was. Like every year since we'd broken up, I'd extended an invitation to Nathan's mom—for his sake—not hers. And she declined, like she always did.

We had an agreement.

I got him full-time but she was allowed to take him for holidays. I'd offered visitation but as he'd gotten older she'd taken me up on it less and less. She had a new husband now, more kids, a life in the suburbs two hours away from ours.

You'd think two hours wasn't that far, but for her apparently it was an unsurpassable distance.

She never fucking saw Nathan anymore, and even though it was shitty of me, and I wished she would treat him better, part of me was grateful. The kid he was when he came back from his mom's was just a shadow of himself.

Like he forgot what it meant to be Nathan, and I hated seeing him shrink down the way he always did.

"Abandoned again," Baxter sighed from beside me. I glanced down at him, startled when I realized I'd spaced out for longer than I'd meant to.

"What?" I grunted, my hands shoving into my jean pockets. The denim scratched as I inhaled the scent of roasted nuts and apple cider in the air. There were hundreds of booths stacked together like dominos inside the indoor stadium. The seats that lined the walls were full of families laughing and munching on Christmas delicacies, their arms laden with bags full of junk.

"The kids." Baxter nodded toward the distant bob of Nathan's head and Becca's floppy bun.

"Where are they going?" I asked, stupidly.

"Something about a tree farm? I didn't catch the rest."

Right. Because Nathan was fucking obsessed with the family business.

Thank god he'd gone off on his own. Maybe I could distract Baxter enough that we wouldn't run into anyone I knew.

"I'm not sure what to do!" Baxter admitted, clapping his hands together and pushing them against his lips as he hummed. "As much as I love Christmas, I've never actually been here before. What do *you* do?"

Why was it cute he was asking me this?

Why was *he* cute?

Why?

Fucking.

Fucking fuck.

"Usually people shop for presents," I said. Stupidly again.

Stupid.

"Right." Baxter nodded. I tried not to be charmed by how the swell of his shoulders filled out his cream colored sweater. He was always in sweaters. Looked fucking fuzzy and soft and…man, when I bent closer I caught the scent of snickerdoodles wafting from his skin like he was made out cookies himself.

I wondered if I licked him if I'd taste sugar.

God, and now my dick was hard.

"Becca is the only one I shop for," Baxter admitted to my surprise. "Everyone else in my family is dead or…." He smiled at me and I stared at him, my jaw dropping. That was…the most cheerful declaration of death I had ever heard.

But then again, I remember what he'd said earlier.

I'm fucking miserable.

I swallowed.

"Or?" I asked, curiously. Baxter's face shuttered and he chewed on his full lip, his freckles scrunching up as he shook his head. He had smile lines. Why was that…ugh.

"Fired? I've fired them."

"Fired them?"

"Yes." He blinked those big green eyes up at me and I shuddered, goosebumps prickling up my arms as I crossed them over my chest to attempt to keep my heart from beating right out of it.

"I feel like that's a long story," I hedged and Baxter just nodded. He chewed on his lip, obviously debating with himself over something.

Then, to my surprise, he latched onto my arm, his fingers tucking up into the crease of my elbow with a soft squeeze. I could feel how cold his hands were even through my flannel. Apparently heated coats were not completely foolproof.

Instead of shrugging him off like I would've before, I let him hold onto me, herding him through the crowd as my heart stuttered in my chest. My cheeks were a little pink, but it wasn't because he was touching me. Of course not. That would be stupid. Right?

Right.

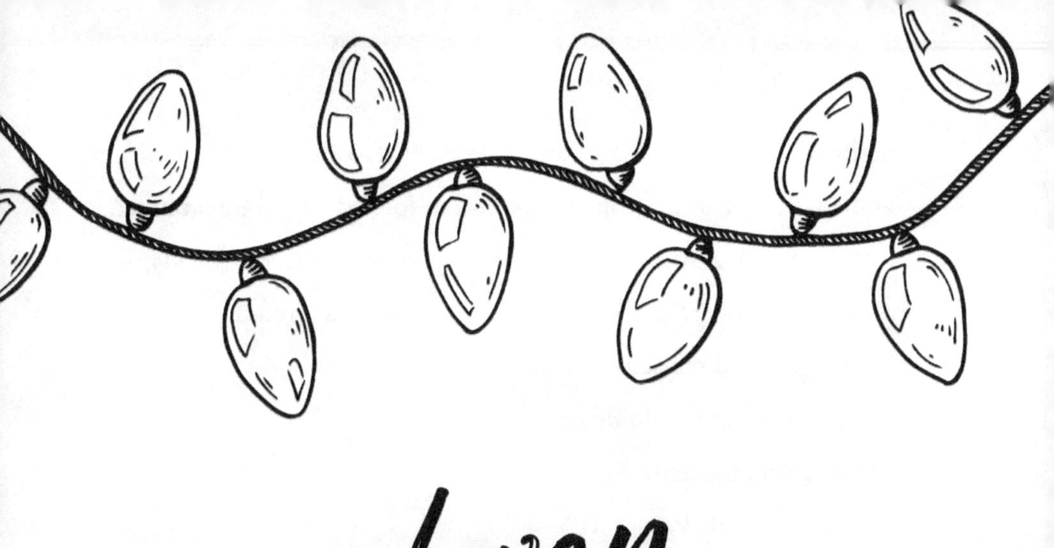

eleven

BAXTER

THE CHRISTMAS MARKET WAS POSSIBLY the most magical thing I had ever seen. Booths glittered, food wafted like poetry through the air, the scent of cinnamon and magic tickled my senses—and Paxton Montgomery was holding my fucking hand.

How we'd gone from elbow holding to hand holding was a mystery.

It had happened somewhere between a custom yarn booth and a wax melt store. So yes. Here I was. Holding hands with possibly the most attractive man I had ever seen, in the most magical place I had ever been. My heart was soaring, my ears pink as I tugged Paxton from booth to booth and loaded up on roasted nuts and chaos.

He kept steering me away from the back corner of the room but I let him.

Figured he was allowed his secrets, just like I was allowed mine.

He looked…gorgeous like that. Dressed in red flannel and wool, his wavy hair tucked into a cap that would've looked silly on anyone else, but on him just added to the whole rugged aesthetic. His hands were massive—as massive as he was. Callused. Warm. Scratchy as he tucked me inside his grip and refused to let go.

I never knew hand holding could be so sensual.

It seemed so innocent.

Tell that to my dick.

By the time we'd looped through all the booths I was feeling overstimulated and overly caffeinated. I shouldn't have whipped back those tester shots of peppermint mocha at the coffee booth as quickly as I had—but alas. Past Baxter clearly hadn't thought ahead. The ride home would be hell down the switchbacks with this much caffeine in my system.

"Where do you think the kids are?" I asked, trying to ignore the way my palm was sweaty and my dick was hard. *Platonic hand holding, platonic hand holding, platonic hand holding,* I reminded myself.

Paxton's eyes were honey as he glanced down at me, his lips twitching.

"Probably with my fucking brother." He shook his head.

"Your…"

"Brother runs the tree farm." He grimaced. "We're avoiding him."

"Oh." I blinked and cocked my head, my pulse fluttering. "Why are we avoiding him?"

"Doesn't matter." Paxton's voice grew all growly again and my toes curled inside my winter boots. Jesus. I wondered what he sounded like in bed? All…gruff and…grrrrr.

Like a big bear.

I bet he had chest hair.

Fuck, I loved chest hair.

We don't date, I reminded my dick. We're just a dad. No dating.

Right.

Oh god, who was I kidding? I would roll over and play dead if Paxton Montgomery told me to.

He was everything I'd fantasized about for the past thirty years rolled into one delicious pine-scented giant. Magic-hands Montgomery.

I wondered if his hands were as talented in bed as they were at fixing things.

Maybe he could fix my lack of recent sexual history?

Ha!

"What are you smiling about?" Paxton asked, arching an eyebrow at me as he pulled me to a stop again in front of a booth full of custom kitchenware. I was momentarily distracted by a loaf pan I saw that had little ornaments etched into the bottom. Would it work? Would the bread bottom really pop in?

What an interesting thought.

"Bread pans," I said, unthinking.

"You're smiling about *bread pans?*"

I blinked. When I glanced up at him I saw that he was chewing on his own smile. He looked…handsome like that. Softer. Like his ice was melting just a little every day. A glacier that warmed beneath the beams of summer sunlight.

I grinned at him, wide and bright, and for the first time in a long time my smile felt real.

That was of course when Becca found us again, tear-streaked and sullen. My hand remained tucked tight inside of Paxton's for a solid two seconds before he dropped it, and I was forced to remember the imprint of his heat as I tucked her into my side and tried to covertly figure out what had happened.

Apparently she'd run into some school friends.

Nathan was still with his uncle and she'd run off to…god knows what.

Clearly something had happened but she didn't want to talk about it so I didn't push, instead I just asked politely if the Montgomerys were down to cut our trip short. My belly was full anyway, the warm nuts making me feel nutty myself as we piled our way into Paxton's truck and he blasted the heater toward our kids in the back seat.

Becca sat closer to Nathan on the car ride back than she had on the way over and I couldn't help but smile secretly over at Paxton when he noticed too.

Cute, I mouthed at him.

His lips quirked upward and I shoved my hands under my thighs so I wouldn't be tempted to reach out and hold his hand again.

"Did you want to head straight home?" I asked, my heart hurting for my little girl where she stared resolutely out the window, her mascara smudged, and her sniffly nose sniffing away.

"I don't want the day to be over," she said softly. "That's fucking dumb."

I sighed and chewed on my lip in thought.

Technically we'd planned on spending at least three hours at the market but…I glanced over at Paxton.

"Do you want to come over and watch a movie?" I asked, waiting with bated breath for his answer.

I caught Becca's smile in the rearview mirror and she covertly gave me a thumbs up.

"I really like that one with the claymation Santa," she told the entire car. "When they meet the…dudes?"

"Snow Miser and Heat Miser?" Nathan perked up beside her.

I chewed on my smile, trying not to be completely fucking charmed as the two kids in the back began to rattle away about the movie. That had been one of my favorites too as a kid, and it always made me happy to see what parts of myself Becca latched onto.

She may not be physically mine but she was my daughter through and through.

"You sure we're not imposing?" Paxton hummed beside me under his breath, his voice a quiet rumble. I felt it vibrate behind my ribcage and I shuddered in response, unable to help the way my heart *thump, thumped.*

It was warm inside the truck, my legs chilled from the brief dash between the market and the vehicle. I could feel the way the denim was heating up before my frigid skin and I rubbed at my muscle with a soft shake of my head, offering him a reassuring smile.

"We want you to come," I reassured him.

He nodded, turned back to the road, and flipped the radio to the Christmas station again.

When my favorite Christmas banger, "Santa Claus is Coming to Town", came on I headbanged to the music and to my surprise caught Paxton bobbing as well.

Maybe we weren't so different after all?

Paxton made us hot chocolate again and I couldn't help but be charmed by the way he existed inside my kitchen like he belonged there. His broad frame looked out of place beside the stove, his arm muscles tensing as he stirred. There was a thoughtful, serious look on his face as he stared into the depths of the hot chocolate like it could tell him the secrets of the universe.

"Becca," I murmured softly, catching my daughter's attention where she sat curled up on the chair beside me, her knees to her chest.

"Why don't I grab some blankets? We can set up in the front room," I offered, giving her what I hoped was a reassuring smile. I was trying. Fuck. Sometimes I didn't know what to do about other people's emotions. It felt like a language I couldn't speak. Which was hilarious, considering the fact that everyone seemed to look at me and think communication came naturally.

Becca nodded, her smile warming up as she wiped away some of the mascara that had smudged under her eye. She had blisters on her fingers and I frowned, dipping my head to get a better look.

"What happened to your hands?"

She blinked.

Her eyes widened and she glanced down at her fingers, surprised to see the fact that several of her bandages had sweated off. She'd been wearing gloves earlier so I hadn't noticed.

"Oh. I was helping put up posters for the student council and the staple gun was like...super finicky."

I didn't get why she'd need to staple posters to the wall but...hell. I didn't know anything about that stuff so I didn't push.

"I've got some Neosporin, let me go grab it and—"

"No, Dad." Becca laughed, shoving at my shoulder. "Just get the blankets. I swear I'm fine."

I narrowed my eyes at her and cocked my head. "You're sure? Because it isn't a big deal for me to grab it."

"I'm seriously fine." Becca smiled at me, and this time it lit up her eyes. I relaxed, some of the tension I'd carried with me since I'd spotted her crying at the market seeping away.

"Nathan should be back soon with popcorn," Paxton grunted, and I startled. For a moment I'd forgotten he was there.

He was watching me and my skin prickled with heat as I nodded.

"Blankets, Dad." Becca shooed me away and I laughed, rolling my eyes at her in the exaggerated way she always did to me just to watch her giggle.

Act normal, I reminded myself.

Act normal.

When I returned, I had a pile of blankets in my arms so tall I had to waddle down the stairs.

Don't trip me, don't trip me, don't trip me, I prayed to the dog gods.

Pogo was bound to be around here somewhere and it would be just my luck if the chubby little creature sent me to an early grave. Somehow I made it to the bottom of the stairs with no casualties. Maybe he was out in the yard? I'd installed a doggie door for a reason.

Nathan returned and we set up shop in the living room, piling onto the two couches with our blankets in tow and our treats scattered across the coffee table. It felt suspiciously like being a part of a family. Sure, of course, Becca and I were a family on our own but…There was something about not being the only adult there that made me feel…not so alone.

Rebecca had been the last person I'd shared something like this with.

When she'd first had Becca their whole family would pile onto my couches for Christmas shenanigans. Her and her husband had fired my parents the same time I had, and well…for a while it had just been us. Until the moment it was…just me again.

I'd always had to be responsible.

Reliable.

Careful.

Don't let them see where you're cracked and broken, otherwise people might start to wonder whether or not you're capable of taking care of your own child.

Even my grief had been shoved to the back burner because suddenly it wasn't just me grieving. It was Becca too. My baby. She needed me to be strong. She needed me just as much as I needed her.

Watching the way she settled with her feet sprawled across Nathan's lap, her favorite furry pink blanket bunched around her body in a cloud of floof made me warm on the inside. It was nice to see how far she'd come. To see the fact that I'd somehow managed to raise a human who wasn't afraid of making friends. Someone who was in tune with emotions even in a way her father wasn't.

It wasn't that I didn't feel.

I did.

I just…

Felt too much sometimes.

I shuffled in my seat, reached for the remote, and hit play. With the music filling the room, the familiar jolly jingles vibrating our sound system, I probably should've felt at peace. But…ever since we'd left the market there'd been this feeling of anxiety building inside me.

I could feel the jittery buzz of it under my skin as I gathered my own blanket to my chest and wondered, not for the first time, why I grew older and yet somehow I never felt as though I grew wiser. I willed the feeling away, but it stayed.

Eating at me.

My chest was tight, my breathing a little shallow as I settled down further into the couch and tried to ignore it.

Why was I feeling this way?

Part of it was the car ride through the switchbacks. Roads as tiny and as perilous as those always made me nervous. It reminded me of things I did my best to forget but no…that wasn't what it was.

I startled when Paxton moved in my peripheral vision. He shifted around to get comfortable, his arms crossed across his chest, his brow lowered, lips twisted into a thoughtful frown. I caught him glancing over at our kids and I offered him a reassuring smile.

Becca could handle herself.

Like I'd told him earlier, I trusted her.

Maybe the fact she was growing up made me nervous but I wasn't about to deny her that growth. It was unfair to expect her to remain mine alone forever. She deserved better than that, and I wanted to be the kind of dad she came to when she was in trouble. Not authoritarian like my parents had been.

However, no matter how many self-help, or parenting 101 books I read, it never truly prepared me for the aching, clawing loneliness that choked its way up my throat as I watched the beginnings of my little girl no longer needing me.

Becca fell asleep about ten minutes into the movie.

She slumped over, her quiet snores filling the air.

I'd never told her she snored.

Maybe that was rude of me but…I didn't want her to be self conscious. I didn't want to be the kind of dad that pointed out things about her someone else might not like. God. Why was my whole life revolving around all the things I did and didn't want to do for my daughter?

Was that really all I was?

Just…

Fuck.

Who even was I anymore?

Did I even *like* Christmas movies?

Or did I just think I liked them?

Was I just doing this so I could chase a normality that didn't exist?

As I had an existential crisis, Nathan settled down, his eyes wide and bright, his gaze trained on Becca's sock-clad feet like they were simultaneously the coming of Christ and a viper about to strike him. It would've been funny if my chest wasn't full of squirmy worms and my heart wasn't about to choke me to death.

I needed to breathe.

"Gonna um." I rose quickly, my hands shaking a little. "Be right back."

I bolted up the stairs and pushed my way into my bedroom, my heart thudding unsteadily as I covered my eyes with my hands and shoved my palms into the sockets.

"*What am I doing?*" I asked myself, my voice quivering.

Fuck.

Pogo jingled as he hopped his way up the stairs and I listened to his approach, my mouth dry and palms sweaty as I lowered my hands and watched him nose his way through the crack in the door and waddle his way over to me. He blinked big brown eyes in my direction, assessing me as his little nubby tail wagged.

Corgis.

Jesus, he was cute.

"I should fire myself," I told him quietly as I reached down to scratch between his ears. It was funny actually that I'd bought him to get closer to Becca and here I was—bonding with him more than she was.

His big bat ears flattened as his tongue lolled and he smiled at me.

"Not a Santa fan?" Paxton asked, his voice rumbling from the open doorway. I startled, my fingers freezing in Pogo's thick fur as I glanced up at him, guilt probably etched across my face.

"No." I blinked. "I mean, yes. I like Santa."

Paxton cocked his head, his brow lowered.

Having him just…look at me felt like too much right now.

The jittery feelings were back and I shoved my shaking hands against my thighs to soothe myself. I watched the way he watched me, observing, contemplating. He stared at my hands, my tense shoulders, the quiver of my lip.

I couldn't move.

I couldn't stop shaking.

"My brother Ben has anxiety," Paxton said softly. "He used to go to this therapist for it when we were kids. Taught him a bunch of coping mechanisms. Think he still has one actually."

"I don't have anxiety." The words left my lips before I could take them back. But…the lie was already there, so I just smiled, wobbling all over.

Liar, liar, liar.

My smile seemed to set him off.

"Cut the shit, Baker." Paxton's whole body tensed up, his eyes growing cold as ice as he glared down at me. "You don't have to tell me anything. You don't owe that to me. But you at least owe yourself the truth." He sneered. "You know, if all you do is smile, the smiles stop meaning shit."

I swallowed.

Pogo, the traitor, didn't attack—or bark, or anything.

He just flopped over onto his back and wiggled his big white belly at me.

I swallowed again.

Even the familiar interior of my bedroom didn't soothe my nerves as I rose to my full height, crossed the minimal distance between our bodies and pushed right into Paxton's space.

I wanted to fight him.

I wanted to—

To—

Cry.

I wanted to cry.

The fight left me with a *whoosh* of breath. My forehead thumped against his chest in defeat, the scent of pine and wood shavings filling my nose as the weight on my shoulders grew heavy enough all I could do was wilt. I curled my fingers tight where they hung limply at my sides, the steady *thump, thump* of Paxton's heart beating against my cheek.

My eyes burned.

It hurt.

The tension in my forehead, the headache behind my temples, the way my heart squeezed tighter, tighter, *tighter.*

"Sometimes I can't remember what it felt like to be a real person." I whispered, my words wobbling in the space between us. My dam had cracked. Maybe this isn't what Paxton had meant when he said to cut the shit but…

His heartbeat was steady.

His scent was a balm on my raw nerves.

"I'm too old to feel this uncertain." My voice wobbled.

Tears blurred my vision and I blinked them away, trying to force down the tidal wave I knew was about to come. I didn't know if he would shove me away. I didn't know why he would let me stay. All I knew was that in that moment Paxton Montgomery made me feel…like Baxter again.

Not a business owner.

Not Dad.

Just…me.

"You're never too old to learn something new," Paxton said, his voice a quiet rumble against my forehead. I chased the vibration, pressing my face against the fuzz of his shirt, my tears flowing freely now as a hiccuping sob left my chest.

"I'm sorry," I choked.

"No." Paxton said firmly, at the same moment I felt his massive palm cradle the back of my head. "You're not sorry." *What?* "You're Baxter."

It took a second for the dad joke to register.

My laughter bubbled up out of nowhere, and that simple joke broke open the dam inside me the rest of the way. My tears were hot where they spilled down my cheeks onto the fabric of his shirt as I pushed my way tighter against Paxton's chest, my fingers tangling around the hem to pull him close.

He was warm.

Solid.

Strong.

Maybe Becca had been onto something with this whole friend thing.

It wasn't half bad.

Paxton let me cry for a long time.

So long my tears ran dry and my sobs quieted to sniffles.

By the time I finally finished, that tight, overwhelmed feeling inside me had ebbed away and I was now achingly familiar with the feeling of Paxton's fingers carding through my hair. I hadn't realized how big he truly was till we were standing pressed up together like this. I wasn't a small man, but I wasn't large either. He made me feel…well, like maybe it was okay to not be the largest presence in the room.

After I'd cleaned up in the bathroom, Paxton led me downstairs again. Pogo followed after us loyally, his thumping little stubby legs plodding along diligently. Without speaking, Paxton heated up another cup of cocoa for me and I sipped at it till my stomach no longer felt quite so empty.

When we returned to the living room Nathan was still staring at Becca's feet, his hands in the air like he was terrified of touching her despite the fact she was actively touching him.

When Paxton sat down I sat right beside him.

I shared my favorite blanket with him, didn't give him the choice really, as I bundled us up inside it and ignored the curious look Nathan threw our way. Today had been…well, today hadn't been the worst day ever.

Despite the fact I'd cried for probably the first time in ten years.

Onto a hot guy's shirt.

Fuck me.

But still.

I dozed off with my face pressed to solid muscle, listening to the steady beat of a kind man's heart. One thing was certain. Paxton wasn't who I thought he was. But, that wasn't such a bad thing, actually.

He was soft.

Kind.

Steady as the tide.

Solid as a mountain.

I…liked that.

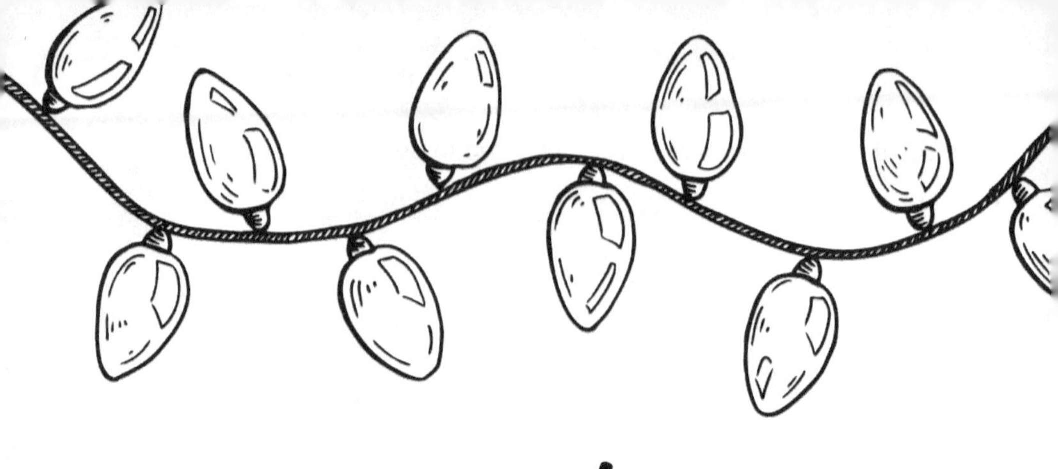

twelve

PAXTON

MAYBE IT SHOULDN'T HAVE SURPRISED me that Baxter showed up to my house the next day with a thank-you basket and a…card?

But it did.

I stared at the paper monstrosity, oddly charmed by the fat rabbit on the front with big green eyes and the caption, *Have a hoppy day!*

Nathan stared at me across the dinner table, his head cocked curiously to the side.

"He left already?" I confirmed, only to be answered by a bob and flop of chestnut brown hair. Nathan's eyes were twinkling, smug little shit. "What?" I asked, though I actually didn't want to know.

"Nothing." He blinked.

"*What?*" I growled, brow lowered. Nathan just shrugged, his shoulders climbing up till they brushed his ears before he hopped to his gangly boy-feet, plopped his dirty bowl in the sink, and scurried away.

When he was halfway down the hallway he peeked over his shoulder and called back.

"I think he likes you."

"Likes me, my ass." I grunted back, flipping him off with an eye roll before I turned back to my…basket.

Cookies.

Santa themed?

Two loaves of pumpkin chocolate chip bread, my favorite.

Six chocolate muffins.

If I hid all of it I could bring it with me to work this week. Ration out the food with my lunch so I'd have something to eat other than Hungry Man TV dinners and Costco chicken cups. I really needed to learn how to cook, but my four rotated meals were enough. Meatballs. Chicken marinara. BBQ pizza (with store bought dough). And spaghetti.

We ate well enough.

The baked goods were…nice though. A nice change of pace.

I opened the note next, not sure what to expect when I did. It felt like disabling a bomb as I unfolded its edges and grimaced with one eye shut as I glanced down at the page.

What I saw there though was…

Well.

Hell.

My cheeks warmed, and my heart did a weird squirmy thing in my chest that I hadn't felt in—god knows how many years. I swallowed.

I shut the card.

Because I didn't want my nosy brat finding it, I brought the basket and the card up to my room to hide. He never went through the shit in my room because I'd told him not to, so I wasn't worried about him finding it.

Every time I looked at the card it made me feel…fuck.

I hid it in my underwear drawer so I wouldn't have to look at it anymore. When even that didn't get it off my mind, I buried it in socks until it was nothing but a memory and I managed to force myself through my usual morning routine.

I couldn't remember the last time someone had said something so sweet to me. My cheeks were hot as I got ready for the day and headed down to my truck to wait for Nathan. Baxter must've been up since ass o'clock if he'd managed to not only bake me the food but deliver it as well, all before school even started.

I swallowed, shaking off the heat in my cheeks as Nathan slipped into the passenger seat beside me with a grin and a waggle of his long awkward fingers.

"You get your C to a B in Algebra?" I asked, switching the heater on as I pulled out of the driveway and tried not to look like…well, like a little kid caught doing something he shouldn't.

Why did the note…why was it affecting me so much?

A simple thank you shouldn't mean so much to me.

But it did.

My cheeks heated again.

"Oh yeah, I've got a solid B plus now." Nathan piped up, rifling around in his backpack, his brow furrowed. I raised a hand to stop him.

"You don't gotta show me, kid. I believe you."

He relaxed, flashing me a happy little grin as he settled down in his seat and rezipped the bag.

When I dropped him off I tried to ignore the fact that I scanned the parking lot for two familiar blonde heads. I didn't see them though, so I just gave Nathan my usual smile and fist bump and watched him wander his way toward the front entrance, his skateboard tucked under his arm.

He'd ride it home like he always did when the roads were clear.

Sometimes in the snow too, stubborn little shit.

I wondered if he'd watch Baxter again after the final bell.

If he'd see him sitting alone in his car, just waiting for his daughter to come out so he could boot up again.

Sweet.

Sad.

Lonely.

I couldn't help but remember the way he'd clung to me the night before. He'd been all sleepy limbs and heavy lashes as I'd tucked him into my arms and carried him up the stairs to bed. I could feel the way his cheek rubbed against my chest, the steady warm puff of his breath heating my overworked heart.

When I'd laid him down he reached up for me, his fingers tangling in my flannel, his hair like spun gold, gossamer and downy soft in a cascade atop his pillow.

I'd had to pry his fingers off, though I'd been gentle.

He'd whimpered and I'd stared at his freckles for a second too long before I forced myself to leave. If I hadn't…well, I wasn't sure what I would've done.

But it certainly wouldn't have been something the me from a month ago would've approved of.

Baxter with his legs sprawled wide, his broad shoulders relaxed, pink lips parted in a sad little whine was just…

No.

I'd escaped down the stairs, my heart in my throat only to discover Nathan staring down at Becca's feet—still—his eyes wide and lost with alarm.

"What do I do?" He'd whispered, terrified of making the wrong move.

I wanted to tell him to stay put.

Let her sleep.

But that was silly. It was a school night. We needed to go home.

The rational thought was easy enough to gather but harder to follow as I forced myself to gently shake the little blonde's shoulder. When she woke she smiled at me, all traces of her earlier sadness gone and I cocked my head toward the stairs, trying not to think about how delicious the way her father's thighs had looked when they lay parted and vulnerable atop the comforter.

"Bed time." I'd grunted, and up she got obediently, waving to us both with a sleepy yawn before she'd stumbled her way up the steps swathed in her ridiculously massive furry blanket.

I'd watched her bun wobble, my ears pink as I turned back to my son.

"Home," I'd said. Though our swift departure didn't stop me from locking up on our way out.

And it didn't stop me from thinking about how warm Baxter had been, bundled up in my arms. Not heavy, but not light either. Solid. Real.

So sweet.

So *fucking* sweet.

Sweet as the things he baked.

Sweeter even.

His hair was honey, his skin was spun sugar, and I couldn't help but crave him in a way that was so terrifying I had no idea what to do with it.

I shook my head to clear it, turned the Christmas station on, and blasted thoughts of Baxter Baker right out of my head with a jolly rendition of "Jingle Bells".

Everything went well. Normal. Fine. Good. Whatever. Work was busy but in a good way. Nothing particularly frustrating happened as I replaced a water heater and inspected Trent's basement. I typically saved family work for the weekends because I refused to take payment for it but…

We were all a little concerned about Trent's house.

I'd warned him again and again that the foundation was shit when he'd bought it. I knew the construction company that built his subdivision and they usually skipped out on things that weren't visible to the naked eye but were incredibly important.

Like tarring the fucking foundation to waterproof it.

Did he listen to me?

No.

So I checked it for the hundredth time, warned him to be ready for shit to hit the fan, and headed home for the night.

Trent usually took longer than other customers. Because he was my little brother—and chatty—I usually spent a good hour catching up with him before I managed to finish what I'd come over to do in the first place.

Chatting exhausted me.

Even with family.

It was for that reason that I was too tired to notice the familiar car in the driveway as I pushed my way through the front door, kicked off my muddy work boots, and grunted my hello into the abyss.

"Dad?" Nathan pounded his way in from the kitchen. Fucking elephant feet. His brow was furrowed, his eyes wide and worried.

Immediately it struck me that something was wrong.

"What?" My voice was a low growl, my shoulders rising, muscles flexing as I prepared myself for battle.

"Um." Nathan peeked over his shoulder, back toward the kitchen, then shuffled in his hole ridden socks. I'd bought him a new pack last week, but he still stubbornly wore the other ones. Something about the difference between Marvel and DC socks? I didn't fucking know.

I'd bought him the superhero ones.

That's all that mattered.

"What?" I repeated, lower this time. He was freaking me out.

"So, Mr. Baker is here?" Nathan blinked, shuffling awkwardly. "I fed him dinner but he said he wanted to see you."

Weird.

He'd been here earlier today too, why hadn't he wanted to see me then?

Maybe he was embarrassed.

Hell, I was.

I'd fucking carried him to bed. Tucked him in practically. Held him as he cried. Imagined again and again what it would feel like to slip my way between the sprawl of his thighs and taste the salty, sweet nectar from the tip of his cock.

With my cheeks hot I just nodded.

"Tell him I'll be down in a minute."

Nathan nodded, smiling at me before he headed back into the kitchen to entertain our guest.

I cleaned up in the bathroom adjoining my bedroom, trying to scrub the heat from my cheeks with cool water. When that didn't work I hopped into the shower for a quick rinse, suddenly self-conscious of how sweaty I got while working.

When I was clean, I smudged a hand through the fog on the mirror, glared at myself, and then proceeded to moisturize my skin and beard liberally till I smelled like pine trees and felt a little less…like a mess.

Nathan was in the kitchen with Baxter when I arrived.

They were sharing cookies.

More cookies.

Jesus. It was like the man fucking popped them out like Yoshi eggs.

"I gotta head up to bed," Nathan hummed with a smile, glancing over at me, *help* clearly written in his eyes. I had no idea why he was being so weird all of a sudden. He liked Baxter. He'd told me that.

So why was he—

Oh.

Baxter turned to look at me, a soft smile on his lips. Except the smile was faker than fake and I could clearly see how pink his cheeks were and the streaks of leftover tears that clung to them. His dark brown lashes were spiky and wet, his green eyes crisp as an autumn morning and I swallowed. Hard.

"Don't forget to do your homework." I grunted, my heart thudding unsteadily.

"I won't!" Nathan abandoned me as quickly as he could, though he made sure to give me an adorable floppy hug on his way by.

"I'll be home early tomorrow," I told him. I always liked to let him know my schedule ahead of time when I could. I didn't like coming home late like this. I didn't make a habit of it. That was probably why it didn't bother him the way I knew it did when he was spending time with his mom and she didn't fucking come home.

Not that he'd seen her in months.

It was hilarious actually, in a shitty way, how serious and career-oriented she'd become after marrying her newest husband. She was a totally different person than the one I'd been with. Some things were better. The stability for one.

I remember how wild she'd been back then, though I hadn't known at the time just how wild. Hadn't known till she was pregnant and I found out she'd been fucking stealing from our bank account and using the money to shoot up until the day Nathan was conceived.

At least she'd stopped then.

But the trust was already lost.

I shook my head to clear it for what felt like the hundredth time that day as I turned back to Baxter with a sigh. My stomach growled and I watched the way his eyes flitted over me. *Flutter, flutter, flutter.* His attention was butterfly wings.

"You still hungry?" I grunted. I didn't have the patience for the microwave and honest to god, I felt hungry enough to eat six TV dinners. Didn't want to cook, so pizza it was.

It made great leftovers anyway.

I pulled my phone out, hit the speed dial for my favorite pizza place, and arched an eyebrow at where Baxter still sat, awkward and tense at my dining room table. It was weird seeing him here in my personal space.

Good, weird.

Weird still.

I could get used to it though.

"Toppings?" I asked, not giving him time to overthink.

"For…?"

"Pizza."

He blinked. Those lovely green eyes swam, a stray tear slipping down his cheek as he reached up and dashed it away. He had nice hands. Slender. Capable. Strong. Calluses from his work—his knuckles thicker than the pads of his fingers. Pretty.

"I like anything vegetable."

I ordered the pizza half and half. My side had every meat they carried and Baxter's had every vegetable. I knew Nathan would eat whatever so I didn't worry as I rattled off my credit card number by memory and slipped my phone into my back pocket.

There was a weird jittery feeling building up in my chest.

Anxiety? Excitement?

Both.

I opened the fridge to give myself something to do as I waited for Baxter to explain why he was here. Why he was crying. It didn't bother me. The tears. I preferred honest emotion over everything else and the way he was opening up to me made me feel…

It just made me feel.

"Beer?" I grunted.

"Sure, thank you."

Beers secured, pizza ordered, I had nothing to do but wait. Man I hated talking. Was I supposed to ask him what was wrong? Somehow it felt too rude to demand why he was here of all places.

I didn't want to be rude to him, not anymore.

When I sat down, the chair creaked beneath my weight, and I crossed my ankles, leaning back with a quiet grunt. I popped my back, stretched my neck, and flipped the cap off my beer by whacking it on the table.

Baxter's bottle sat untouched in front of him, the condensation dripping slowly, slowly down.

I waited.

There was another snow flurry outside and I watched the fat flakes flutter their way through the inky black of the long winter night till they settled atop my porch.

"Becca and I fought," Baxter said after what felt like an eon.

Normally I didn't mind the silence but this was a different situation.

"Yeah?" I grunted, taking a sip of my beer to give myself something to do. I couldn't look at him.

If I looked at him again I was sure I would do something stupid, like drag him into my lap, tear his sweater in half, and torture his sweet little nipples till he had something real to cry about.

My cock perked up and I shifted till the lip of the table would hide it from view. God. What was wrong with me?

"She lied to me," Baxter said softly. His words caught my attention and I stiffened a little. Of course I was concerned for him, concerned as to why he was so upset. Everyone fought. Parents. Couples. Siblings. Friends. It wasn't the end of the world. But trust? Once broken, it could never be unbroken.

Baxter didn't need someone to preach at him, even I could see that. His sweet eyes begged for someone to listen. The bruised hollows beneath them crying out for kisses I knew I didn't have the right to give him.

"She isn't on the cheer team this year," Baxter told me softly. "I don't know…what she's been doing," he choked out. "All this time. Every time she said she was at practice I just—I just believed her?"

"Do you think she's doing something bad?" Now I felt like shit, because it didn't take a genius to figure out where Becca had been in her spare time. Helping me. Fixing her dad's bakery.

Should I tell him?

No.

And spoil it all?

He could wait.

Right?

Fuck, I didn't know what the best thing to do would be in this situation. I wasn't used to…looking out for someone's interests that weren't my own—or Nathan's.

This was new.

"I don't think Becca is the kind of girl to get into trouble," Baxter said softly, chewing on his lip. He reached for his beer but he didn't open it; instead he just picked at the label. Pick, pick, pick. Pieces of paper littered the table beneath his hands, his eyes lost as the murky water at the center of a hurricane.

"Then what's the problem?"

"The problem is that she lied."

"Okay." I grunted, cocking my head to the side as I took another sip of my beer and contemplated what to say. Navigating this conversation was like traveling across a minefield. One misstep and bam. It could blow up right in my face. "You trust her, don't you?"

"Well, yes." Baxter nodded, then paused. "I…did, at least."

"Okay." I set my beer down.

Pick, pick, pick.

Paper fluttered to the table. He was halfway through the label. I watched his hands shake, his lovely broad shoulders tucked in tight. His chest shuddered with a sharp inhalation, his cream colored sweater swelling with the breath.

"It seems to me you have two choices."

"Right." Baxter looked at me—finally. His eyes were wet, his brow furrowed. The freckles on his nose were less noticeable in this light but I counted them nonetheless. One, two, three, four—ten, twelve, fifteen.

Constellations.

"You can either choose to trust her, or choose not to."

He blinked.

"Chances are if she's as good of a kid as you say she is, she's got her reasons for not telling you."

"Right."

"If you trust that she's not getting into trouble then you should trust that she's old enough to make her own decisions."

"But I'm supposed to watch out for her, it's my job," Baxter blurted, his eyes a little wild. His wavy hair was a mess like he'd run his fingers through it and I squeezed my hands tight atop my thighs to stop myself from reaching over and smoothing it down.

"Sure, but it's also your job to raise a functioning human." I nodded. "How is she supposed to grow into a proper adult if she can't be trusted to make her own decisions?"

Baxter blinked.

I wondered if his wet lashes felt cold where they brushed his cheeks.

I wanted to lick up his tears.

Weird.

Fucking weird, Paxton.

"Your job as a dad is to set an example for the rest of the world. She learns from you how she should be treated. If you're distrustful. If you're distant. If you're controlling—that's what she's going to expect from everyone else. What will happen one day when she moves away?"

"What do you mean?"

"She'll date. Probably. Make friends. All that shit. And she's going to decide who is worth her time based on the example you set."

"So you're saying that I need to blindly trust her, because she needs to know what to expect from other people?" Baxter's brow furrowed.

"It would be different if you hadn't raised such a good kid." Weirdly enough, I meant what I was saying. Becca was sweet. I'd been spending a lot of time with her lately as we fixed up the Bakery and her serious nature, her kindness, and her drive were obvious in everything she did.

She was quiet.

Well-mannered.

Resourceful.

She always meant well.

Even I could see that and I barely knew her.

"You raised a good kid, Baxter." I picked up my beer again, my cheeks hot as I shuffled in my seat. Baxter's eyes got caught on my chest and I flexed it, curious to see his reaction. It was only because I was so closely observing him that I got a front row seat to the absolutely gorgeous red flush that spread across his splotchy cheeks.

I flexed again.

He inhaled sharply.

Muscles, huh?

Interesting.

I took a sip of my beer, suddenly parched.

"You're really smart," Baxter said softly, his gaze snapping from my chest to my eyes again. "I…guess when you put it like that it makes sense."

"'Course it does."

"What if…what if something is happening? Something bad? And I'm just too stupid to see it?"

"You're not stupid, B." I grunted, shocked as the nickname slipped from my lips. B? What the fuck. I was not a nickname kind of person. Hell. I'd never even given Nathan one. Nathan was just…Nathan. "You've got some extra…"

"Anxiety?" he offered, cringing a little.

Pick, pick, pick.

His label was nearly gone.

I reached over and grasped his fingers, giving them a tight squeeze. My palm entirely enveloped his and that same squirmy feeling I'd felt earlier came back full force. My chest was tight as I pulled back, ignoring how badly I wanted to smooth my fingers over the delicate lines decorating his wrist, or play with the silvery golden hair that peeped out of the edge of his sweater sleeve.

I licked my lips.

"I think…" Baxter shook his head, his voice quaking. "I think I have a problem?"

"Yeah?" My heart thudded.

"I think that…" Baxter chewed on his lip and I was half tempted to reach across the table again and rescue it. If he gave it the same treatment he'd given the beer bottle, hell—I'd have to. "I think I have some problems. Multiple. With anxiety. With…emotions."

"We all have problems, B." Fuck. Again.

At least I hadn't slipped up and called him baby.

The thought made my insides turn molten.

My cheeks grew hot.

"I know, but…" He shook his head again, hair flopping. "I think I have a lot of trauma I haven't dealt with since my sister's death." His poor lip got caught by his teeth again and I licked my own in sympathy. "Ever since she died—ever since I got Becca, it's like…I've been just waiting for the other shoe to drop."

I nodded.

Baxter reached for the label on his beer again and I didn't stop him this time.

I let him cope, aware now that that was what he was doing.

There was a time for soothing and there was a time for listening.

This was the latter.

"Rebecca—Becca's mom—was my entire family. The one that doesn't hate me, at least. She was…proud of me."

Oh.

Oh.

My heart gave a lurch in my chest. So that's what he'd meant at the market when he'd said he fired his family. Maybe they…hadn't loved him the way he was so clearly meant to be loved. The way he *deserved* to be loved.

He'd taken himself out of a bad situation.

That was so fucking brave.

It was one thing to stand up to a bully but when that bully was your own family? Well.

I realized I'd judged him too harshly. He was braver than I'd given him credit for. So much braver. My family had always accepted me, flaws and all. They'd never wanted to change me, even at my surliest, most secretive, most angry.

"It must've been hard," I said softly. "Becoming a dad."

"I wasn't ready." Baxter laughed, though the sound was brittle and bitter. "I wasn't ready, but it was the best thing that ever happened to me. I needed Becca. She…she's *everything* to me."

I nodded, my heart hurting as I thought of my own little boy. The way he'd cried the first time I held him. The way I'd smoothed my hand over the fuzz all over the top of his head. The way his skin had been pink, his little fingers chubby and strong as they'd gripped my pinky tight.

He'd claimed me then.

As I'd searched his face I'd found religion in the way people spent years hunting chapels for.

So I could understand better than anyone what Baxter meant when he said his next words.

"When life became hell, Becca was my angel. She still is." He swallowed and I watched his throat bob. The light flickered and I made a mental note to check the bulb after he left. "I'm always terrified I'm going to fuck it all up, you know? I'm not stable. I'm not the person she thinks I am. I'm just…fuck. I'm forty-two and I still feel like the same scared kid I was just out of culinary school trying to figure out how the fuck to survive.

I feel like I'm flying blind all the time. I try, but…how can I know what I'm doing is right?"

"Baxter." I interrupted him, reaching out again, my fingers wrapping around his wrist. The bone was fragile, waifish despite the taper of his frame. Broad shoulders. Tiny wrists. Long fingers. Perfect. "There's no parent on this goddamn Earth that knows what they're doing."

His eyes were wet, his free hand shifting till he could curl it on top of mine. It was a little sweaty, warm, and clammy too. I covered it with my own till our hands were sandwiched together. The touch was sweeter than the last time we'd held hands like this at the Christmas market. "You're a good fucking dad, okay? The fact you're here right now, instead of blowing up at her is testament enough to that."

"I'd never blow up at her," Baxter said softly. "I just…"

"You just?"

"Shut down?" He bit his lip again, searching my gaze for reassurance. Clearly he found it because I watched the tension seep from his shoulders bit by bit, trickling away as he scooted closer to me, chasing connection with a twist of his soft bitten-pink lips.

"Where is Becca now?" I asked, because I knew he needed to tell me.

"She went to her friend's house." He blinked. "I…wouldn't have left her if she hadn't left me first."

"I know, B." My thumb stroked his knuckles and I soothed the silky smooth skin. "She's safe though?"

"Yes." He nodded.

"And you're safe," I reminded him. I watched the way his breath fluttered, his eyes glancing guiltily to the side because deep down he didn't know whether or not what I was telling him was true. Anxiety could be a bitch that way. I was suddenly overwhelmingly glad that he'd come to me with this—where I could help him. Where I could make sure he was safe.

Somehow I doubted anyone was looking out for Baxter the way he looked out for his kid.

"I thought about what you said? About your brother. And how he had a therapist." Baxter swallowed. "I think…"

"You think?" I urged when he trailed off and didn't continue.

"I think I want to do that." Baxter glanced up at me again, his eyes wide and sweet as he searched mine for approval. I swallowed the tightness in my throat. "I think I deserve…better than how I've been treating myself." He bit his lip. "I think that I deserve a chance at getting better."

"Mental health isn't that way, sweetheart." The term of endearment slipped from my lips before I could catch it. I hurried on, embarrassed, hoping to cover it up. "Therapists aren't there to 'fix you' they're not… magicians."

"I know…" Baxter said softly.

"They teach you how to cope. They can help you get the tools you need. The work comes from you. It's something you have to choose to do every single day."

"Forever?"

"Forever." Hell. Ben still went to a therapist regularly and he was thirty-nine now. It was an uphill battle. But seeking help had made all the difference for him. It had taught him how to exist inside himself, how to not be ashamed of how his brain worked. Even the medication he was on helped loads with his coping.

"I want to put in the work," Baxter said softly, though his voice swelled with conviction when he added. "I want to help myself. I…deserve that."

"That's good." I nodded, offering him a smile that felt far too raw—far too real. I'd never felt this pull toward someone else like this. My heart fluttered unsteadily. "That's real good. I'm proud of you."

Baxter nodded. He squeezed my hand. His lips quirked up and his eyes lit up like Christmas lights. "I'm glad I came to you," he said softly. "Thank you, Paxton."

Oh Jesus.

Those simple words meant more to me than I could ever fucking explain.

My heart beat right out of my chest when I nodded. "I'm proud of you." The repeated words were a quiet croak, answered by Baxter's sunny grin.

It wasn't fake this time.

It was sunbeams, summer days, and new beginnings.

The doorbell rang and I answered it, unable to stop the flutter of my pulse or the way my stomach flipped as I remembered the way his nose scrunched when he grinned. I tipped the delivery man in a daze, returning to the kitchen with my heart in my throat.

Fuck.

I was fucked.

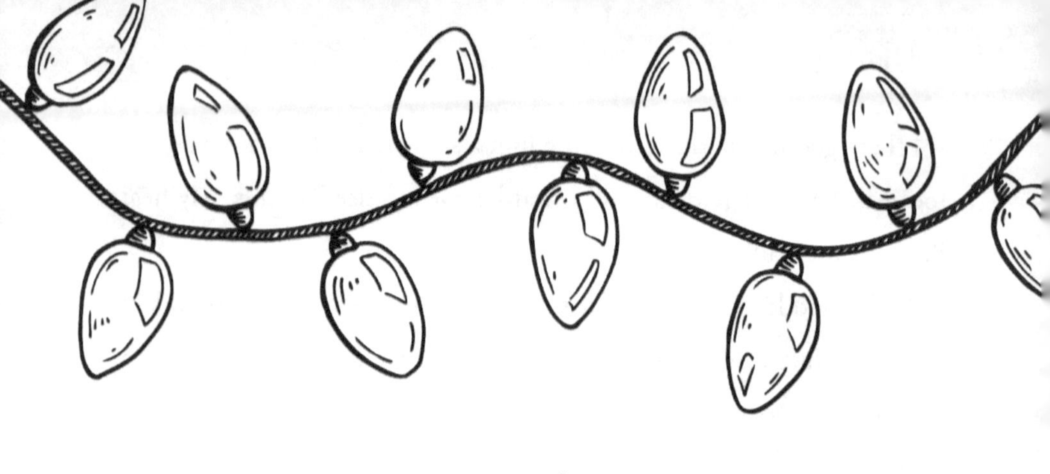

thirteen

BAXTER

BECCA AND I WERE FINE again. I didn't push her to tell me the truth like I wanted to. Instead I listened to Paxton's advice and chose to trust her. Though I did make sure she knew she could talk to me—that I was here for whatever she needed.

We'd hugged it out, watched a cheesy Hallmark movie that made me grin, and I'd sent her up to bed with my heart feeling lighter than it had for a long, long time.

I called up a therapist the next day and made my first appointment for the following week. To say I was nervous would be the understatement of the century. But…like I'd told Paxton, I knew I deserved better than the way I'd been treating myself.

I wasn't just "Dad" even though I'd been trying to convince myself for years that's all I was.

Beneath that, beneath the layer of responsibility, love, and structure—I was just a scared man who had been teetering at the edge of a precipice for years just waiting to fall.

The rest of the week was uneventful.

I stressed about the bakery, like I always did. Freaking out about it was planned for ten minutes a day in my schedule. Wake up at 4:30 a.m., go for my morning run with Pogo, make breakfast, pack Becca's lunch, stress about the bakery, then get started on my orders for the day.

I was trying not to focus too much on it though, even though as December crept up, it became more and more clear that I wasn't going to be able to host my annual Holiday Hullabaloo.

I was trying not to be depressed about it.

Trying.

But…it was hard.

I looked forward to it every year. I looked forward to giving back, to feeling like I was doing something good for others. I loved their smiles. I loved the way the kids snuck extra muffins and didn't think I saw. I loved the laughter as my shop was full of life and for that single night it felt like I had a family again.

Not this year though.

The oven beeped and I pulled my loaf pans out, sighing as I moved them to cool and scrubbed my hand over my sweaty brow.

Becca made her way into the kitchen with a yawn.

She was dressed impeccably as always as she gave me a jovial salute and snatched the plate of pancakes I'd left out for her. The microwave whirred in the background as I stared blankly at the oven and tried to get my brain to reboot.

Last night had been…a lot.

Good.

But a lot.

"Dad?" The microwave beeped and I turned around to face my daughter as she grabbed her food and flopped down at the table. She dug in with a happy hum and I arched a brow at her, waiting for her to continue her thought.

"Yes?"

She blinked at me, brow furrowed in confusion. "What?"

"You're the one that called my name."

"Oh." Becca blinked again, then her confused expression cleared. "Right! Sorry. Forgot. I was going to tell you that tomorrow is Nathan's birthday."

I didn't bother asking why she knew this.

Instead, plans began to hatch in quick succession inside my mind.

We'd need a birthday cake.

Ice cream.

Oh fuck.

Food?

Definitely food. No more pizza for me. Man, last night had been delicious but also incredibly strenuous for my insides. As I aged, dairy got harder and harder to handle in large amounts.

"Did he invite us over?" I asked, already seventy miles ahead of the conversation.

"No, but I figured we could drop something off?"

I cocked my head at her, lips twitching up. "Do you…liiiiike him?"

"What? No!" Becca flushed and jabbed her fork at me. "He's my friend."

I nodded, though my smile only grew more shit-eating.

"Stop looking at me like that." Becca growled, shoving a fork full of pancakes into her mouth before sniffing prissily. "He's my friend—and you always make cakes for my friends so I just figured I'd tell you."

"Riiight." I waggled my eyebrows at her but ultimately decided she'd been teased enough for one day. "I'm going to bake something extra special." I couldn't help but remember how seriously Nathan had decorated his cookies just a few weeks ago. The kid was adorable. His attention to detail was insane; if there was anyone that would appreciate the intricacy of the design I had planned it would be him. "What does he like?" I asked, curious.

"Um…like flavors?"

"Yes."

"I don't know."

"What about like…video games? Does he like those?"

Becca's whole face scrunched up like she was sucking on a lemon as she thought. She clearly drew a blank though because she shrugged. "Sorry, Dad. I'm not sure."

Hmm.

This made it a bit trickier.

He liked sledding.

Hot chocolate.

I often saw him at school too while I was waiting for Becca. Maybe he had a club he attended? An activity? Photography or…

Oh.

Oh!

"Skateboarding!" I perked right up with a grin. I'd seen him zooming around on his skateboard more times than I could count. Why hadn't I remembered?! It was perfect.

A skateboard cake.

"Oh my god, Dad, that's so brilliant!" Becca grinned at me, her soufflé bun wobbling. "Hell yes. Okay. Skateboarding! He'll love that."

"I can make the cake shaped like a skateboard and—"

"Oh my god, can you like…put flames on it?"

"Flames?"

"Yeah!"

We threw ideas back and forth for another twenty minutes before I took her to school. By the time I headed home from running through my deliveries I was feeling lighter than I had in years. A birthday. How fun!

Because I was feeling frisky, I stopped by one of the local clothing boutiques on my way home. As much fun as cakes were, I felt like Nathan was…more important than most of Becca's other friends. As stupid as that sounded. It was a gut feeling—something I couldn't explain but felt right.

I wandered the shelves searching, searching, searching until I found it.

A beanie.

With flames.

Perfect!

Barbara at the front grinned at me as she rang up my order and I fidgeted with the button on the inside of my heated coat. My eyes kept catching on one of the scarves they had proudly displayed up front. It looked thick. Warm. Made of fleece and what looked like wool but was probably sherpa.

With a red checkered pattern and tasteful black tassels at the end I couldn't help but…

Yes.

I bought it, cheeks pink as I watched Barbara package up my order with a grin.

"Have a nice day, Mr. Baker!" she called and I smiled and waved back at her before skipping my merry way home.

Was it weird to buy Paxton a thank-you gift?

No, right?

Hopefully.

Oh, well.

It was done.

There was no use crying over spilled milk.

fourteen

PAXTON

"SHE'S SUCH A FUCKING BITCH, Trent." I hissed under my breath, my phone clutched tightly to my ear as I listened to the squeaky pipe that signaled Nathan was still showering. "He's turning eighteen and she couldn't be bothered to show up for five fucking minutes."

"Paxton—"

"Look, I know I shouldn't be surprised." I was incensed. "It's not that I am. I just… Fuck. You didn't see the look on his face when she answered the phone and said she wasn't coming. Didn't even call him. He had to call *her*!"

"Paxton, bud. We all know how much of a raging dickbag Tracy is."

"Fuck."

"It's not your fault."

"It is though." My heart hurt. "Why did I… God."

"You didn't know she'd be like this. Stop beating yourself up about it. Besides, If Trace hadn't been the one you knocked up, who knows what little gremlin child would've popped out. Be grateful you have Nathan. Kid's a solid dude. He'll pull through."

I knew he was right, but it still…

The frustration of watching my little boy be tossed aside like yesterday's trash was just… Fuck. Fuck. Fuck. There were so many conflicting emotions inside me. Anger that she hadn't shown up for him. Fear that the emotional fall out would hurt him irreparably. Guilt for giving him a mom that didn't give a shit. Guilt for being glad—in a small way—that I didn't have to see her.

Maybe I was a shitty dad.

As much as I had preached to Baxter before I didn't know what the fuck I was doing either. We were both blind here. But like I'd told him, that was just a part of being a parent. Growing up meant realizing the adults you idolized were just as freaked the fuck out as you were; they just knew how to hide it better.

Which was why when Nathan came down the stairs again, freshly showered and bright eyed, I decided to pretend like nothing was amiss so he could have the birthday he deserved.

"What do you want for dinner? Whatever you want." I grunted, folding my arms over my chest.

I'd dressed up a bit today.

It was his birthday after all.

It was tradition.

He got to decide whether or not we ate out or stayed in—most years he chose eating out. It wasn't something we did often. I didn't like people and Nathan didn't like making me uncomfortable.

For his birthday though—hell. I'd fucking hike to Mordor if it was what he wanted to do.

"Um." Nathan blinked, chewing on his lip. "Can we just…"

"Pizza? The Diner? Rudy's? They've got those meatballs you like—better than the ones I make. We could even pick it up and take it ho—"

"Can we just like…not do anything?"

"What?" I stared at him. It felt like my jaw had taken a vacation on the floor as I watched his cheeks flush.

"It's not a big deal, Dad. We can just…you know. Pretend like it's a normal day."

"Like hell." I glared at him. "Like hell. Is this because of your mom?"

"No—"

"Because if it is—"

"Dad!" Nathan reached out, his hands laying gently on my shoulders. I hadn't realized how much I'd tensed up. I was probably red as a fucking fire engine. My pulse was throbbing, the muscle in my neck tensed tight enough it twanged like a bowstring. "Dad."

"Nathan—"

"Mom sucks." Nathan gave me a gentle squeeze, catching my eyes with a soft smile. He looked like me. I knew that. But it was still weird seeing it up close. Like looking down at my younger self. A glimpse inside a time machine. "She does, but…you don't? It's not. It… Ugh."

I swallowed, waiting.

Sometimes he needed time to piece his words together.

Like they were just out of reach and he was gathering them carefully, one by one.

"I don't need us to make a big deal out of today, not when I feel…ugh about the whole thing."

"Can I make you feel less 'ugh'?"

"You can't *make* me feel anything, Dad. That's not how feelings work."

I nodded.

I swallowed.

I waited.

"I just think…I'd rather celebrate another day. Like a do-over? Maybe this time we won't invite Mom. Maybe this time we could…"

"We could what?"

"We could invite the Bakers over or something? You know. Um. They don't even need to know it's my birthday. We could go sledding again—or to the movies. Drink cocoa. Like…" Nathan's cheeks grew red and I stared at him, my heart thudding unsteadily.

"Like what?"

He was interrupted as the doorbell rang.

The sound was loud enough it made both of us jump, and I turned my head to look, glaring at the intruder as the words that lay unspoken between us filtered through the air.

Like a family.

I was sure that's what he'd almost said.

But now I'd never know.

Nathan shook out his shaggy hair, the water droplets leaking onto the towel he had slung over his shoulders. He flashed me a little smile, gave me one last squeeze, and then hurried back toward the staircase.

It hit me then that he'd come down before getting dressed because he was worried about me.

My heart hurt.

"I'm gonna get changed. Will you get the door?"

I nodded, gave him a reassuring smile and did as I was told. Taking orders from an eighteen-year-old. Jesus. I opened the door with a sigh and was met with two bright blonde heads and matching sunny grins.

The Bakers.

Of course.

"Hi!" Baxter beamed, all summer and sunset. His cheeks were pink from the cold and his eyes were bright. It wasn't fake. Wasn't a mask. He was...excited about something.

"Surprise!" Becca waved jazz hands in my face, her pink fuzzy gloves waggling in an almost exact mimicry of the way that Nathan had greeted them that day we'd gone sledding. The day I'd decided to take the stick out of my ass.

"Where's Nathan?" God, if Baxter had a tail it'd be wagging. He was practically vibrating out of his skin, bouncing on the balls of his feet, his hands tucked behind his back like he was...hiding something?

"What've you got there, B?" I asked, the nickname rolling off my tongue like honey. His cheeks grew redder and I ignored the way that Becca paused, cocking her head curiously at me.

Baxter hadn't shaved today. I could see the hint of a golden five o'clock shadow peeping along his jawline and the sudden desire to drag my tongue across it just to feel the rasp of it overwhelmed me. I was distracted, however, as I realized he really truly was hiding something behind him.

He squirmed.

"Nathan's inside." I pushed the door open wide, let Becca through, then leaned up against it, blocking the entrance enough that Baxter was forced to press up against me as he passed. God. That two second brush of his warm body against mine was enough to make me pant.

I forced the intrusive thoughts aside in favor of peeping over his shoulder at the surprise he had hidden behind him.

"Stop!" He commanded, glaring up at me with the most adorably grumpy little expression I'd ever seen. "It's a surprise."

"For me?"

"For Nathan." Somehow those words meant more to me than anything he could've said. Fire lit up inside my chest, my heart a throbbing, shuddery mess as Baxter scurried his way into the kitchen after his daughter, his surprise hidden from view. All I'd seen was a glimpse of what looked like a…plate?

Maybe he'd made more bread.

I liked bread.

Loved it, actually.

Not that I'd told him that.

Yet.

Nathan came thundering down the stairs again, this time fully dressed. His hair was half dried already, the tops wispy, the bottoms dripping as he hopped the last two steps and landed with a loud thump and a slide on his slippery socks.

I'd bought him more socks for his birthday.

The correct kind, apparently.

I'd also gotten him a new skateboard covered in flames and little skeleton men marching in a parade of death. It was macabre but also… pretty fucking cute. At least I'd decided it was after he'd thrown his arms around me, gave me a squeeze, and giggled his way out onto the driveway to test it out.

Watching him zoom around like a little kid had been the best gift he could've ever given me.

It reminded me of how far he'd come.

But also simultaneously that despite his large frame, deep down, he was still that same tiny boy I'd carried on my shoulders and taught how to whistle all those years ago. He was my Nathan, no matter what sized package he came in.

"Bakers are here." I told him, cocking my head toward the kitchen.

The whites of his eyes flashed as he reached up to pat down his hair. "Did you call them?"

"When? They knocked when you and I were talking."

"Right!" Nathan nodded, looking down to check his zipper and the button on his jeans. When he was positive he was presentable, he looked back up at me. "Right. Okay." He cleared his throat, gave me a salute and spun his way down the hallway.

I watched the way he puffed his chest up as he moved through the kitchen doorway and I tried not to laugh.

Showing off.

Posturing like a peacock.

The little lines on the doorframe I'd carved laughed at me as I passed, brushing my fingers along them as I counted the inches between how big my little boy was now and how small he'd been when we moved here. My mother had cried the day we moved out of her basement, but I'd never been more glad for the freedom, even though I loved and appreciated all her help when he was a baby.

"Close your eyes!" Baxter demanded. The light switch was flipped off the moment I entered the room and we were suspended in darkness. I bumped against Nathan's back. He was giggling, and the noise made my heart sing.

"They're closed!" Nathan sing-songed. Apparently he'd given up his macho front. He was too excited. Cute, cute, cute. I ruffled his hair and listened to him groan as he shoved me off of him. I wished I could see his face.

"Paxton, are your eyes closed?" Baxter called, a threat in his normally cheery voice.

"Definitely closed." They were not closed.

"Paxton." Baxter growled, and I laughed, the sound startling from my chest.

I closed my eyes.

There was rustling, whispering, and the creak of one of my dining chairs moving around before whatever the Bakers had cooked up—probably literally—was ready.

I don't know what I expected.

My eyelids lit up red as I listened to the flicker of a lighter clicking on.

I only recognized the sound because Trent was a heavy smoker and I was used to taking his smoke breaks with him just so I could listen to him talk.

"You can open," Becca told us with importance.

I opened my eyes, my gaze traveling first to my little boy before the surprise they had in store.

Nathan's eyes were bright, wet with unshed tears, a sunny grin lighting up his features. Candlelight flickered across his face as I watched a wayward tear slip down his cheek. And then it started. The soft crooning of a scratchy voice—honey sweet—and honest.

"Happy Birthday" rang like magic through the air.

My heart hurt.

Baxter wasn't the best singer. He missed half the notes. His pacing was all wrong. Becca's voice joined in, higher than his and just as bad. But god…that song was the most beautiful thing I had ever heard in my entire fucking life.

My eyes stung as I stared at the two blondes. I watched their heads bob. I watched the way they grinned at each other, like they shared a secret only they knew. I swallowed around the lump in my throat and joined in, rumbling quietly as my gaze snapped back to Nathan so I could watch the ice that had built around him since his phone call with his Mom melt away.

When the song finished my heart hurt.

It hurt.

It hurt.

It hurt.

Becca flipped the lights back on and Nathan leaned in close. It was only then that I noticed the cake they'd brought with them. The thing was massive. I was surprised Baxter had been able to hide it so effectively behind himself.

It was shaped like a skateboard, two tiers tall at least, covered in enough candles you could hardly see the intricate flames that had been painted with icing all over it.

Flames.

Just like the ones on the skateboard I'd given him this morning.

Nathan's laughter lit up the room as he blew out the candles, the puff of his breath louder than it needed to be. He popped back up from his crouch, and his smile was brighter than the summer sun as he turned to me and gave me a double thumbs up. "Got 'em all!"

"Fuck yeah." I grinned at him, my heart fluttering as I stared at where Baxter rocked eagerly on his heels, back and forth.

"Happy Birthday!" He cheered, clapping his hands together. "I didn't know what flavors you liked so I made all of them."

"All of them?" Nathan's eyes bugged out of his head.

"Yes! Well. This part," Baxter gestured at the left side of the skateboard. "That's chocolate. The middle is strawberry. The other end is vanilla." He was smiling and god…looking at his dimples made my palms sweaty and my cheeks hot. "I hope you like it! I also have something for you in the car. But I didn't have time to wrap it because I got wrapped up in baking the cake." He blinked his ridiculously long lashes, glanced at me, and grinned expectantly. "Get it? *Wrapped* up?"

"I got it, B," I murmured, my voice hoarse. I smiled at him and watched the way his cheeks flushed.

"I'll go get it!" Becca scurried off and I let her pass, feeling more than a little dazed myself as Baxter scrounged through my cupboards with Nathan's help, found two plates, and placed them on the table.

"You're not staying?" I asked, because suddenly the idea of them leaving was the worst tragedy I could think of.

"Oh!" Baxter blinked, cheeks flushed. "We didn't want to impose."

"Stay." The words rumbled their way out of my throat. I wasn't sure if Baxter truly understood how serious I was. I glanced at Nathan and he nodded at me eagerly. "Stay, Baxter. We want you to stay."

After cake, dinner, and a movie, I sent Nathan upstairs. He was smiling the whole way, his hands on his distended belly, nerves completely gone. I'd noticed lately—around Becca especially—he'd been growing more comfortable and it made me happy.

Becca and Baxter waved at him from their spot by the front door and Nathan paused at the top of the stairs to wave back.

"Thanks for coming!" he called, more than a little giddy and hyped up on sugar. I bet in less than fifteen minutes he'd be up in his room, blasting his way through one of the video games I'd bought him from his wish list. I didn't have the heart to deny him that, not after the day he'd had. Even though it was a school night and I knew he'd be tired tomorrow.

He disappeared and I turned back to our two guests, my heart thudding unsteadily.

Baxter stared at me.

I stared at him.

Becca cleared her throat.

"I'm gonna go wait in the car." She was gone a moment later with the soft click of the front door shutting behind her and I couldn't help but be charmed by how easily she'd read the room. Did she know how badly I wanted her dad? God, I hoped not. That would be awkward as hell.

Baxter shuffled, rolling onto the balls of his feet, his heels, then the balls again.

He blinked up at me through his lashes and my heart stuttered, my throat tightening.

He looked so cute like that, in a green sweater today—the exact shade of his eyes. His coat was draped over his arm and I couldn't help but feel charmed once again as I remembered the fact it was heated.

Genius little bastard.

I swallowed the lump in my throat.

"Thank you for coming." The words left my lips without planning, a quiet rumble in the space between us.

Sweet.

Gentle.

Two things I never was, unless I was with him apparently.

"Thank you for letting us stay." Baxter countered, his lips tipping up into a soft smile. He continued to do his awkward shuffle dance and I watched him, that pent-up feeling of want building, building, building until suddenly it was too much all at once.

Too much to contain anymore.

Too—

Too—

Much.

I had him against the door half a second later.

His body was warm, his skin even warmer. My hands dug into his hips, biting till I felt the give of his flesh as our noses bumped and our breath mingled. I could feel my heart about to beat right out of my chest. "If you don't want this, tell me now," I growled. It was an escape I hoped he wouldn't take.

Baxter didn't hesitate.

He kissed me.

His lips tasted like sugar.

Sweet as the cookies he baked.

Delicious.

Addicting.

Magical.

He was tentative at first despite his obvious desperation, and I soothed any fears he might have with the slip of my tongue along the seam of his lips. I licked inside—hungry, desperate, drunk on his taste—as my hand shoved up the back of his shirt and his hard nipples scraped up along my chest where we pressed tightly together.

He was smaller than me.

Leaner.

Willowy.

It would be so easy to move him where I wanted him, manipulate him into place with my bulk and get high on the way he surrendered.

With a groan I latched onto his wrist, dragging it up behind my head till he got the picture and held tight as I grabbed his supple thighs and hoisted him in the air. With his back to the door, and his cock against mine there was nothing I could do but grind into him and chase his tongue in a wicked dance.

Baxter was whining.

He wasn't quiet about it either.

This desperate little broken sound that echoed between us as I grabbed his ass and squeezed tight enough he sobbed. I wanted to sneak my hand into the back of his pants like we were teenagers. Feel his cheeks bounce, creep between them and play with the slutty hole I knew was just waiting to be teased.

I bet he'd cry.

So fucking pretty—

So ready for me.

Obedient. Sweet.

My pretty little sweetheart.

God, if I had more time I'd show him everything.

Show him the fucking world.

Grind up against him till his head tossed back, his cock spurted, and his eyes crossed.

Oh, fuck.

"You're fucking delicious, B." I crooned as I dragged my lips over his stubble, nibbling at his jaw till he tossed his head back and let me suck at the fragile skin on his neck. "I wanna eat you."

"Hopefully not all of me?" His voice was ragged and breathless as he joked. Barely there. Just a whisper. The fact that I'd made him sound like that was headier than any drug.

"Not all of you, sugar." I crooned, nipping at the tendon in his neck till he whined again. So pretty. So fucking pretty for me. "Just the naughty bits."

Baxter laughed, though the sound got caught in his throat as I found his Adam's apple and gave it a hungry bite. I could see where beard burn was starting to form on his fragile skin and the thought of him wearing my marks around should've made me nervous.

Instead all it did was make my cock leak where it pressed needily against my boxers. I wanted to fuck. The natural instinct buzzing inside me as I ground against Baxter, chasing friction. His heels dug into the meat of my hamstrings and he tossed his head back, golden curls catching on the door behind him. I watched his throat bob, fascinated.

The way Baxter whined when I released one of his ass cheeks and shoved my hand up the front of his shirt would haunt me till the day I died. His chest arched toward my touch, needy, greedy, desperate…

Everything I wanted him to be *all the time.*

Fuck.

I'd spoil the hell out of him if given the chance.

That was of course when a car horn blared outside.

I froze, my thumb brushing one of Baxter's pebbled nipples under his shirt. He was twitching. Fuck. Twitching, twitching, *twitching*. Needy little thing.

The horn blared again.

Motherfucker.

I was going to get a noise complaint if this kept up.

Baxter laughed, though the sound was really more of a groan than anything else.

"I think that's my summons?"

"I hate your daughter right now," I joked softly and Baxter snorted. His fingers curled in the back of my hair, giving it a gentle tug as he bumped our noses together. I'd have to let him down. I didn't want to.

He felt kinda perfect in my arms like this.

"No you don't," he murmured softly, pressing a gentle kiss against my lips.

It was sweeter than the ones we'd just shared, without the desperation.

I sighed, pressing into his touch with a gentle rumble.

"I don't," I agreed, kissing him again. And again. And again.

The horn blared.

"Jesus fuck." I groaned.

"No thanks," Baxter joked.

I set him down with a chuckle, missing his weight in my arms the second his feet touched the ground again. His fingers stroked over my wrists, chasing my tattoos like he was memorizing them. "Thank you."

His voice was soft.

I kissed him again.

Slipping my tongue inside his mouth felt like coming home. He didn't push me away, he just sucked eagerly, pliant—obedient.

Good little pet.

I grabbed his chin and held him in place, letting him chase his way inside my mouth so I could play with him just a little longer.

He pulled back this time, his pupils blown wide and dark, his lips cherry red. Kissable. So fucking kissable.

He had beard burn all over his neck and looking at it made my cock twitch. I wanted to rub all over him, mark him up. Come on his porcelain belly and rub it in. Fuck. I bet he'd eat that up. Bet he'd let me mark his hole too—fill him up till he twitched and shuddered, unable to keep it all in as it slipped down his creamy thighs.

I shoved the heel of my palm against my cock. Baxter watched. His lips parted, a little whimper escaping them.

"Thank you," Baxter repeated again, dazed. When I chased his lips again he turned away.

I groaned, thunking my forehead against his cheek.

He laughed, the bastard.

Then he kissed my cheek and all was well again. My skin tingled and I pulled back, helping him right his sweater where I'd rucked it high enough up I could play with him. He picked his coat up off the floor, dusted it off, and smiled at me.

"Oh!" Baxter shook his head, cheeks pink. "I have a gift for you."

I stared at him, brow furrowed in confusion.

Hadn't he just brought a bunch of gifts?

"You already—"

"No!" Baxter shook his head. "This one is for *you.*"

For...*me?*

I couldn't remember the last time someone had bought me something just because they wanted to, Baxter's baked goods aside. He opened the door and I followed after him dopily, hiding behind him and willing my cock to go down.

Down boy, bad.

When we reached the car Becca was grinning at us. The shithead had been honking the fucking horn and yet here she was acting innocent as punch. It was a good thing she was cute.

I stared at Baxter's ass as he opened the trunk and rifled around inside it. It was a nice ass. Round. Bouncy. Just the right amount of muscle. I'd gotten to feel it earlier but touching it was different.

I licked my lips, my cock perking up again.

Baxter popped up, no longer wagging his ass in my face, taunting me into a quick fuck inside his tight hole.

"Found it!"

It took me a second to realize what he was holding.

He offered it to me, a shy twist to his lips. "I wanted to say thank you for the other day... I didn't know where to go. I knew you would...um. I knew you would help. You're honest. Blunt. But...kind? And you didn't have a scarf when we went sledding, so I just thought..."

He blinked those big green eyes up at me and I swallowed the lump in my throat as I accepted his gift.

"To keep you warm," he said, as if it was that simple.

But it wasn't.

Because the scarf meant far more than any other gift I'd ever received.

It was a promise.

Friendship.

Companionship.

A future.

"Thank you," I murmured, more than half tempted to lean down and kiss him again. He must've read my mind because he laughed and shoved playfully at my chest.

"Go to bed, Paxton," he teased. I stared at the pink rash on his neck and I grinned, wide and unrepentant.

"Sure thing, sugar."

I went to bed.

fifteen

BAXTER

TO SAY I WAS SURPRISED by this recent development in my life would be a massive understatement. I'd never seen Paxton date—but like everyone else probably did—I'd just assumed the fact he had a son meant he was straight.

I shouldn't have assumed.

Honestly, it was wild that me of all people had thought that, considering the fact that I had a kid too and I was most definitely not interested in the opposite sex.

Becca was Rebecca's through and through. She'd even been named after her.

Though looking at her wouldn't tell you her lineage. We looked alike—incredibly so. She'd taken after her mom and subsequently our side of the family. The Bakers were always blonde. We always had green eyes. Freckles.

So, that was just another reason I shouldn't have assumed shit about Paxton.

I forced aside my surprise however and basked in the memory as my lips tingled and I wandered through my nighttime routine in a daze. Becca had been staring at me the whole car ride home, probably because I couldn't stop smiling.

I felt like a teen again.

Young.

Excited for what the future might have in store for me.

I was looking forward to the mandatory ski trip that was part of the Christmas Buddies program even more now. We were only two weeks away and, wow! The thought of being stuck in a room with Paxton just made me…

Mmmm.

Best not to think about that now, not when I had deliveries to—well, deliver.

I finished up my last drop off, gave Rudy a hug and a squeeze, and dodged his concerned well wishes before I hopped my way through the snow on the sidewalk to where I'd parked on the side of the road.

Becca was out of school today. Something to do with student council. They'd had some sort of field trip into the city to one of the museums and the fact that I wouldn't need to pick her up from school greatly freed up my schedule for the day.

What to do though…

Hmm.

The optimist in me wanted to pop by the Montgomerys' and see if Paxton was home.

The realist knew Paxton was no doubt working.

I climbed into the car and shuffled in front of the heater, rubbing my hands together to heat them as the chill from outside seeped out of my fingers. They were pink with cold and my knuckles were all wrinkly. I snorted, rubbing them more vigorously to get the feeling back.

My phone buzzed in my back pocket and I ignored it at first, figuring I'd call whoever it was back when I was done thawing.

It buzzed again though.

And again.

Confused, I wiggled till I could get it out of my back pocket and flipped it open. The fact it was an unknown number didn't alarm me. I got new customers every day. Word of mouth in Belleville was the most powerful marketing I could ever have.

It was probably someone trying to get in the last week before Christmas.

I had a deal going for families who wanted cookies for Santa without the hassle of baking themselves.

Christmas Eve was already scheduled to be the biggest day of the year for my business.

With a hum, I swiped right and brought the phone to my ear.

"Mr. Baker?" Nathan's sweet voice trickled through the speaker and even though it was slightly tinny, I could still hear the anxiety vibrating through it.

"Nathan?"

"Um."

"What's wrong?" I sat up straight, my heart racing as my palms grew sweaty.

"I'm…" He cleared his throat. "I skipped school. And…I have Dad's truck. But I got a flat tire—and I'm stranded. And I only had half a tank of gas. And I'm worried I'm going to be stuck here for like eternity. And the gas is going to run out. And then I'll freeze to death."

Wow. Okay.

That was a lot to unpack.

"Where you at, buddy?"

He texted me the address and I was on my way before I could blink. The plows had come through that morning so the roads were clear for the most part. Though the snowbanks were brown with salt and slush. This was going to be cold.

Very cold.

At least it was sunny out, right?

When I arrived, Nathan rushed toward me, his brows knit together, his floppy hair shoved inside the fucking—

The beanie I'd got him.

He was wearing the beanie I got him.

My heart thudded unsteadily and before I could overthink I launched myself at him and gave him a hug.

"I'm gonna take care of it," I promised.

He nodded.

His nose was cold and a little wet where it brushed against my neck. He was taller than me, which wasn't a surprise considering the fact his dad was half mountain. But it still shocked me a little. I didn't see an adult when I looked at him, just like how when I looked at Becca all I saw was my little girl staring back at me.

Nathan hugged me back.

He was shy at first but he warmed up quickly as I gave him a tight squeeze and patted his back reassuringly.

"Why don't you get in my car, huh?" I urged, pulling back and pushing him toward the passenger seat. "Get warm."

He handed me his keys and offered me a wobbly but grateful smile. Sweet kid.

I smiled back and gave his shoulder a gentle squeeze, cocking my head toward my car. "Go on, I've got this."

He nodded again and did as he was told.

Half an hour later I was shivering, my knees were wet, and my hands were frozen stiff. But the spare tire was on the truck and Nathan was watching me with wide grateful eyes. The way he looked at me made me feel like I'd hung the moon—and not fixed a flat tire.

"My dad says he'll be here soon," Nathan told me, shoving his hands in the pockets of his coat. He looked cold already and he'd just barely stepped out of the car. Poor thing.

"Why don't we wait inside the car?" I offered, pushing him back toward the passenger side he'd exited.

The heater was on full blast and I rubbed my hands together in front of it, ignoring the way I had oil smudged across my fingers. I wasn't even sure where it had come from actually but I supposed it didn't matter.

"You hungry?" I offered, already reaching between the two seats to the back where I had stashed a spare loaf of bread I'd brought with me to snack on. I hadn't gotten into it yet—which ended up being fortunate because Nathan ate half of the thing in basically a single bite.

There were crumbs all over his lap and chocolate smudged at the corner of his lips by the time his dad arrived.

I had no idea how Paxton was going to show up considering the fact we were currently rescuing his car.

The question was answered, however, when a large red truck pulled up and two men exited. Paxton I recognized right away. All six foot five of him. Big, big, big. Thick thighs, testing the seams of his Levis. His massive chest splitting his wool coat wide. It was parted over a hoodie that had one of the local college logos on it. I wondered if he'd gone there, or if maybe he just liked the school.

Maybe that's where Nathan was planning on going?

I'd have to ask.

Nathan was out of the car quicker than I could blink. Despite the fact he'd been breaking the rules, he had absolutely no qualms as he launched himself at his dad, waving his hands and talking a mile a minute. The fact he wasn't afraid of him, even when he'd done something wrong said a lot about their relationship. I was a lot slower, my legs creaked, and my frozen knees felt like they'd need some rubbing and a bit of oil to get working again.

With a groan I popped my back as I exited and then headed toward the other two adults.

The second man—the one that had been driving—looked like Paxton. Bearded. Lumber-jacky. Sexy as all hell. Though his hair was black and he didn't have the salt and pepper that Paxton sported.

He grinned at me and winked.

"Paxton didn't tell me how cute you were," was his greeting. I just blinked at him, confused. I glanced down at myself, noting for the first time I'd gotten that same mystery oil all over my favorite cream sweater. Oh well.

I could buy a new one.

Clothes were meant to be worn, after all.

"I'm Baxter." I hadn't met this man, though it didn't take a genius to figure out he was one of the elusive Montgomerys. They lived spread out around the borders of the town. Becca had informed me of this after our market disaster, though despite her upset she'd been eager to relay to me all the juicy gossip surrounding the tree farm Paxton had grown up on.

How I hadn't known about it boggled my mind.

Though I supposed I'd always been a plastic tree sort of guy, so maybe that was why.

"Trent." Trent shook my hand, flashing me a slick grin that made me want to laugh. He was cute. Not nearly as grumpy as his brother.

I released his hand and turned back to Paxton with a soft smile.

He was staring at me.

I could feel the way it heated up my body, my cheeks tingling, my toes curling inside my boots.

"You alright?" he asked, his voice a quiet rumble.

"I'm great." I bit my lip, my smile threatening to break through the clouds of my expression. "I'm tire-d, but wheel."

He blinked.

He cocked his head.

The laugh that rumbled its way out of him warmed me all the way to my bones. I couldn't help but grin right back, ignoring the way the other two Montgomerys were staring at us both.

"Tire-d, but wheel." Paxton shook his head, chuckling darkly. His whiskers twitched when he laughed and I couldn't help but be charmed all over again.

"Thank you, thank you." I bowed and he just laughed harder.

"Be car-ful with those puns," Paxton grinned. "They're so sharp someone might get hurt."

I grinned so hard my cheeks burned.

Paxton sobered after a moment, his honeyed gaze flickering over to his truck where it was parked on the side of the road. He shook his head, turned back to me, lips pressed into a gentle twist that was equal parts sweet and amazed.

His eyes said, *thank you.*

They said, *thank you for taking care of my boy.*

They said, *you don't know what it means to me.*

Five minutes later while Trent and Nathan were chatting beside the truck, Paxton grabbed onto my wrist. He pulled me away from them, his eyes dark, the sun catching the copper in his hair and making it glow. It didn't escape my notice that he was wearing the scarf I'd given him the night before.

Like father, like son.

He brought me around the back of Trent's red truck, his grin turned wicked as he pressed me up against the cold metal with his hands bunched in the back of my shirt.

"You're like a little Christmas Elf, aren't you B?" He murmured, crowding up against me till we were pressed flush together and I could enjoy the heat of his body exuding through his many wind-chilled layers.

"What do you mean?"

"Santa's little helper." He laughed, leaning down to flutter a barely there kiss against the sweaty hair at my temple.

"I'm not sure I follow."

"Doesn't matter." Paxton's lips dragged across my skin, kissing my cheekbone, my jaw, the cold shell of my ear. His voice rumbled as his wet-hot tongue traced my sensitive skin. I shuddered, tingling all over.

I'd never been touched like this.

Hell, the last time I'd hooked up with anyone was in culinary school.

It felt like being a virgin again.

I swallowed the lump in my throat as Paxton's fingers grew greedier, sliding around my body till he could give my hips a possessive squeeze. I could feel his thumbs digging into my hip bones and my lashes fluttered as I groaned.

Despite the cold my dick came to life.

It's aliiiiiiiive, I inwardly cackled.

"Thank you for being here for him," Paxton said, his words a prayer between us. "Thank you for answering when he called."

"Of course." I blinked. It hadn't even occurred to me that it was an option not to help. "I'd never leave him."

"I know, honey bee." Paxton gave my hips another squeeze. The pressure went straight to my dick and I was having a hard time following the conversation at all anymore. I just wanted him. Preferably naked— preferably somewhere a lot warmer than this.

It was relieving that what we'd shared the night before was clearly not a one-off.

Maybe it was as special to him as it was to me?

It meant…so much.

Too much.

Honey bee, honey bee, honey bee.

"Honey bee?" I questioned, more than a little distracted as I listened to the murmur of Nathan and Trent's voices carrying over the wind. I hoped they couldn't hear us. God. They better not be able to *see* us.

Paxton was a lot more daring than I'd expected.

This was practically voyeuristic! Never mind the fact that we had trees in front of us and a truck at our back. And all we were doing was… hugging? Whatever you'd call this. It was definitely a prelude to some sort of frot-tery that was for sure. Was that even a word?

Frot-tery?

"Cuz you're sweet as honey. And you're always buzzing around. Yellow too." Paxton reached up with one of his hands to pluck at my hair and I laughed, more than a little charmed.

Honey bee.

That was cute.

Really fucking cute.

I often thought of Becca as a bee herself but I'd never stopped to realize someone else might think of me that way as well.

"I want to kiss you," Paxton murmured, dropping down so I could feel the tickle of his beard again. I shuddered, tipping up like an eager slut toward his mouth. My lips parted and my lashes grew heavy.

"Kiss me."

"Just a little," he teased, a twinkle in his eyes that was more than a little naughty as he leaned down and closed the distance between our lips. His mouth was hot, hungry, and delicious. Big, meaty fingers stroked along my neck, teasing the sensitive skin till I opened up and let the slick twist of his tongue inside my mouth.

We kissed.

We kissed, and kissed, and kissed.

We only stopped when the sound of footsteps approached and Nathan's chatter rang through the air, suspended on the chill like snowflakes. Paxton pulled back, straightened my sweater where he'd rucked it up to get at the skin on my lower back, and turned away from me.

"That's very fascinating," he hummed, giving me a wink as he turned to his approaching son. "Never knew that about…"

"Yeast," I supplied helpfully.

"Yeah." He grunted, brushing along my side as he stepped away. "Yeast."

"Very fascinating thing, yeast." I added, fumbling to get my mind back on track as I stumbled after him, my cheeks bright red. "Did you know it's technically alive?"

"That so?"

"Oh yes."

Paxton's eyes twinkled as he glanced down at me and I was—not for the first time—floored by how handsome he looked with silver flickering through his beard and at his temples. He had a nice nose too. Strong. With a bump in the middle—like he'd gotten into a fight as a kid and broken it once or twice.

I bet he'd won every fight he'd ever been in.

He'd be noble about it too.

He was just that sort of guy.

"Come over for dinner," Paxton commanded, his voice a quiet growl that sent shivers through my body all the way down to my cold little toes.

I swallowed.

"Sure!" I followed after him obediently, my hypothetical tail wagging.

It was one in the morning when I heard a knock on my window and my heart decided to yeet itself from my body (yeet was a new word I'd learned earlier that week from Becca. I was still figuring out how to use it.)

I gathered my blanket around myself, terrified of ghoulish possibilities as I tipped my head toward the window, expecting to see a ghost or something equally horrifying. Could ghosts even knock?

I guess the better question would be, why would they?

But no.

What was at my window wasn't a wayward tree branch, a ghost, or a demon.

It was…the last thing I would've ever expected. *He* was the last thing I expected.

Paxton was outside my window. Frost tickled along the glass, his breath fogging it up as he grinned at me from his perch on top of my roof. To say I was shocked to see his thick body settled there as he gently rapped on the window pane a second time would be a gross understatement.

I stared at him, my jaw agape.

He had to be cold.

His cheeks were flushed red, his nose even redder. I rushed to the window, my heart in my throat, my blanket fluttering to the ground behind me as I threw it open with laughter bubbling up inside me.

"Paxton!" I gasped, latching onto his cold shoulders the moment the window was open wide enough he could slip inside. The winter chill had seeped into his jacket, and I tugged at him, the whisper of wind tickling my sleep-warm skin. "Get inside. *Jesus.* Haven't you heard of a door?"

"Where's the fun in that?" he teased as he slipped inside the room. It still surprised me every time he joked with me. I hadn't known he was capable of emotion other than disapproval but here he was. Playful. Cold. Pink from the winter chill.

He shrugged his backpack off, draped it over my reading chair, and turned to watch me as I forced the window shut again. My nipples were hard, sensitive where they pushed against my silk pajamas. I shuddered, gooseflesh dancing up my arms as I finally got the latch shut and turned back to him with a surprised, but pleased, grin.

"It's one in the morning!" I reminded him, breathless and excited. I was careful to keep my voice down, terrified Becca would wake up and hear me talking from her room down the hall.

"So it is," came Paxton's quiet rumble as his lips twitched up, and his toffee-colored eyes twinkling merrily. I noticed his laugh lines for the first time and I had to bite back the urge to reach out and trace over them with reverent fingers. I wanted to kiss them. Kiss his lashes, kiss his dimples, kiss the years of laughter right from his face.

I hadn't known he could laugh like this.

I hadn't known anything about him at all.

Paxton picked his backpack up again and I watched in fascination as he rifled around inside it, the pink tip of his tongue poking from between his lips as he focused. Despite being massive, hairy, and made of granite, he was surprisingly soft like this. His shoulders shifted, the muscles in his forearms flickering with tension and I marveled at the fact that all I felt was a rush of lust and affection. He wasn't intimidating like I'd once thought. Not intimidating at all.

It was crazy how much could change in just one short month.

"I have something for you." Paxton's voice was a low murmur, its normal scratch rumbling through the space between us suspended like frost in the air.

"You…have something for me?" I blinked, shocked.

He snorted, but continued digging in his bag.

When he found what he wanted, he paused, his thick brow knit, the moonlight flooding through the massive bay windows painting his beard in a gentle haze. The silver that trickled at his temples, hidden beneath his beanie glistened and my heart gave an unsteady thud.

My mouth was dry as Paxton raised his head, catching my gaze with his own.

His eyes said, *be gentle.*

They said, *I've never done this before.*

They said, *you don't know what this means to me.*

I swallowed the lump in my throat.

"Your sweater got all messed up earlier so I thought—" Paxton withdrew a plastic bag, reaching delicately across the short distance between us to place it inside my hands. I blinked down at it, shocked into action only when I realized how rude it was to stare.

I scrambled inside it, twisting cool plastic between my fingers before I touched fabric softer than a cloud itself.

The plastic bag fluttered to the ground as the sweater was released and I stared down at it, my jaw slackened in awe.

It was the color of homemade whipping cream or buttercream frosting. Nearly the same shade as the one I'd tossed in the trash when I'd come home earlier that day. The feeling of the fabric alone was spectacular, but most amazing of all were the cute little embroidered honey bees that danced around the collar and cuffs. I could practically see them buzzing as I traced over their round little bodies and child-like wonder warmed me from head to toe.

How had he…

How had he gotten this?

I'd never seen anything so soft before. So expensive, so…wow.

There was nothing like this in Belleville.

"My sister-in-law has a sweater making business," Paxton grunted after a moment. "Wasn't that big of a deal to call her up and ask if she had anything with bees." He downplayed his own effort so easily but I refused to accept that.

He'd planned this.

Planned the bees.

I should've assumed, but somehow I was constantly surprised by sweetness when directed toward me. Like I didn't deserve it, even though deep down I knew that was a silly notion. Everyone deserves a little love. Even broke bakers with hollow smiles.

My eyes were wet as I clutched the sweater to my chest reverently.

"Thank you."

"You're welcome." Paxton's lips twitched up and he took a step toward me. With him came the remainder of the winter night. It clung to his clothes, blowing my way in a flurry of chilled air that made the hair on my arms rise and my nipples perk up all over again.

"You look cold." Dad mode officially activated. I gingerly set my sweater in a place of honor on my reading chair before I turned back to my lumberjack with a wry twist to my lips. "Get in the shower."

"The shower?" He cocked his head, clearly surprised.

"Yes." I shoved at his massive chest, unsurprised when he didn't budge. How was it that I had never once considered my own height until I'd met Paxton Montgomery up close? And why did his extra bulk make me shivery all over?

I couldn't help but remember how easily he'd lifted me from the floor earlier that week. He hadn't even broken a sweat, like I wasn't a middle-aged man and was instead light as a feather.

I swallowed.

This time I was less sure.

"Shower?"

"Why?" He cocked his head again.

"You're cold—"

"Why don't you warm me up then?" Paxton took another step closer and automatically I stepped back, even though all I wanted was to press forward. My heart was thudding unsteadily, my palms sweaty as he advanced. With each step he took I stumbled backward. Inch by inch. Foot by foot.

Soon enough the mattress met the back of my knees and I was forced to still as my belly did an eager little flip and my fingers tingled where I'd pushed at his chest and yielded no response.

"I…" I flushed, the heat traveling from head to toe.

Paxton grinned. "Not very sweet of you, honey bee. To ignore me when I'm cold like this." He gave an exaggerated shiver and I tried not to laugh. Somehow despite being silly, the seduction was weirdly doing it for me.

"I'm not ignoring you."

Why was I feeling so shy?

What was wrong with me?

I wanted him.

I wanted him more than I'd wanted anything in my entire fucking life.

Maybe it was…

Oh.

I bit my lip.

"What's wrong?" Paxton's hand rose to cup my cheek, his thumb brushing against the hollows beneath my eyes. I knew I looked bad. Knew they were bruised from exhaustion. I'd been running myself ragged for months trying to pick up the slack—trying not to suffer because my business was my livelihood and without my bakery I had no choice but to soldier onward.

I was so close to having enough money for at least Becca's Christmas present.

The bakery would have to wait but…

"I want you," I told him softly. "I really do."

"Then what's the problem?"

"I don't…" I swallowed. "I don't know how to seduce you…or to give you what you want. I don't know if I'm good at sex. I don't know what it's like to be with someone who wants me when I want them in return. I don't want to fuck this up—whatever we are. I don't want to disappoint you. I don't want to disappoint myself. I want this to be as good as I know it can be. I want—"

Paxton leaned down and kissed me.

His kiss quieted my worries.

Despite the chill of his fingers, his lips were warm.

His tongue was warmer.

Paxton kissed me. He kissed me, and kissed me, and kissed me. By the time he stopped kissing me, I'd forgotten why I'd been freaking out in the first place. We were on the bed. I wasn't sure when that had happened, I'd been too caught up in his big hands, the heat of his mouth, the way his beard tickled my cheeks.

I was already out of breath, my lashes fluttering as I lay sprawled on my back, his massive form perched overtop of me in a way that felt almost respectful.

Instead of speaking I just pulled him down into another kiss, my leg hooking round the back of his thigh, heel digging into the supple muscle so I could force him to sink his weight on top of me. I wanted him to squash me. I wanted to no longer be able to breathe. I wanted—I wanted—*I wanted*—

"You're a greedy little thing, aren't you?" Paxton murmured as he nipped at my lips and I squirmed beneath him. He followed my unspoken plea for more as he settled his hips against mine, his bulk pressing against the swollen weight of my cock. I groaned, bucking against him to feel the swell of his own matching arousal.

His cock was big.

Proportionate.

Fuck.

I wanted to wrap my fingers around it and measure it through the denim. I wonder if he was the kind of man whose cock leaked when he was horny? I was. I'd stared at my fair share of digital cocks over the years on my favorite website but nothing compared to the real deal.

Maybe I was greedy.

"You're big," I murmured, stupidly.

Paxton chuckled. "Too big?"

"Just right." I tugged on his belt loops till he ground his cock against mine and my eyes rolled back again.

"Alright, goldilocks." Paxton teased, a quiet rumble against the shell of my ear as he bit his way along the fragile skin. His tongue traced the tendon that ran to my collarbone and I tossed my head back with a whimper.

"Greedy, greedy." He hummed, and I realized belatedly I'd been grinding up against him like a desperate teen.

Then suddenly Paxton's weight was gone.

He sat up on his knees, looming above me, his honeyed eyes blown black with lust. I watched the flush of his lips as he licked them, fascinated by his pink tongue. My cock twitched and I squirmed as he stared down at me. His gaze was made of spun sugar and honeycomb. Sweet. Cloying. Delicious.

"What are you doing?" I asked, my voice wobbling.

"Just looking, sweetheart."

Just looking, he said.

Like I was anything to look at.

Maybe in his eyes I was?

I swallowed, doing my best not to squirm anymore, though I gave up that particular goal only seconds into the decision. I couldn't help it. My balls had drawn tight and I could feel the sticky-wet spot on my boxers where my cock rubbed eagerly against them.

Paxton's silhouette was framed by moonlight as he spread his fingers along the outside of my thighs and ran his hands slowly, inch by inch up my body. He settled at my hips, his thumbs rubbing circles in the sensitive skin where my silk pajama top had rode up.

I shuddered, the weight of his gaze making me dizzy.

"Sweet little thing, aren't you, sugar?" Paxton murmured, one of his hands slipping beneath the hem of my shirt. He played with my treasure trail, scratching along it till he could trace over my ribs one by one. It shouldn't have felt as sexy as it did, but god, I was like a live wire.

"Sweet?"

"So sweet." Paxton growled, the sound low enough it barely registered. And then—the world flipped. In a feat of physical majesty he somehow managed to hoist me into the air, tug me forward, and flip me all in one fluid movement.

My breath left me in a startled woosh and I whimpered, shocked and more than a little turned on as I felt Paxton's breath ghost the back of my neck.

"Wha—"

"You've been teasing me with this ass," Paxton murmured, one of his meaty hands slipping from my hip till his thumb dug into the crease between my ass cheeks. The skin was sensitive there and the silk of my pajamas did nothing to hide the sensation of him pressing into me. "Waving it around like you thought I wouldn't notice."

I hadn't actually thought that at all—but now that I knew he'd been looking…

I waggled my ass at him a little and Paxton huffed an amused breath before his other hand crept to my other cheek and I felt his thumbs settle in mirrored positions at the bottom. He gave me a squeeze that made me breathless before his voice echoed behind me again, "How loud can I make you, sweetheart?"

How loud…? Oh. Oh. My kid. I had a kid. I flushed and flailed a little, panic bubbling up inside me for the moment it took me to remember that Becca slept with the TV on and we had an entire hallway to separate us.

The soundproofing wasn't perfect but it would work well enough.

I relaxed.

"Medium?"

"Medium it is." Paxton growled. His hold on my ass grew even tighter, more possessive. He played with the meat of my cheeks, looking his fill. My cock was leaking, my head spinning as I shoved my hips back only for him to give one of my cheeks a playful swat in retaliation. "You're going to get what I give you and nothing more."

"Okay." I didn't even recognize my voice, that's how far gone I was.

I'd never been touched like this.

My boyfriends in school had never held me like this, never grabbed me, moved me—claimed me. With Paxton's hands on me it was like I became his property and I had never in the history of ever wanted to be anything more.

His thumbs dug in and with a quiet groan that rumbled between us Paxton pulled my cheeks apart. He couldn't see my hole but it was easy enough to imagine. It twitched needily and I whined, surprised by how badly I wanted him to put something inside it. Anything really. I wasn't picky.

"How much do you like these pajamas?" Paxton asked after a moment of me humping the mattress then shoving back into his hands so I could feel my hole twitch again.

"They're not my favorite, why?"

He answered my question as I felt his fingers bunch in the fabric, then tug. It only took a second for it to give in to the pressure, the sound of the fabric *riiipping* echoing through the room as I gasped and cool air met the backs of my thighs where my boxers ended.

I probably looked ridiculous—face down, ass up, with my pants ripped open to expose me—but Paxton didn't seem to think so.

His growl of approval was the only warning I got before he ripped through my underwear too and his heated mouth met the top of my ass. His breath tickled between my cheeks and I was so breathless with lust I couldn't help but whine.

"I wonder if this part of you is as greedy as your pretty cock." One of Paxton's hands yanked my cheeks open, the cool air meeting my fluttering hole as I pressed back toward his face, suddenly eager for a taste of something I'd never had before.

He laced a few fluttered kisses against my skin, toying with me. Teasing till I was breathless and my cock was leaking against my now ruined pajamas. Worth it. It was so worth it. "Naughty little thing," Paxton purred. That was the only warning I got before his hot tongue was tracing tentatively over my quivering, needy hole. I gasped, the sound muffled by the mattress. He did it again, though this time the stroke was broader, slicker, hungrier.

"Oh fuck." I shoved back against his face.

Paxton chuckled, low and dark.

"That's the idea," he growled, giving my hole what I could only describe as a filthy suck. He played with me, teased me, toyed with me till I was nothing but a sobbing mess. By the time one of his hands wrapped around my throbbing cock I was so far gone I hadn't even noticed the way I was humping his tongue like a whore.

It wouldn't take much to make me come.

I was close.

So, so close.

Paxton played with my tip, rubbing around it, teasing my slit through the layers of fabric as his tongue speared inside me and warbling whimpers tore their way through my throat to get lost among the sheets.

"'M close—" I whined, shoving back against him, desperate for more.

"Mmmmm." Paxton hummed, his tongue vibrating inside me in a way that made my body ignite as electricity zapped all the way from my weeping cock to my toes.

"Oh fuck—" I pressed toward him, my hole slackening for his tongue.

All I needed was one more twist of his fingers, one more fuck forward of his slick hot muscle and I'd—

He pulled away.

He pulled away, he pulled away, *he pulled away.*

The sob I let out was nothing short of anguished. Paxton chuckled, pressing an apologetic kiss to one of my cheeks, then the other. I could feel his spit drying cool on my skin as I hiccuped my displeasure, my cheeks wet with tears.

"No, no, no, no, no."

"Patience, sweetheart."

"No!"

Paxton swatted my ass, though the tap was gentle. A reminder of who was in charge here. His fingers left my cock and I was forced to hump against the mattress, searching for the friction I'd just lost.

Paxton rose from the bed. I felt the way the mattress lifted, his heat no longer behind me and another broken sob tore its way through me. Lonely, empty, sad-sad-sad-sad—I hiccuped my displeasure only for

Paxton to return a moment later, his massive body covering my own.

He crushed me gently into the mattress, his elbows braced on either side of my head as he let me take enough of his weight that I no longer felt like I was about to float away.

"Just grabbing my bag, baby," he murmured against the shell of my ear. He smelled like pine trees, winter air, and wood shavings. I inhaled greedily, settling once again as I felt his thick cock press against the meat of my ass. I could feel the soft cotton of his boxers and realized he must've unzipped himself.

I could feel how big he was.

Bigger now that he was fully hard.

I wanted to savor him, taste his salty-sweet pleasure. I wanted to trail my lips down the vein that throbbed on the underside of his cock, I wanted to suck on his soft sac till he was groaning and whimpering above me. I wanted him to smother me till all I could breathe was his sweat and the scent of his pleasure. He could crush me with those powerful hairy thighs, trap me between them, suffocate me on his cock till I was sobbing around him, eager as he claimed I was.

"There you go," Paxton murmured, sucking a mark in the sensitive skin at the hollow beneath my ear. "Back with me, huh, sweetheart?"

I didn't know what he meant, only that he was right.

It felt like I'd been floating without a tether before but I was back now, grounded again.

I nodded, the anxiety settling as Paxton shifted his hips, rubbing his arousal against where my ass still twitched needy and empty.

"How do you feel about fingering?" Paxton asked.

Maybe we should've had this conversation before. But my answer would've been the same either way.

"Love it."

"Great." Paxton hummed, his cock slowly grinding against me. I could feel the way even clothed his crown wanted to pop inside me. Oh fuck. I hadn't been fucked in years. Maybe the idea should've made me nervous but all I felt was eager anticipation.

"Now?" I asked, hopefully.

"Mhmm." Paxton's voice was a quiet growl as he gave my neck one last sloppy kiss before he pulled up and away from me again. "I wanna see your sweet face." He flipped me over again. My breath left in a woosh, though this time being manhandled felt less surprising and more…thrilling.

Paxton spread my legs wide and I wiggled against the mattress, enjoying the way the fabric scratched along my sensitive skin where my shirt had rode up. Paxton grinned down at me, his teeth flashing white in the dark as he gave my hips a greedy squeeze before his hands slid slowly, deliberately up to my chest.

"You like this?" He asked as his callused palms rubbed across my nipples.

I nodded, probably more enthusiastically than I needed to.

Paxton's eyes darkened.

Watching him was almost more pornographic than feeling him. He looked like he'd stepped straight off the pages of my favorite porn website. His massive shoulders blocked out any light from the window, his muscular thighs shoved up against mine so he could force me to spread. He was so much thicker than I was—thicker chest, thicker belly, thicker hips, thicker thighs. Built like he was meant to last.

Dear god, I hoped that was true.

"I'm gonna tear these off of you," Paxton growled, his words more of a threat than a promise. "I'm gonna suck on that needy cock of yours—"

"Yes," I gasped.

"And then I'm gonna fuck your ass silly with as many fingers as I decide I want to."

I liked that he wasn't asking me.

I liked that I didn't have to choose.

Though there was a question in his eyes that meant all I had to do was say the word and he'd stop.

I said nothing.

I just nodded and whined, shoving my hips up toward him. My cock hurt. I could feel the wet spot where it had leaked through my clothes and I had half a mind to reach down and grab onto it so I could fuck my own fingers.

But no.

I could wait.

I could be patient.

Paxton's eyes glimmered, glowing softly in the dark as he hummed his approval and reached for the front seam of my pants. *Riiiip* the sound tore through the silence as he split the pants the rest of the way from back to front. The fabric lay in tatters on either side of my needy cock as he repeated the process on my underwear and suddenly cool air was caressing the overheated skin of my needy dick.

I was leaking more than I'd anticipated, wet and hard, my cock slapping against my golden pubic hair.

"Mmmm," Paxton hummed, clearly pleased. I watched the way his lips twisted upward, a satisfied sort of smile. "Such a slut for this, aren't you?"

"Yes—" I moaned.

Paxton's smile disappeared and he growled at me, a sound that made my head spin and my cock drip. "Not you."

Not…me?

Then who?

He dipped his head down till his nose brushed the soft skin of my belly, his breath fluttering against the eager red tip of my cock. "I was talking to you, wasn't I, sweetheart?"

Oh fuck.

Why was that so hot?

Paxton's hand found the back of my thigh and he shoved it upward, his fingers digging into the meat of it as his lips traced barely-there kisses along my pelvis. He didn't touch my cock though. No. That would be too easy.

"Needy little thing," Paxton purred. And then he was sucking me down. My crown hit the back of his throat before I could even blink and a noise unlike anything I'd ever made before left my throat. He was thorough, eager, demanding as he sucked me down.

I couldn't help the way my hips snapped toward his face, chasing friction. Paxton pulled back, his brow furrowed, eyes glinting dangerously.

"Who said you could move?" he purred, and I whined.

"Please—"

"No," he denied, quicker than I could blink.

He sucked me down again and this time I held still. I squirmed, my whimpers growing needier, breathier as his free hand found my crease and began to slide up and down, up and down. Never stopping for long where I needed him the most.

The hand on my thigh moved, and I heard rustling before it was back again, this time slick with something cold.

Distantly I realized it was lube.

"Relax," Paxton threatened, though the words were more a quiet croon as he leaned down to suckle on the head of my cock again at the same time his slick finger traced a circle around my twitching, needy hole.

I wanted him inside.

I wanted him inside so bad it hurt.

But I remembered his admonishment so I held still, my toes curling, my lashes wet with tears.

"I was right," Paxton murmured quietly to himself after another minute of pleasure-torture that felt more like an eon. "You're beautiful when you cry."

And then he slipped inside me again and I was…lost.

One finger became two, became three, became four.

By the time his pinky had tucked up inside me I was whining loud enough I'd had to grab my pillow and gag myself with it to get myself to stop. Every time I lifted it I glanced down to watch Paxton's face. His eyes were dark, hooded with lust, his tongue peeking out between his lips in a mimicry of what he'd done weeks ago when we'd been decorating cookies together.

It had seemed so innocent then.

Now it was anything but innocent.

That tongue had been inside me—just like his fingers were now.

I ground down on his knuckles, my sobs growing loud enough I had to gag myself again.

The pillow muffled my sounds but they didn't stop me from listening to Paxton's quiet crooning.

"That's right, baby," he growled as he slipped out till only the tips of his fingers remained. The stretch felt smaller like that and my loose hole trembled, sucking at him, eager to bring him back inside. Every time I got close to coming he'd back off just long enough the orgasm would float away.

He stared at my gaping hole hungrily, his eyes dark, a predator over its prey.

This was the longest most amazing tease I had ever had and I was loath to stop him even though at times it felt almost like torture.

"Let me in," Paxton hummed, easing his fingers back inside me till he was deep enough I saw stars. My prostate throbbed, the pleasure spot aching as he rubbed liberally up against it, his tongue sucking at my foreskin till my eyes rolled back and precum leaked against his lips.

Paxton's movements grew more hurried, his wrist surer, his fingers greedier as he fucked up inside me. Every so often he'd add more lube and the obscene squelching noise would make my dick spurt against his tongue.

It was filthy.

Filthy and fucking amazing.

By the time he finally let me come I was a floaty mess. My whole body was tingling, my belly wet with my own desire, my hole aching and deliciously stuffed. I hadn't realized how thorough he was being until my cock spurted and my orgasm rushed up toward me.

I could hear the bed frame creak beneath us as endorphins flooded my system. My eyes squeezed shut as a pleasure unlike anything I'd ever felt before rocketed through my body. I came, and came, *and came.*

Even after I'd finished coming, the sensation remained for several long blissful seconds.

By the time I was coherent enough to speak again, I tossed my pillow aside and stared in rapture as Paxton's cum-slicked fist gripped his own cock tight. All I could see was the eager pink head where it peeked out of his fist on each downstroke and I was suddenly desperate to taste.

He was cut.

His crown dripping, red and eager.

I shimmied down, though my body refused to cooperate more than a few inches. It felt like I'd lost all motor control as my lips parted and a needy whimper escaped my lips.

"Open," Paxton commanded. I didn't know what he wanted me to open so I just opened everything—spreading my legs, parting my lips, my lashes fluttering as I stuck my tongue out and waited.

His groan was worth any embarrassment I might have felt.

When he looked at me I felt like porn.

I watched his cock through my lashes, my thighs straining as I let him look his fill. The bed was shaking, the noise getting louder and louder as he shuffled forward till he was straddling my chest. All he'd have to do was sit back to crush me but he didn't. My hands snuck up his thick hair-covered thighs and I whined as my tongue twitched and my eyes crossed so I could watch the drip of his precum gather at the tip of his cock.

I wanted to taste him.

It looked like I'd be getting that wish.

He came with a grunt, the sound nothing more than a deep huff of breath that set all my nerve endings on fire. Salty-sweet pleasure dripped onto my tongue, my cheeks, into my hair. I shuddered as Paxton worked himself through it, his hips rocking into his fist, his mouth parted, pink tongue panting.

By the time he was finished, I was thoroughly marked.

I wasn't sure what I expected to happen next.

My skin was buzzing, my body floaty. I didn't want to move, much less wipe the cum from my skin. So I didn't. I just blinked up at him, a lazy smile decorating my face. Paxton looked glorious above me, his jeans parted, his now softening cock thick and heavy where it lay between the parted folds of his zipper. He was panting, his chest heaving, eyes dark as he stared down at me, enraptured.

I let him watch as I drew my tongue back into my mouth and swallowed his spend.

He groaned, his hand sliding up to grasp in my hair. He gave it a gentle but slightly painful tug that made my hole clench up and my toes curl as he bent down to whisper, "Such a naughty little thing, aren't you?"

I smiled at him, watching as his pupils expanded again and his lips curled into an answering grin.

And then the worst possible thing happened.

A horrible creaking sound filled the room and I stared up at him in confusion for all of two seconds before the sound increased in volume and then—*crack*!

The bed frame broke.

The mattress fell the short distance to the ground as the wood snapped and the thud of our weight caused a small earthquake to shake the room. I gasped, shocked, and more than a little relieved that hadn't happened with his fingers inside me.

And then…

The laughter hit.

I couldn't help it.

Paxton was staring at me, his jaw dropped, eyes wide with panic.

But the laughter wouldn't stop and I reached up for him with my wobbly fingers, curling around his tattooed forearms till I watched his alarm disappear and amusement climb like sunrise across his face.

His laughter wasn't as loud as mine.

It was a quiet sort of chuckle, sweet as dark chocolate, tart as cherries.

"Dad?!" Becca's voice echoed from down the hallway and I had to slap a hand over my mouth to stifle my giggles. Shit. Shit, shit, shit.

The laughter still wanted to escape though despite my efforts and I beamed at Paxton as I gathered my wits about me enough to answer.

"Bed broke! I'm fine."

"You sure?" Becca sounded concerned and sleepy. Mostly sleepy.

"Go back to bed! I'll call Paxton and ask him to fix it in the morning." I grinned at my handyman and he rolled his eyes heavenward though that didn't stop him from dropping down and fanning kisses across my marked cheeks.

"Alright. Night, Dad!" I listened to Becca's footsteps retreat before the giggles came back full force and I hid my amusement in the collar of Paxton's now warm shirt.

We laughed for a long time.

Long enough my heart lifted and I was lightheaded all over again.

There were butterflies flitting around in my belly as I reached up to card my fingers through the soft hair of Paxton's beard. "Are you warm now?" I asked him, a play on the conversation that had gotten us into this mess in the first place.

Not that I'd really call it a mess.

Not the first part anyway.

"Mhmmm." Paxton hummed against the hollow of my throat and I smiled. I smiled so hard it hurt.

We discarded the rest of our clothing and five minutes later we lay huddled under the covers, my mattress settled firmly on the floor, broken bits of wood fragments laying on either side of it.

Paxton's weight was heavy on top of me. He glommed onto me like a starfish, his prickly hair tickling my body as he hooked a leg around mine and his soft cock pressed into my hip. I wiggled, just to feel his length and he hummed with a pleased grumble.

"Sleep," he growled.

I slept.

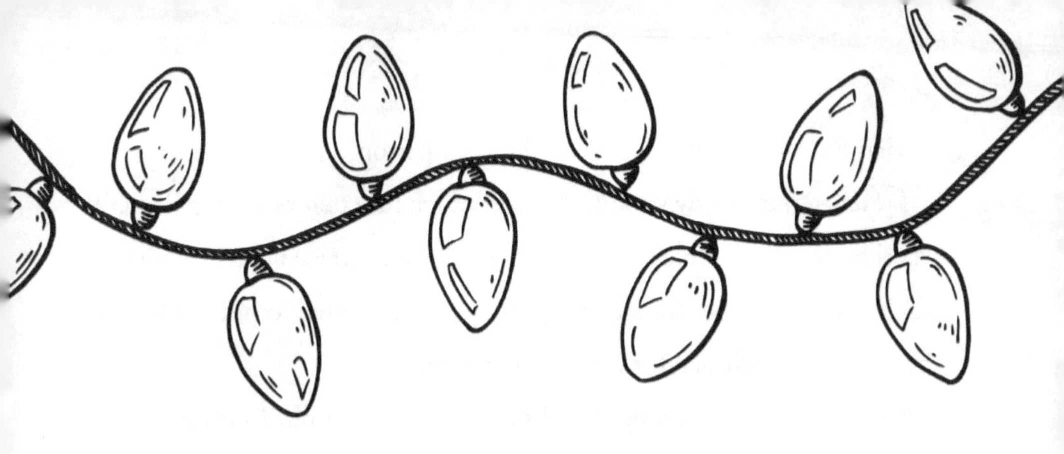

sixteen

PAXTON

THE NEXT MORNING I WOKE up with a sore back and a flip in my belly. Baxter was sprawled beside me, naked and gorgeous, the downy fur on his arms and legs flickering in the soft indigo of the early morning.

The sun hadn't risen yet, and for that I was grateful.

I wasn't ashamed of what we were doing, but I was conscious of the effect this could have on our children, especially with it being so new. I didn't know what to call what…this was. All I knew was that my heart hadn't felt this light in years.

In fact, I'd never felt butterflies like this.

Twisting, trembling, writhing in my belly as I stared down at the flutter of Baxter's lashes and I tried not to fall completely in love with him.

How was it possible that just a few weeks ago I'd abhorred the thought of spending time with him?

That Paxton felt like an entirely different person.

I reached out, gently stroking the soft peach fuzz that ran along Baxter's cheekbone. His stubble was darker now, thicker. I traced over it with my thumb and watched the way his pretty pink lips parted, echoing the way he'd held himself open for me the night before.

I shuddered at the thought and my cock began to fill. Mornings were always a good time for me and my self-pleasure routine, but today… today I wanted something softer. So I ignored my dick as I settled over him and placed a gentle kiss against those sweetly parted lips.

Baxter made a questioning little noise.

I kissed him again.

And again.

And again.

This was new for me.

I'd never spent the night with someone before, not since Tracy, and well…even with *her* it had never felt like this. I'd always had this unsettled feeling—a feeling at the time I had written off as love. I realized now, however, that it was different. I'd felt…paranoid, distrustful. I'd grasped at straws, looking for the reason I was feeling that way. One that didn't mean I had completely wasted three years of my life with the wrong person.

I was older now, wiser too.

This feeling I had for Baxter was nothing like that. It was exciting, it was pure, it was champagne bubbles and the glimmer of lights strung like stars on a pine tree.

Baxter woke slowly, his cloudy expression shifting till his pretty green eyes flickered open and I watched his pupils dilate as he adjusted to the light. The smile that greeted me the moment he recognized me made my heart lurch and my toes curl.

"Good morning," he murmured sleepily.

"Morning," I rumbled back, burying my face in his still sleep-warm skin, my nose rubbing up along the underside of his jaw so I could smell the sugar that clung to him like cologne. Baxter's fingers curled in the back of my hair and for a moment I just breathed him in.

Let his warmth soak inside me like sunbeams.

"Breakfast?" Baxter offered softly. "I've got muffins, orange juice, and I can whip up some eggs."

I couldn't remember the last time someone had made me breakfast.

"What time is it?" I didn't normally wake up this early. Maybe it was my back that had woken me. Or maybe it was that giddy feeling that had fluttered inside since the moment I'd decided to sneak into Baxter's house.

I felt like a kid again, happy—ready for adventure.

Sure of myself in a way I'd only felt when I was young.

Baxter wiggled, probably to check his watch, and then gave my hair a gentle tug. "Nearly five."

"Five?"

"I slept in," Baxter sighed.

This was sleeping in?

Jesus.

"What time do you usually wake up?"

"4:30?" His voice came out as a question and I couldn't help but laugh. Clearly he expected me to judge. Which I was. Silently, since I wasn't a dick.

"I'll skip my run today, though I do need to take Pogo out."

To be honest I'd forgotten he had a dog at all. The creature was surprisingly polite. We shuffled around and Baxter urged me into the bathroom with a pleased little shove to get ready. He assured me Becca wouldn't be up till seven so chances were I wouldn't see her. I was still nervous though, and I had my excuses ready.

Every time I looked at his broken bed frame a laugh threatened to break from my chest but I stamped down on my glee as I showered off the night before and plotted what I was going to work on in Baxter's bakery that day.

It was crazy to me now how far it was coming along. Weirder though, was the fact that I'd started the project before I'd had any sort of amorous feelings toward its owner. It was interesting how the universe worked that way.

I borrowed some of Baxter's lotion and aftershave, enjoying the scent of sugar cookies far too much as it clung to my skin. I'd think about him all day. I didn't give a fuck that Trent was bound to make fun of me, or that Becca might notice I smelled suspiciously like her father.

They could all suck it.

I didn't flip the lights on as I headed down the now-familiar stairs, though that ended up being a mistake because I nearly brained myself dodging the last step where the chubby corgi lay belly up.

He woofed at me in annoyance and I just patted his back in apology.

Baxter fed me breakfast and the entire time I watched him flit around the kitchen in a new set of pajamas and an adorable 'kiss the cook' apron, I had a hard time containing the desire to pick him up, hoist him onto the counter, and fuck him silly.

I whistled my way out the door, my cheeks pink for reasons other than the cold.

I'd parked a few blocks over, not wanting to deal with the gossip I was sure would follow my truck remaining in the Bakers' driveway all night. I still had an hour before I needed to head home to take Nathan to school.

He, no doubt, had no idea I'd even left.

I still felt guilty though.

Was that bad of me?

No…right?

He was eighteen.

I trusted him to take care of the house alone.

Instead of making up demons, I just shook my head and shrugged off the paranoia. He would've called me. He was fine. As I stopped at the bottom of the driveway and contemplated the snow that decorated the lawns on either side, my gaze slipped to Baxter's mailbox.

The dent was even more obvious in the morning light like this.

I wondered if Becca had hit it.

Baxter had never mentioned it, in fact I doubted he'd even noticed.

He seemed to live in his own little world most of the time, exhausted and pushing-pushing-pushing through his own struggles with his head held high and his dark circles slowly growing darker.

If there was one thing I was good at, it was fixing things.

So I made the trek to my truck and drove it back over, a mission in mind.

Twenty minutes later, Baxter wandered out of the house with his arms laden with bread loaves. He was in the sweater I'd bought him and god, he looked delicious. All creamy and soft. Snuggly. The best kinda teddy bear. He was surprised to see me; I saw the glimmer in his eyes as he packed up the back of his car for his morning deliveries and made his way toward me.

"What are you doing?" he asked curiously, his green eyes sparkling in the morning light. He was flushed from the cold and I had to squeeze my fist to stop myself from reaching out and tracing the curve of his sweet upturned nose.

"Fixing your mailbox."

Baxter blinked, his eyes narrowed, and he cocked his head.

"It was broken?"

"Bent."

"Oh." He watched me for a few seconds, then started to shiver. His hands climbed to his arms, crossing so he could rub himself warm. "Do you…need help?"

I could tell he was confused.

Hell, I was too.

Why I felt the need to fix everything in his life for him was a mystery.

Maybe it was because I cared about him?

My cheeks flushed.

"I'll bring you more coffee." Baxter darted away and I groaned as I watched his long legs eat up the sidewalk. When he took the steps on the porch his ass tested his khaki pants and I had to force back another noise of pleasure. I probably looked ridiculous, crouched with my tool box outside his house, thirsting after him like a dog in heat.

Things were escalating, but I wasn't mad about it.

It felt like the water between us had been simmering for far longer than it had taken to reach a boil. I had every intention of enjoying every second of it for as long as he'd let me.

By the time Baxter returned I'd finished fixing it up. Good as new. He handed me a thermos covered in reindeer heads.

"Cocoa and coffee," he told me with a shy little smile. His nose was pink. I wanted to bite it. Fucking cute, cute, cute. "The best combo."

"Thank you, baby." I rumbled as I forced myself once again not to grab him, even though my fingers itched to latch onto his hips and pull him close. He was wearing the cutest little tennis shoes. Dad shoes, I thought fondly as I squeezed the thermos tight.

"I'll fix your frame when I come back; I'll need to bring some extra stuff."

Baxter waved me off, "No need. I don't mind the mattress on the floor for a while."

I stared at him, my eyes narrowing. The words that left my throat were little more than a growl. "You're not sleeping on the floor."

"Well, technically the mattress is the one sleeping on the floor," Baxter joked.

"No partner of mine is sleeping on the goddamn floor."

Baxter's jaw dropped a little and I watched his flush grow ruddy and red. His freckles looked more pronounced like this and I couldn't help myself as I dipped low enough I could place a brief little kiss against the tip of his cold nose.

He scrunched up, but his eyes were happy as he shoved playfully at my chest.

"Fine," he murmured, clearly swayed.

"I'll bring Nathan."

"Please do." He grinned at me and I vibrated with the need to touch again.

I forced myself to leave because if I stayed any longer, I was sure to pounce him into the snow. While I drove away, I stared at my rearview mirror, trying to ignore the throbbing of my heart as I caught him watching me from the end of his driveway. He shivered, his broad shoulders encased in the sweater I'd bought for him and I couldn't help the way my heart stuttered as I turned a corner and he was out of view.

Mine, my heart promised.

Mine.

We got a lot done at the bakery the rest of the week, though Christmas was creeping up on us and I already knew there was no way I'd finish in time for Baxter's usual Hullabaloo. I pushed aside the guilt though, because I knew at this point it was more important that I do a good job than rush it so he could have his annual party.

It was clear how sad he was that the bakery was still out of commission, however.

Ernie had only been able to claim the bug excuse for a few weeks so we were running out of things to keep Baxter away. Becca had a lot of creative ideas but none of them seemed plausible. Hell, now that I truly cared about Baxter, I felt bad for the bug lie anyway.

Maybe the surprise would be ruined but…

I couldn't freak him out like that again.

The bruises beneath his eyes got darker each day as his exhaustion grew. I wondered if he was pushing himself because he wanted to fix up the bakery, or maybe…maybe he just didn't know how to stop.

After his first therapy session he'd given me a call, his voice shy, his words wobbly. He'd told me it had gone well—as well as he could guess anyway, considering the fact he'd never been to therapy before. He liked his therapist. He said she was funny.

Which, I supposed for him was a ringing endorsement.

I was proud of him.

The hardest thing in the world was having the courage to face your own insecurities. Baxter was brave. I made sure to tell him this and his response had been a nervous laugh that sounded wet even over the phone.

I didn't want him to cry.

God, never again.

So I'd driven to his house and distracted him…thoroughly. We'd been interrupted though when we'd both had to climb into our vehicles and pick our kids up from school.

Nathan had stared at me, his eyes catching on the smile that wouldn't seem to leave my face.

He'd just smiled right back, a knowing glint in his eyes.

I wondered if he suspected…but. No.

We were being careful.

Besides, he didn't know I was bi so why would he?

By the end of the week, I'd finished the flooring in the bakery, as well as the electricity. I had to patch up some of the drywall. It'd gotten a fair bit fucked after we'd torn down the eons-old puke-green wallpaper. How anyone had ever actually chosen that for the walls was beyond me. Becca had assured me it hadn't been their fault. That her dad had simply been so busy spending all his money trying to repair appliances that broke every other week that they'd never had time to fix up the interior like they wanted.

That wasn't going to be a problem for long.

Every day someone would come along to check on the work inside the bakery, chat for an annoying fifteen minutes, and drop off a donation to either our supplies or our ever growing basket full of money.

Jesus.

The amount of people that were hell-bent on helping Baxter get back on his feet was just…amazing. I hadn't realized Belleville's community was so tightly knit. Or maybe…maybe I'd just spent so long glaring from the outside I hadn't realized how easy it was to be accepted among them.

The second they heard what I was doing for Baxter they welcomed me like I was an old friend.

We had an entire storage closet full of gifts, and Becca had quite literally burst into tears when she counted the money and realized that we were only a thousand dollars away from replacing Baxter's freezer. The fucking thing cost ten thousand dollars. Christ.

Did they think bakers were made of gold?

Greedy bastards.

The fact that we'd had nearly nine thousand dollars in donations was just…amazing.

I didn't mind the chatting anymore, not after I'd realized how much people actually cared about Baxter.

About me too.

I couldn't count how many times we'd had casseroles or food dropped off to us while we were working. And somehow—still—the secret hadn't gotten out. People popped by to help too. Trent was my most frequent visitor. At first he'd been a bit surprised by how enthusiastic I was about the whole thing, but he soon warmed up to the idea.

After a whispered conversation with Nathan one morning, they both gave me knowing looks and after that…well, he showed up for at least an hour every day.

My other siblings showed their support with donations and daily "how's it going" texts that I ignored. Jesus. As if I had time to have a whole conversation about work when I should be working instead.

They all got the same one-worded replies.

Paxton: Good.

Christmas break started the next week and Becca was practically bouncing off the walls that Friday after school as she chatted my ear off about the ski trip. It was a mandatory part of the Christmas Buddies program and every family that participated would be staying at the lodge in the same wing.

It was also fucking expensive, even though the lodge had given a very generous discount.

Baxter and I had opted to share a suite to save on the extra cash, and where before I'd been apprehensive about the sleeping arrangement, now I was a little giddy.

The money though?

Jesus.

But seeing the way Becca and Nathan screeched their excitement about the trip made it worth it. The way they were warming up to each other made my heart hurt. Nathan was no longer the nervous kid he'd been when we'd met up for the first time. He was himself around her—giggly, goofy, and adorably dorky.

My little boy.

I watched them giggle together for another lingering moment before I sighed and thought about what was going to happen tomorrow.

A bus would be picking the kids up from the school parking lot and they'd all ride together early. There was some sort of activity they were participating in that the parents were apparently not allowed to know about.

Becca and Nathan both were being very secretive about the whole thing but…to be honest, I didn't care. I was just excited for the two-hour drive I'd get to spend alone with Baxter. Sure we wouldn't be able to get frisky while I was driving but…just talking to him was enough to make my heart beat double-time in my chest.

He was funny, clever, and always thought the best of everyone.

I liked talking to him.

More than I liked talking to anyone.

I suppose that shouldn't be all that surprising considering the fact that as a general whole, I hated people. Chit-chat. Pointless small-talk. Feelings. None of those things were my cup of tea.

With Baxter though—he could ask me about the weather on repeat for eternity and I'd still find him endlessly fascinating.

"Fair warning," Becca popped up beside me, still far chattier than she normally was. She was actually really good about following my "silence" rule, so I didn't begrudge her excitement as she chewed on her lip and narrowed her eyes at me.

With her nose scrunched like that, she looked just like her dad and it made me bite back a smile.

She may not have been his physically but she sure as hell looked it.

"Dad is really, really freaked out about driving in the snow."

"I'm driving," I reassured her.

She nodded, but it was clear she wasn't done. "He's…" She shook her head, struggling for words. "Ever since mom died in a car accident he's been really weird about cars. Especially with snow though. He might act…weird or jumpy—or like…I don't know. Nervous? But can you… just be patient with him? I know sometimes he's a lot but he's really just feeling too much all at once and he struggles getting it all processed."

That was an incredibly eloquent way to put it, and I didn't want to give too much away so I just nodded and gave her a reassuring grunt.

Relieved, she turned away again.

"Oh and don't let him drink too much hot chocolate. He'll only get more jittery because of the sugar."

Jesus.

I suppose to be fair I'd fed him hot chocolate basically every time we'd all been together.

I rolled my eyes at her retreating back but then turned back to the spackle I was currently layering over a particularly nasty hole in the wall. I whistled a merry tune as I worked, my mind entirely in the gutter.

I dropped Nathan off at home after we were done for the day and turned to the other side of town to take Becca home. She'd climbed into the front seat the second Nathan had vacated it and I watched her through the corner of my eye as she fiddled with her seatbelt in a parody of the way her father had all those weeks before.

"Dad's happy," Becca told me after a moment of silence. I grunted. "He's…" She shook her head. "He's always been really sad. He just thinks he's good at hiding it. But he's actually really not. I worry about him a lot. But…"

My heart hurt as I remembered how I'd brushed off Nathan's comment weeks ago when he'd told me how he saw Baxter just sitting in his car sometimes.

Becca fumbled with her words for a second but I let her take her time, my heart beating unsteadily as I stared out at the snow-packed sidewalks.

"I'm worrying less about him now," she murmured softly. "I'm glad he has a friend like you."

Jesus.

My heart hurt.

"I'm gonna take good care of your dad, kiddo." I promised quietly, reaching out to give her shoulder a gentle squeeze. "You don't gotta carry it all anymore."

She sniffed a little and my heart lurched.

Her hands wobbled as she reached up to swipe at her eyes. I hadn't even realized she was crying. Silent crier, like her father was. Jesus, these two were adorable little blonde messes. How had I never noticed before?

They wore their hearts on their sleeves.

Open books.

"He works so hard for everyone but himself," she said softly, reaching out so her tiny little fingers squeezed my wrist. "He told me the other day he went to a therapist and I just…" she sniffled and I exhaled, my heart thudding. "I'm just so happy that he's taking care of himself."

"Your Dad is a good man, Becca." I told her softly, my voice a quiet rumble. The echo of Christmas music from the radio blanketed the silence in the cab as I chose my words carefully. "He's sweet. A fighter. A hard worker. Everyone goes through rough patches. But he's pulling through."

"Because he has you now," she nodded. We pulled up to a stop sign and I glanced over at her, noting the pink twitch of her sniffly nose and the way her makeup was already starting to run.

I shook my head.

"No, Becca. It's not because of me." I swallowed, unsure how to convey what I was trying to say. Feelings were complicated, slippery things. I didn't want to get this wrong. Especially when my own kid didn't ask me questions this complex. I was out of my depth here. "He made the choice for himself. I was just there to show him which direction he needed to take the first step." She nodded. "But he started walking all on his own." I repeated quietly. "I'm not going anywhere, but even if I did—he'd still be moving forward."

"That…that's good, right?"

"Real good, kiddo." I agreed, a quiet rumble. "Real good."

When we arrived at her house, her father's car was missing. He'd had some last-minute runs for deliveries before the trip and Becca smiled at me as she let me in and her dog came waddling his way toward us from the kitchen.

"You sure it's okay if your brother watches him?" she asked me, her voice still a little wobbly from our earlier conversation.

"He's a dog lover. I'm sure Pogo's gonna have the time of his life," I reassured her. It didn't take long for her to gather up all of her dog's shit and we piled it into the passenger side before loading up the corgi himself.

He panted at me, a king atop his folded up dog bed, brown eyes glistening with intelligence.

"You have short legs," I pointed out and he just woofed in reply.

Becca waved goodbye from the driveway as I drove away, my heart in my throat.

How was it that the Bakers had managed to whittle their way so quickly under my skin? They made room inside my heart where I hadn't known there was any vacancy. As I made the drive out of town toward Trent's house, I couldn't help but think about how different my life was now.

It hadn't been long but I'd changed.

Baxter Baker was changing me, and I couldn't even find it within myself to be mad about it.

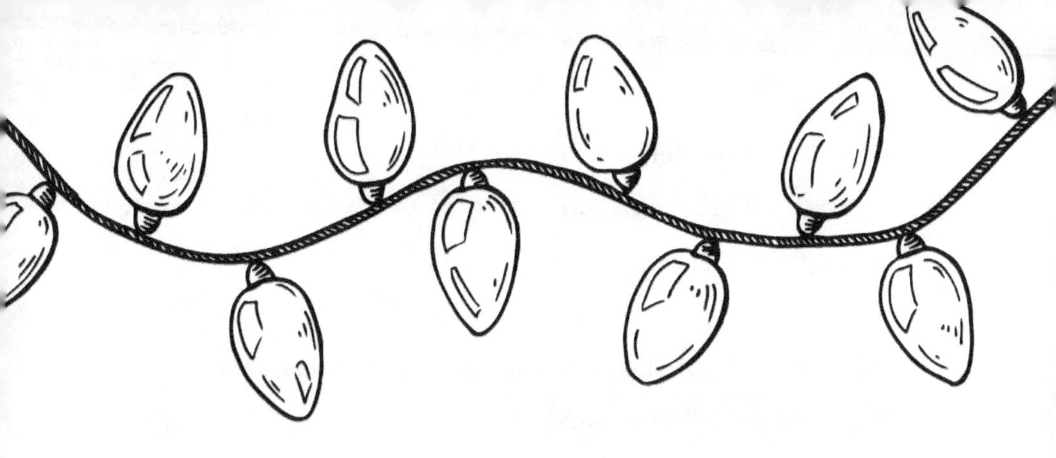

seventeen

BAXTER

NERVOUS EXCITEMENT BUBBLED UP INSIDE my chest as we peeled our way out of Belleville and began the half-hour-long journey toward the base of the switchbacks. We'd have to go up the mountain, down again, then up another to reach our destination and I was honestly terrified.

I hated the switchbacks on a good day but today the weather forecast had hinted at hell on Earth and I couldn't help the way my pulse fluttered every time I thought about it.

Paxton was dressed in a thick hoodie that left absolutely nothing to the imagination, his coat parted overtop of it because even with the heater in the car, it was cold as fuck today. I caught the scent of snow in the air and the overcast cloudy skies only seemed to solidify the fact that soon enough it would come down.

At least the kids had left before us, though now I was frightened the snow had hit them before it hit us.

They were two hours away after all.

Had they gotten to the lodge safely?

Christ.

Don't think about it, don't think about it, *don't think about it.*

"What's wrong?" Paxton asked after a few minutes of tense silence. He had the radio on and the quiet rumblings of Frank Sinatra over the speaker should've soothed me but it didn't. I felt like I was quite literally ready to bounce off the fucking walls.

"Nothing," I promised, even though I was lying.

"Baxter," Paxton growled, his voice a warning. I wilted, slipping a little in my seat as my fingers fumbled for my seat belt and I scratched at it in a nervous gesture to soothe myself.

Scratch, scratch, scratch.

"Baby," Paxton implored, this time lower—growlier. My heart flipped and my toes curled as I turned to look at him, my fear probably obvious as my lips wobbled.

"It's supposed to snow," I told him, more than a little breathless but not in a good way.

"I know." Paxton nodded, surprisingly patient as he reached across the space between us and closed one of his big warm hands around my own. My fidgeting stopped and I melted a little, the familiar brush of his calluses making my cheeks warm.

"I don't…" I shook my head. "I hate driving in the snow."

"That's alright," he rumbled quietly. "I've got you."

I've got you.

Those simple words were enough to make some of the tension in my shoulders bleed away.

But I couldn't…I couldn't stop thinking about the kids. The fucking kids, and their bus, and the fact that Becca hadn't texted me back in nearly two hours and god—was she already there? Was she safe? Had the storm hit early? Were they stranded?

Had they crashed?

Oh fuck, oh fuck, oh fuck.

"Baxter," Paxton murmured my name. "Talk to me."

"What if they crashed?" The words ripped through me at the same time the first flurry of snowflakes hit our windshield. As soon as the words were out, the fear became real again. Suspended between us was the possibility of death and my hands began to shake at the same time my heart gave a sickening lurch. "What if…"

"They didn't crash," Paxton reassured me, but I was too far gone to listen.

"What if…the storm…what if—"

"Baxter." My hands were slick with nervous sweat as Paxton gave them a tight squeeze. He held me tight enough my bones creaked and a broken, terrified little laugh left my throat.

"I should've made them ride with us."

"They had to go up early," Paxton reminded me.

"Oh god." I was going to be sick. "Did…did they text you?"

"The kids?"

I nodded, my phone screen still black where it rested on top of my thigh. I'd texted Becca again. Six texts now and nothing. Realistically I knew she was probably busy with her friends, or the activity that they'd gone up early to do but…I couldn't help the way fear crawled up inside me and made a home, gripped like a vice around my heart.

I couldn't breathe.

"Check my phone." Paxton passed me his phone, though he kept his movements careful and slow, his eyes never leaving the road.

The snow was beginning to come down harder and I swallowed bile as he rattled off his password and I swiped up to open the screen.

Nothing.

No new texts.

Paxton flipped the switch for the windshield wipers and they began to move quicker. The faster they moved the more rapidly my breath wooshed out. *Wipe, woosh, wipe, woosh.* My hands were shaking as I pocketed his phone.

If this had been any other situation I would've marveled at the fact he trusted me so easily with not only his phone but his password as well, but I was staving off a panic attack, so all I could do was choke on my own feelings.

Man.

Why hadn't I asked my therapist about this?

All we'd done was quick introductions and we hadn't gotten into coping mechanisms yet. I should've asked. I should've told her what I was about to do—about the lodge. The possibility of snow. The two-hour drive.

There was a reason I hardly ever left Belleville, and fuck.

Here it was.

Paxton was going to run away from me the second he got the chance. I was clearly unstable, and even though I knew this, I couldn't stop myself from shaking, my body cold all over as his hand returned to mine.

I almost wanted to shove him off.

I didn't want him to feel how cold I was, how much I shook, how my palms were sweaty and my hands were limp.

"Sweetheart," Paxton tried again, his voice quiet. "They're fine."

"But what if they're not?"

"Mmmm," Paxton rumbled in thought. He was concentrating on the road, which was fair. Because honestly I didn't want to die either. I was trying not to focus too hard on the fact that we were also driving through a potentially deadly storm. At least we'd opted to drive his truck and not my own modest van.

I stared out at the torrent of snow where it was now coming down in the beginning of what I knew was going to be a blizzard. We were only forty minutes from home. Maybe we could go back? But no. No.

Becca was waiting for me.

I swallowed bile.

"Try calling again," Paxton urged softly, giving my hands a gentle squeeze. I should've been more concerned that he was driving one-handed, but I needed him so badly it hurt. I pinched my eyes shut and tried to get my breathing under control.

Wipe, woosh. Wipe, woosh.

"Breathe, baby," Paxton urged, his warm hand only growing warmer the colder I became. "Breathe and we'll give them a call."

"What if they don't answer?"

"We'll call one of the teachers."

Oh.

Okay.

That…that was a solid plan. I hadn't thought of that.

I relaxed fractionally as I grabbed my phone with my free hand and wobbled my way toward Becca's number. Her profile picture bobbed at me as I hit the button and listened to the rumble of the call not connecting.

No service.

No fucking service.

"We'll get to the bottom of the mountain and try again," Paxton promised.

I knew he was right.

There was nothing we could do at this point but wait, but that didn't stop me from growing cold all over. *Breathe,* Baxter. I reminded myself. *Breathe.*

The first few breaths were stuttery and uneven.

I pinched my eyes tightly shut, focused on the swoop of the wipers on the window, and the quiet swell of Paxton's breath.

Listening to him helped more than I could explain.

He was calm.

Steady.

A mountain, a boulder, a tree.

There was no fear on his face when I peeked at him through my lashes. I watched the way his golden eyes stayed trained on the road, my heart in my throat. He looked handsome like that, confident, unbothered. He gave my hand a gentle squeeze.

"Match my breathing," Paxton urged in a quiet rumble. "Watch my chest, and try to mimic me."

I nodded, because what else was I supposed to do?

It took me a while to get the hang of it but eventually my breath was no longer rattling and I was able to calm myself down enough that I could think rationally again. The thick swell of Paxton's chest tested his hoodie as he inhaled, then exhaled. Slow and steady.

With each breath I matched, I relaxed infinitesimally.

I was so focused on the warmth of his hand and the flutter of his breath that I hadn't even realized we'd reached the end of the switchbacks and were firmly on the other side of the valley. This time when I peeked out the window, the white blizzard that fluttered in a torrent around us looked less deadly and more…pretty.

We were caught in nature, just like our ancestors of the past.

I swallowed, surprised when I realized the lump in my throat was gone and my eyes were no longer burning.

"Try again, baby." Paxton urged, giving my hand a gentle squeeze. "But use my phone. My service is better." He flashed me a teasing little smile and to my surprise I was able to return it with nothing more than an eye roll.

I tried again, fumbling my way through his password and pulling up Nathan's contact with barely a wobble.

It rang once, twice, three times.

He picked up.

The relief I felt was visceral. I felt it all the way down to my toes as I practically collapsed back into my seat, my fingers squeezing Paxton's so tight his fingers turned white.

"Nathan?"

"Oh hey, Mr. Baker." Nathan laughed, his voice merry. Not at all like the sound of someone who was stuck in a fucking blizzard. "Are you and Dad on your way yet? We got here like an hour ago."

My belly flipped and I released the breath I hadn't realized I'd been holding.

"We're halfway or so," I said quietly. "But the snow is bad out here, so it may take us longer to get there."

"Oh, no problem. Drive safe."

"Is Becca with you?" I asked quickly, because I could tell he was about to hang up. "Can I talk to her?"

"Oh!" Nathan made a sound and then I heard some rustling and what sounded like vigorous, waving? "Here she is."

"Hi, Dad." Becca's voice filled my ear and the relief I felt at the sound of it would've made me fall to my knees if I'd been standing.

"Are you safe?"

"Ugh. Yes!" Becca laughed. "I'm fine, silly. Are you safe?" She parroted back to me. I laughed, though the sound was brittle.

"I'm safe."

"Okay. Good." Becca was smiling. I could hear it. The sound soothed my soul and I relaxed as I released another tense breath. Paxton squeezed my hand tight. "I gotta go now Dad. Try not to think about the snow too much."

"Okay." My breathing felt more under control now and I smiled a little as I listened to the call disconnect. I tucked Paxton's phone safely inside my pocket and I turned back to him, the relief I felt clearly written across my face.

"See?" He murmured, his thumb rubbing circles along the top of my hand. "Nothing to worry about."

"Nothing to worry about," I repeated, marveling at how simple he made things seem.

Nothing to worry about at all.

Fifteen minutes later we were forced to pull over onto the side of the road at the base of the next mountain. The snow was coming down too quickly and it would be unsafe to travel the switchbacks before the next plow came through.

When that would happen though…we had no idea.

"It won't be long," Paxton reassured quietly, reaching over to give my shoulder a gentle squeeze. "They usually come through these parts an hour or so after the worst of the snow hits."

Until then, however, we were stranded.

Maybe if we'd left earlier we could've avoided this.

But…

It was too late now.

As my grandma used to always say, there was no use crying over spilled milk. We were stuck now, for good or for bad. I tried to ignore the piercing anxiety that was eating away at my chest. After talking to Becca and Nathan, I was feeling loads better. But that didn't stop the instinctual feeling of fear from creeping up on me as fat snowflakes hit our windshield and the quiet rumblings of Christmas music echoed through the air.

I figured…

I figured Paxton deserved an explanation for my odd behavior.

Hell.

He deserved a lot more than that.

"My sister died on a day just like this one," I told him quietly, fiddling with my seat belt, my heart in my throat. "She just…" I swallowed, my eyes burning. "She was just trying to get home to Becca."

"I'm sorry," Paxton's words felt like a blanket as they wrapped around me and I turned to him, searching his honeyed gaze for comfort.

"They'd been visiting a friend," I said softly, chewing on my lip. "I was at home. I'd just gotten the news about the bakery going up for sale and I was so, so fucking excited. It felt like everything was going right."

My heart was in my throat as I remembered the call I'd gotten. The way it had shattered me. The way the ground had fallen out from beneath me and I'd crumpled to the floor like I was made of paper.

Rebecca had been there all my life.

Loved me when our parents couldn't.

Grieved with me when Gram passed away.

Supported even my wildest dreams.

She'd been there every day—for as long as I could remember—until suddenly she wasn't.

And the Rebecca shaped hole in my life would never be filled.

It got easier as the years passed by but I never forgot the emptiness beside me where she should've been had she not gone out all those years ago.

I told Paxton about it.

Maybe for some, it was simple to explain.

Maybe for some, it wouldn't have meant what it did.

But I had never told anyone how I felt about that day. How I felt about what had happened. How every day I struggled to pretend normalcy when even just the slightest reminder sent me into a tailspin of grief.

Rebecca hadn't just been my sister, she'd been my only family.

I'd loved her with my entire heart.

And it had been torn right out of my chest.

I'd always had anxiety before that day. It was a part of who I was. A part of what made me...me. Another thing on the long list of reasons my parents found me intolerable right after *sucks dick* and *likes to take it up the ass.*

But after Rebecca was gone, my anchor had been severed and I'd been forced to swim for the surface. I had to pretend like I wasn't drowning because I knew the moment I acknowledged how deep I'd sunk, I'd no longer know which way was up anymore.

Paxton didn't say anything.

He didn't need to.

With the truck parked and the heater blasting, he just reclined his seat, slid it back as far as he could, reached for me and yanked me right into his lap. He was warm. Solid. Strong beneath me. I settled on top of him, my heart in my throat as he threaded one hand in my hair and the other smudged the tears away from my ruddy cheeks.

"Thank you," he murmured, like it was that simple.

Like sharing what I went through was enough.

Like all he wanted was to know me.

Like I was…

Like I was enough, faults and all.

"I got you," Paxton murmured a moment later and I stared into his golden gaze and wondered how the hell I'd gotten so lucky. His lips twitched up and I reached out with desperation, threading my fingers through his incredibly soft beard. The position we were in wasn't the most comfortable, especially on both of our backs but I ignored the twinge as I leaned down and our lips brushed gently, sweetly.

It felt like coming home.

Paxton's tongue slipped inside my mouth and I sucked on it, eager and desperate for more of him. He made a quiet rumbling noise in denial, slowing me down when I tried to speed up, kissing, sucking, licking until I got the picture and relaxed into his leisurely pace.

Maybe this—whatever it was between us—should've caused anxiety, but it didn't.

It was a break from the monotony of what ifs.

We kissed for what felt like ages before it was clear the snow wasn't letting up any time soon and we were both too hard to ignore the way our cocks rubbed together. I trembled, aching for him, aching for more, aching to be touched in a way I'd never felt before.

Our night at my house felt too far away, like a lifetime ago as I tugged at his hoodie and tried to get it high enough I could touch his skin.

"Slow down, B," Paxton said, his chest vibrating against my questing fingers. He reached down to the side of his seat, fumbled for a moment, and then with a click and slide his chair scooted back till it was in a fully reclined position.

I rocked a little, losing my balance, but Paxton caught me by the hips and held me steady.

Like this I could move more freely.

I rucked his shirt up as far as I could, my mouth watering as I stared down at the rolling, flexing muscle in his chest and abdomen. There was a swath of gorgeous dark curls that crested between his thick pecs and trailed deliciously down the center of his abs where it disappeared beneath his waistband.

I swallowed, my mouth suddenly dry.

"Like what you see?" Paxton rumbled, stretching out, flexing his chest at me in a way that made my dick hard and my eyes want to roll back. His round brown nipples peaked from the cold and I wanted nothing more than to give them each an apology suck and feel his muscles flex toward my lips.

"Fuck yes," I breathed, overwhelmed and more than a little turned on.

Paxton growled his approval, his fingers biting so tightly into my hips I was certain he'd leave bruises. I shuddered at the thought, my cock painfully hard where it twitched against the seam of my jeans.

Why had I worn jeans again?

They were incredibly difficult to get off, even when it wasn't fucking freezing out.

I shuddered and watched as Paxton's lips curled into a sexy little smirk. He released my hip with one hand and shifted to cradle the back of his own head, his bicep bulging as he watched me through hooded eyes.

"You gonna give me a show, B?" Paxton purred, his low voice doing something to my insides that I had no idea how to describe. I was breathless, hot, and more than a little eager as I reached for my zipper with shaky fingers.

I hadn't been lying when I'd told him I didn't know how to seduce someone, but he didn't seem to mind. In fact, he seemed to like the idea of me fumbling through this more than if I'd been a siren ready to take him to sea.

"Pull your shirt up," Paxton demanded, still calling the shots even though I was in the position of power here. I swallowed and complied, more than a little eager as I rucked my sweater up into my armpits and cool air hit my already shuddering chest. My nipples perked up immediately.

Despite the heater blasting in the car, I could still feel the cold exuding from the frosted glass. The closer we pressed together, the foggier the interior became. I was suddenly worried we might be spotted. We were pulled to the side of the road after all—no cover in sight.

"No one's going to see us, baby," Paxton hummed, the hand still on my hip giving it a circular rub that sent shivers all over my body. It was like he could read my mind. "I'm not reading your mind, you just keep looking out the window." He was teasing, but I wasn't convinced.

I narrowed my eyes at him.

"Uh uh," Paxton hummed, his brow lowering, his cocky grin dissipating. "None of that."

"None of what?"

"That attitude." He released me for a moment, only for his hand to return, fingers snapping gently but firmly against the fleshy part of my left ass cheek. I jumped a little, but the groan that left my lips was nothing but authentic as my skin tingled and I tossed my head back to whine.

"Sorry," I mumbled, wiggling on his lap, more than aware of the fact that I was sitting almost directly on top of his hard cock.

"S'okay," Paxton said, his voice nothing but gravel. "You gonna be good for me now?"

I nodded frantically, reaching for him with greedy hands that he swatted away. His pecs were heaving with each of his breaths—the only indicator aside from his cock of how turned on he was by all of this.

I wondered if he did this with all his boyfriends, but then I felt stupid. Paxton was like I was.

A dad first.

I'd never heard of him dating in all the fifteen years I'd lived in Belleville with him. The grapevine here was extensive and thorough, I was certain I would know.

I figured that was a question for another day though.

Right now I was far too focused on the way that Paxton had reached for my hips again and was giving my ass a slow sensual grind with circles of his powerful pelvis. He was lucky he had such a large truck otherwise this would've been entirely impossible.

"How far do you want to go?" Paxton asked, his honeyed eyes blown black with lust. His tongue flickered out to wet his lips and I had to force myself to hold still for fear that I would lose control and begin begging like the slut he made me whenever he was near.

"Fuck me," I breathed, more than a little eager.

"Mmmm." Paxton cocked his head, eyes narrowing, assessing.

His cock betrayed him. I could feel the way it twitched beneath me at the thought. I ground against it in thanks and watched as Paxton gritted his teeth and his brow knit in pleasure. He pressed his hips up against me, encouraging the movement, so I repeated it. Again, again, *again.*

"Pants off." Paxton's voice was nothing but honey as he suddenly hoisted me off his dick in a move so powerful it made my head spin. I sat suspended, shuddering as my head bumped the roof of the car and a quiet whine of my own echoed through the air.

It took some doing, both of our hands, and a good few minutes of swearing, but eventually I got us both naked. Paxton was eyeing me, a predatory glint to his eyes as I settled my naked ass atop his thighs again and he drank me in.

His eyes were heavy-lidded as they dragged up my thighs, across the v-line that led to my swollen cock and up to where my chest shuddered and heaved with each labored breath.

"Turn around." He raised a finger, wagging it in an exaggeratedly slow circle as I caught my breath, enjoying the brush of his thigh hair against my own. I did as I was told.

This new position was embarrassing, but I ignored the feeling as I leaned my arms against the steering wheel and held myself perfectly still. From this angle he'd have a front row seat to my ass and…well, I wasn't sure how I felt about that.

"Stop overthinking," Paxton hummed, reaching out for my hips. I expected him to grab me, to manhandle me again, to force me out of my negative mindset with eager kisses and the slick press of his cock, but he didn't.

Instead his touch was gentle as he smoothed his hands across my skin. He caressed me. That was the only way to describe it. His fingers trailed along my legs, across my hip bones, the gentle swell of my belly. He dipped for a moment into my belly button, tickling me there till my cock jumped. His fingers traced across my ribcage and the movements stopped with his hands fanned across my waist, and then he repeated the process all over again.

Paxton's hands were scratchy and hot, far hotter than the heater that now blew directly at me.

Outside the world was pure white.

Fat snowflakes flickered across the window and I watched enraptured as we sat safely tucked away inside the flurry. Close enough I could taste the frost in the air. It looked like heaven. Felt like it too.

The longer Paxton stroked my skin the harder my dick became. I could feel myself leaking and I had half a mind to reach down and touch my cock but I somehow refrained. I wanted him to do it for me. I wanted to feel the scratch of those fingers on my heated skin—to fuck his fist till my eyes rolled back.

There was a rustling sound behind me as one of Paxton's hands released my body. The other one remained firmly placed on my hip where he continued to pet me, almost like I was a spooked horse he was trying to soothe.

Maybe that's what I was?

Just an animal, ready to be tamed.

Why didn't that thought bother me?

eighteen

PAXTON

BAXTER WAS DELICIOUSLY PLIANT BY the time I got the lube out of my bag. He'd jokingly called me a boy scout earlier and I'd given him a playful salute. I figured now he'd be grateful for my forethought.

"I'm going to move you now," I warned, giving him a second to protest—he didn't—before I grabbed his hips and hauled him back far enough in my lap that his back was forced to arch and his lovely ass was close enough for me to really play with.

God it was nice.

Thick, bouncy.

Muscled but soft in the way only a man who ran and enjoyed his fair share of cookies could be. I ran my hands along his heated skin, testing the give, squeezing till I heard him gasp and only releasing when I knew he couldn't take anymore.

His pretty pink hole winked invitingly at me and I had to bite back a moan as I remembered what it felt like to taste him there.

I licked my lips, my cock jerking.

"Relax," I murmured, one of my hands smoothing over his hip again. His broad shoulders were tense. "Open up for me."

He did.

So beautifully.

Baxter's lovely hole fluttered as he released a broken sigh and followed my command obediently. He melted in relief like he'd just been waiting for me to tell him it was okay. God, he had no idea how much power he was giving me. My tongue felt too big for my mouth, my cock aching painfully as I uncapped the lid of the lube, squirted some on my dominant hand, and moved into position.

"If it's too much you tell me." I commanded, my fingers twitching as I watched the muscles in Baxter's back tense and flex as he got comfortable.

"What if someone sees us—"

"I'll protect you." I could've told him again that no one was going to see. We were in the middle of nowhere after all—in a blizzard. Hell. We couldn't even see out of the vehicle. How the hell was someone going to see inside it?

But he already knew all that.

It was his heart talking, not his head.

"I'll protect you," I promised again, and then I got an idea. I reached over to our discarded pile of clothes, trying not to shift too much on the seat, and not smear lube everywhere with my other hand as I grabbed my discarded hoodie and shoved it at him.

"Put this on."

It wouldn't hide what we were doing, on the very slim chance someone might see. But it would help him feel better. Hidden. Safe.

Baxter donned my hoodie without protest and I watched the twitch of his sweet ass as he moved, more than a little slack jawed. My fingers twitched, desperate to sink inside him, the lube glimmering as I stared enraptured.

With my hoodie pulled on Baxter looked…well.

Fuckable.

Jesus.

It hung on him, at least three sizes too big. Too long. Too wide. Too everything—Jesus. He was so fucking cute I couldn't wait to stick my cock inside him. As if his sweet little ass knew exactly what I was thinking his hole gave another eager twitch.

I groaned at the thought of him wanting something inside him just as much as I wanted to *be* inside him.

Needy little slut.

"Arch your back for me, baby." I reminded him. He did as he was told, incredibly obedient as he leaned his arms on the steering wheel for support and waved the supple globes of his ass in my face again.

God, maybe it was a filthy thought but I wanted to lick him where he was cherry red and eager to be filled.

There wasn't room though.

My back was already aching and I hadn't even gotten to fuck him yet.

The idea of sinking inside him again was just…fuuuuuck.

I was over eager as I played with his hole, rubbing the lube against it till he glistened, and the sweet little muscle gave beneath the press of my fingers. Sinking inside him felt like heaven. He was hot. Tight. Sucking at my fingers like the slut I knew he was.

My cock jerked where it pressed against his inner thigh and I groaned when I felt Baxter reach down. His fingers twisted around the head of my dick, playing with it, pulling at it till I saw stars and the two fingers I had sunk inside him started to move quicker than I'd meant to.

It was an accident really—only it quickly became more than that because Baxter's grip on my cock slackened and a desperate, needy whine filled the air.

So he liked it rough then.

I could do rough.

I had him riding my fingers like a cowboy in a few short minutes. Every time he sunk down on my hand he made this punched out little sound— broken and wet—like it felt so good he couldn't help but cry.

Sweet baby.

I curled my fingers and rubbed, stroking along his swollen prostate till he was humping my hand like a bitch in heat, his voice a needy warble as he hiccuped greedily for more.

Putting the condom on took what felt like eons.

It was worth it though because the first brush of his slack hole on the crown of my covered cock had my eyes rolling back and my balls drawing up tight.

This was Belleville's Baxter Baker.

Uptight little sunshine boy.

Everyone's favorite golden child.

And I was about to fuck him silly.

Sinking inside him felt like heaven. He clung to my cock, hot and tight, sucking me in with an eagerness I couldn't help but rival as I flexed my hips and ground up against him. With each snap of my hips Baxter only got louder.

By the time I was riding him hard he was moaning into the dashboard, his delicious ass bouncing, the muscle rippling as my pelvis slapped against him over, and over, and over. The harder I fucked him, the whinier he got, all breathy and sweet, my hoodie covering him in my scent as my cock split him open.

"Look at you," I purred, grinding up hard just to hear the way he cried. "Such an eager little slut, aren't you, sugar?"

Baxter let out another sob, his head bobbing with enthusiasm.

"You like my big cock, don't you, sweetheart?"

"Fuck—" Baxter's voice dropped an octave, breathy and broken as he ground down against me in response.

Interesting.

"I like your sweet ass too, baby," I hummed, my fingers biting hard into his hips as I continued to grind deep inside him. Watching the way his hole parted for me, slick and pink, dripping with lube as my hard cock disappeared inside him was the single hottest experience of my entire fucking life.

I'd fucked before.

Of course I had.

But I'd never fucked Baxter.

"I think you can do better," I purred, just to hear him sob. "I think you can ride me better, don't you?"

Baxter shook his head, his muscular thighs trembling so hard I was sure if I hadn't been supporting him he would've collapsed.

"You need help?" I asked, knowing he would say yes, knowing this was what we both wanted.

He nodded rapidly, his golden hair flopping, his body silhouetted by the flutter of the blizzard on the move.

Without asking again I sprung into action.

I grabbed him tighter, my grip bruising as I anchored myself into the sweat-sticky seat, pulled Baxter up off my cock by my hold on his hips, then slammed him back down.

The noise he made went straight to my head.

Both of them.

My cock spurted a little and I growled, an animalistic desire to claim, mark, bite roaring up inside me as I watched his pink little hole part for the thick head of my cock. An obscene squelching sound filled the air as I drew him up again, let him hover till he started whining, and then dragged him down *hard* on top of my cock.

In. Out. In. Out.

He was wet with lube, the sound of our joining filthy as salty-sweet sweat filled the air. I couldn't help myself. The louder he got, the harder I fucked him. I liked the way he trembled. I liked the way he squeezed around me every time I was almost all the way out—like he was trying to suck me back inside.

God.

I just liked *him*.

I liked him.

By the time I was ready to come Baxter was a sobbing, trembling mess.

"Touch yourself," I commanded, more than ready to hear the way he cried out his pleasure. I wished I could see his cock. See the way it bobbed when I fucked him. See the way it leaked all over, eager and wet. He was probably hard enough to pound nails.

Fuck.

I should buy him a flesh light. Tuck his pretty cock up inside it and force him to fuck it while I fucked him.

Baxter's hand snapped to his own cock and I watched enraptured as his arm blurred, his thighs tensed, and with one last snap of my hips he spilled with a cry across his fingers. I'd lick them after. Force him to let me clean him up—but for now I concentrated on the task at hand.

I fucked, and fucked, and fucked till my eyes rolled back, his breath caught—and I spilled inside the condom with a quiet groan.

By the time we were back in our respective seats, cleaned up, and no longer out of breath, the snow plows had come by. I turned to Baxter with a grin, ignoring the twinge in my back as I caught him watching me.

His pretty green eyes were still clouded with lust, though his earlier anxiety was long gone. He was too well-fucked to worry, apparently.

Best medicine ever.

"You okay, honey bee?" I asked, surprised by how gentle my voice was as I reached out to stroke over his still ruddy cheeks. He turned his gaze to mine—really looking. The dazed expression on his face fading away as his pink lips turned upward and the smile wrinkles at the corners of his eyes winked into place.

"I'm…" Baxter paused, his brow furrowing in thought. For a second I worried—worried I'd gone too far, that I'd pushed him too much. I shouldn't have been though, because his smile came back full force and he shook his head. "I was trying to think of a good sex pun, but…you fucked the puns right out of me."

I laughed.

Baxter kissed my palm.

And we headed out again, sweaty, sated, and happy.

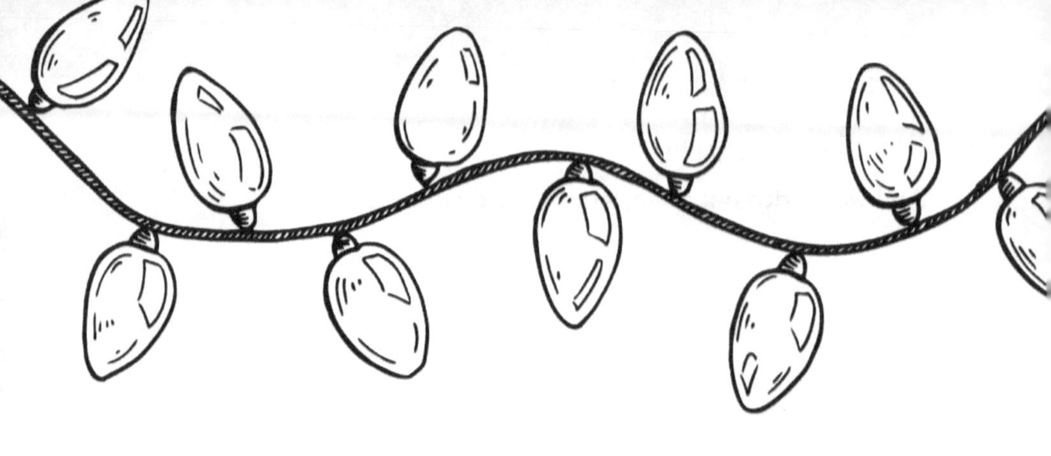

nineteen

BAXTER

THANK GOD I DIDN'T GET a leg cramp. My ass was sore in the best possible way, my thighs still trembled, and I couldn't help but be grateful my body hadn't decided to give out on me even though I had demanded acrobatics of it I hadn't performed in—well—ever.

I was sated and dopey the entire ride to the ski resort.

Paxton smiled at me fondly and my heart gave a fluttery sort of lurch as I remembered what we'd just gotten up to.

The anxiety was only a memory, I was too well-fucked to pay attention to anything other than the twitch of my greedy hole, still eager for more despite how thoroughly it had been taken care of.

The kids were waiting at the front entrance when we arrived and Becca shooed us toward the parking lot.

Paxton and I groaned in unison as we stepped out of the truck. I popped my back—or tried too—it was too fucking sore to do much of anything with. I couldn't help but laugh when I glanced over and saw the mirrored grimace on his face.

"Worth it," I hummed with a grin and Paxton just smiled back, a shy little thing that made his eyes spark.

He pulled a beanie over his ears and I ignored the fact that I'd stolen his hoodie.

I wasn't going to give it back.

Everyone could look at me and think what they wanted but…fuck. I'd never had the opportunity to wear around someone else's hoodie and I wasn't going to pass it up. Hell, if they asked I'd just lie and say I'd gotten cold.

Paxton's fingers closed around my shoulder, giving it a warm, firm squeeze before he released me and we headed on our way.

It turned out the surprise the kids had rode up to the resort early for was a dance. On ice. In the ice rink that was situated in the middle of the resort. It was really more of a cluster of hotels than anything else, though the outsides of the buildings were made entirely with rough-hewn wood made to look like log cabins.

The fresh snow made the place feel like a winter wonderland and I couldn't contain my excitement as Becca tugged me toward the ice rink with a wicked grin.

We'd had a chance to change and get warm before being forced out again and I tipped my head up to admire the way the sunset bled pink through the overcast sky. Night would come soon and with it a malicious chill would follow. I ignored that inevitability, however, as I sensed the retreating snow in the air and inhaled the crisp clean breeze that tickled the tip of my pink nose.

"It was my idea!" Becca cheered and I grinned at her, following her around as she pointed out all the decorations that she'd planned. As head of the Student Council she'd gotten to be in charge of a lot of the planning for the trip and she was more than a little excited as she chatted away at me.

I couldn't help but be warmed by her words.

It had been a long time since we'd just…talked like this.

Without the anxiety of the bakery hanging over us. Without my own fear. Without her age getting between us because I didn't know how to talk to the teenager that held my little girl hostage inside her.

I realized now that the distance between us had been mostly my fault.

Becca hadn't changed.

She was still the same little kid that threw up a lemonade stand at the end of our driveway every summer and saved all her money up so she could throw an even bigger stand the next year. She was still the same kid that had given all her Barbies haircuts, then insisted she cut mine. The same kid that skinned her knee at the park and instead of crying, she just told me with importance that "it would heal, daddy. Don't cry."

She was…

Mine.

As she always had been.

"It's beautiful, Becca." I told her as I reached out to pluck at her little soufflé bun. It bobbled and she laughed, dodging my hands, though her green eyes were brighter than the flickering lights that decorated the edge of the ice rink.

There were silver paper snowflakes hung from wooden beams that spanned the top like an open roof. Christmas lights glimmered, dipping like fallen stars. The sound of Frank Sinatra's sweet crooning echoed through the mostly empty space as I tucked Becca against my chest and gave her a happy little squeeze.

"You smell like Paxton," Becca complained and I just laughed.

"He smells good though."

"Yeah." She sniffed me, clearly having noticed my borrowed hoodie immediately. "It suits you."

I smiled at her, tucked her into my chest, and we headed toward the booth where the rental skates were being held hostage.

By the time we hit the ice the rest of the parents and families had shown up. I tried not to be obvious about the fact I was checking over my shoulder constantly for the moment Nathan and Paxton would arrive.

"I don't think Paxton's gonna come on the ice, Dad." Becca told me. She saw right through me and I blushed bright red, more than a little embarrassed. She just laughed and gave my elbow a pinch as we zoomed around the outer edges of the ice rink.

We'd spent a lot of time skating when she was younger.

I'd been poor, so most of our Christmas activities had to be things where I could get a membership. The movie theater really had been the only thing we did that I wasn't able to get a discount for.

Becca was graceful. She looped around me in easy circles, her round cheeks pink, her eyes bright as we chatted about school, work, and things that meant nothing, yet…meant everything in that moment.

It was the boring things that built stability.

I couldn't help but be grateful that I'd lived a life blessed enough that I could enjoy my daughter complaining about the monotony of school activities.

The sun sunk low and the inky indigo sky bled blue, dappled by winking stars that laughed above us. I bumped into another family, mumbled an apology, and spun my way around them to catch up with my daughter where she whipped around the arena like an ice dancer on crack.

Becca was giggling as I chased her down and my heart was in my throat, cheeks flushed as I finally caught up and we spun to a stop. The way the ice kicked up beneath my skates was more than a little invigorating. I could feel the blades sink into it, building friction and speed, smooth as butter as we spun our way around the rink once more. Twice more. Three times.

"Nathan!" Becca called, waving her hands in excitement as we approached the opening to the rink once again. There was a little plastic lip that stopped people from gliding in and out and I paused, stepping up onto it, then onto the rubber padding as I wandered my way after Becca as she chased Nathan down.

It wasn't hard to spot the Montgomerys.

They towered above the crowd.

Nathan was waving at us, all gangly limbs and sunshine smiles, and I couldn't help but wave back with just as much enthusiasm. The kid was fucking adorable and it was just…rude not to give back the effort he expended.

Paxton's smile was softer, sweeter.

Just for me.

With my skates on I was taller than normal and I could feel my pulse stutter as we came to a stop only a few feet in front of the two men and I realized I could almost see directly into his eyes.

It felt weird.

But good.

In the way all things did when you experienced them for the first time.

New.

"You gonna come onto the ice?" Becca asked Nathan. It didn't escape my notice that she hadn't offered the question to Paxton.

"Yeah! Just gotta get my skates." Nathan grinned at her and for a moment I was shocked because…fuck. I hadn't realized how close they'd gotten. Seeing how comfortable they were now made it obvious how awkward he'd been when we'd first started meeting up.

I didn't get those same fluttery vibes anymore though.

His eyes were warm.

His smile was honest.

I wondered if he still liked her or if maybe…his crush had turned into something more…platonic?

Becca snagged Nathan's arm and dragged him off. She abandoned us without a glance over her shoulder as she chattered away and my heart gave a throb in my chest at the thought of how comfortable she was with him now.

Becca, as much as she razzed me about it, also had difficulty making real friends.

It came with being friends with everyone.

You were never really friends with anyone at all.

I turned to Paxton, shocked all over again by the fact that when I looked I didn't have to look up to catch his gaze. At least not by much.

"How's your back?" I asked, because it had been clear he'd been favoring it all the way up the steps to our shared hotel room.

I swallowed the lump in my throat when I thought about the fact they'd only given us three beds. Two separate rooms for the kids. And for us…well.

We'd either have to make use of the pull out bed or…get creative.

"Sore," Paxton grimaced, but then his expression softened and he reached out to gently run his thumb across my lower lip. His hand was warm and I sighed, my lashes fluttering happily as I let him play with me for a moment before lacing a gentle kiss against the pads of his finger. "How's yours?"

"Sore," I parroted.

He snorted.

His finger released my lip, but instead of moving away he slid his hand to the back of my hair, scratching along my scalp till a shiver of pleasure shuddered its way through my body.

"Anything else…?" Paxton rubbed up behind my ears and I had to stop myself from purring. "Sore?"

Oh.

My hole gave a sympathetic twitch and I whined, unable to help the needy noise as it left my lips.

If I hadn't been paying close attention I probably would've missed the way Paxton inhaled sharply in response. His pupils dilated. His lips parted as he rumbled out an answering groan.

"Don't get me started again," he growled softly. "I don't have enough self-control."

I didn't want him to have self-control.

I didn't say that though, because that was a lie.

We were literally in public. As much as I loved his voyeuristic streak, there were places that were better left pure.

"Come skate with me," I urged, tipping my chin back so I could lean into his questing fingers.

"Can't."

"Your back?" I blinked.

"Can't skate."

Oh.

Why had that not occurred to me? I'd just…assumed everyone knew how.

"I can teach you!" I offered, reaching out to catch Paxton's wrist as he dropped his hand from my hair and his brow lowered into his, now familiar, grumpy scowl.

"I'll look ridiculous."

"C'mon, grumpy." I urged, latching onto his hand and giving it a little tug. "You won't look ridiculous."

"I will if I fall on my ass."

"Everyone falls at least once when they're learning. Hell. I fell at least fifty times."

"Doesn't make me feel better."

"Paxton," I said softly, ducking so I could catch his gaze. He had a stubborn twist to his lips and the muscle in his jaw was jumping beneath his immaculately manicured beard. The starlight flickered in the silver at his temples and I had to bite back the urge to lace kisses along them till he gave in.

I gave his hand a gentle squeeze instead. Even through his gloves I could feel how warm he was. I craved him, like a drug. Suddenly wishing we were anywhere but here. Somewhere…private.

Warmer.

"Please?" I asked softly, gently. "If you don't want to, that's fine but…I would love to teach you. To help you. I don't care what anyone else thinks."

I watched his throat bob, his toffee-colored eyes flooding with heat once again.

"You might change your mind when I take you down with me," he said softly.

"I'll go wherever you go, happily."

"Even to the ground?"

"Especially to the ground."

Paxton grinned at me, so bright and fierce I was sure it could set me on fire. He was so handsome like this. Carefree. The breeze lifting the tips of his chestnut brown hair where it stuck out of his beanie. His ears were pink from the cold—the tip of his nose too—and I couldn't help but want to kiss him.

I didn't though.

My heart throbbed.

"I admire that kinda loyalty," Paxton told me, leaning down to bump our cold noses together. I laughed, gave his hand a tight squeeze, and pulled him toward the rental stand.

Paxton was not at all gifted when it came to ice skating. He was stiff as a board, terrified, and more than a little angry as he swore up a storm, waddled around, and clung to me with desperation written across his handsome features.

Despite this, I had more fun helping him around the rink than I'd had in years.

He fell.

He took me down with him.

The ice was slippery and cold as we skidded, careful of our skates, and I couldn't help the way laughter bubbled up inside me so violently I had no choice but to tip my head toward the sky and release my joy for the rest of the world to hear.

When I stopped laughing, Paxton was staring at me. His eyes flickered with what could only be described as awe as he flashed me a grin and then began the arduous process of climbing to his feet again.

We fell three more times by the time the night was over.

But Paxton had smiled at me more during that brief two-hour period than he had in the entire time I'd known him.

In some ways it was almost like I was teaching him what it felt like to lean on someone else. Which made me incredibly happy—considering the fact that lately it seemed all I did was search for his steady presence like a compass drawn north.

Paxton looked at me like I was spun from gold.

It was frightening.

Amazing.

Wonderful.

I'd never had someone else look at me that way before.

Later that night after the kids had gone to bed, Paxton and I made our way quietly down to the outdoor hot tub. It was situated at the back of the lodge, in a private area that faced toward the mountains. Though it was technically outdoors, it was still blocked from prying eyes by walls made of rough hewn wood and that same canopy of fairy lights that had decorated the ice rink.

"Ouch," I hissed with a wince as we began the painful process of undressing in the changing room. It was empty, probably due to the late hour, and I couldn't help but be grateful as I grimaced my way through painfully pulling my shirt over my head.

There was a reason we were at the hot tub after all.

And it had nothing to do with sex.

And everything to do with the fact we were both feeling battered and bruised and more than a little sore from our earlier exhibitionism.

Paxton grunted in sympathy, the clenching of his jaw the only indicator that he was just as affected by our mutual back pain.

He somehow undressed even slower than I did, so I stood there and watched him, a towel wrapped around my shoulders, admiring the view.

Paxton's back flexed and flickered as he stretched his arms above his head. I watched, enraptured, tracing my eyes down the dip between his lats to the dimples that flickered at the top of his waistline. God. His ass was glorious. Thick, muscled. Not an ounce of fat in sight. His tattoos were entrancing, nature scenes that spanned his lovely skin like his body was a museum.

The muscle though…fuck. It was beautiful.

I figured it must come from his job.

He was thick. Capable. With curly, nearly red, chest hair that danced between the massive swell of his delicious pecs. God. I wanted to bite them. Suck on them and smash my face between them till he smothered me with his lovely chest.

"Ready?" Paxton hummed, nodding his head toward the heated walkway that would lead the twenty or so feet to the hot tub enclosure.

I hoped we'd be alone.

Even though we were there for relaxation, I couldn't help but optimistically slip our discarded bottle of lube into my swim trunk's pocket. They were really more cargo shorts than anything else, but they had flamingos wearing Hawaiian shirts all over them, so I figured they were vacation approved.

Paxton eyed me from head to toe, his lips twitching up, his eyes flooding with heat as he looked his fill. He stepped close enough I could feel the heat emanating from his body, his chest nearly brushing my own.

Somehow, when he stared it felt less creepy than when I did.

My toes curled and my cock gave a needy twitch.

Fifteen or so years without sex with another person had made my libido more of a whore than I was.

Paxton's grin turned feral, his eyes flickering golden in the dim light as he reached out with one massive palm and curled his hand around my covered cock. He didn't stop there. With his palm flush to my needy dick, our breath mingling, he slipped his fingers lower, rubbing behind my balls, his grip firm but almost clinical.

Like in a way he was checking whether or not I was taking good care of his property.

I licked my lips, a needy noise escaping me unbidden.

"Tell your thirsty little cock to behave," Paxton threatened, leaning down till his hot breath caressed the shell of my ear. I could smell him. The scent of wood shavings, sweat, and power trickling off his lovely skin.

He gave my dick another squeeze.

My hips fucked toward his grip, unable to help myself as I leaned heavily against him. Paxton easily took my weight as he played with my now fully hard cock.

The throbbing in my back cut our little exchange short, though as a pained gasp left my lips and Paxton pulled back quickly, his eyes wide with concern.

"Hot tub?" I urged, gently cocking my head toward the door.

"Whatever you need, B."

When he released me my dick gave him an unhappy twitch goodbye. Paxton chuckled.

The hot water did wonders for my back as I sunk inside its heat. Paxton groaned beside me and I sighed, stretching my arms so I could casually— sneakily—adjust the lube bottle inside my discarded towel on the side of the tub. We weren't alone, like I'd hoped. So my plans to get fucked again had to be thrown out the window.

Paxton arched a brow at me but I clammed right up.

We had an audience, after all.

The man sharing the hot tub with us sat with his legs slung wide, his head tipped back, as he enjoyed the rush of the heated jets just a few feet away from where we sat. I felt Paxton's foot bump up against my knee and I reached down to give it a gentle squeeze in warning.

Though it had a much different effect than I'd expected because the moment I touched him Paxton groaned, a quiet, unplanned little noise that sent shivers all over my body. Interesting. I gave his foot another squeeze.

He opened his eyes, dark lashes fanning to highlight the molten glimmer of his iris as he cocked his head at me, brow furrowed in his usual pissed-off way. Though, this time I thought it might have more to do with the fact that he hadn't expected to make a sound when I touched him.

"Your feet sore?" I asked quietly, watching as his face performed a ballet of emotion. Denial. Embarrassment. Desire. Resignation.

"The skates were too small," he admitted, voice a quiet rumble that made my belly flip.

Oh.

Oh.

I blinked, my heart fluttering. Like a freight train the realization hit me that not only had Paxton indulged me for several hours of ice-skating humiliation, he'd also done it wearing skates that were far too tight. He hadn't... *Why hadn't he said anything?*

"You were having so much fun," Paxton grumbled quietly. "They were the largest ones they had. I didn't want to..."

The words remained unspoken but they hung like a gift in the air between us.

He didn't want to disappoint me.

My eyes burned a little as I realized just how far this man would go to make me happy. He supported me—in more than just my lowest moments. He was kind, fair. Sweet. His affection was quiet as a winter morning but warm enough to burn when you knew where to look.

I rubbed the hell out of his feet in thanks.

Ten minutes into the foot massage the man next to us seemed to come to life. For the most part he'd ignored us, though now I could feel his gaze prickling over my skin. He was a handsome man. Tall. Broad-shouldered. Not nearly as handsome as my lumber jack but definitely not hard to look at either.

His attention made me flush, my skin crawling as my heart gave a nervous flutter.

"You a natural blond?" He asked me, his voice a quiet drawl.

I glanced over at Paxton, my fingers stilling where they caressed the insole of his foot.

He was watching me, a dark glimmer in his gaze.

I didn't know what to do.

I didn't want to be a dick.

But…

"Um. Yeah." I said quietly, not wanting to encourage the conversation but not really sure how to stop it either. It wasn't like I got hit on all the time. *That's what this was, wasn't it?* Or maybe…god. Maybe I was being stupid.

Maybe he wasn't interested.

Maybe this was all in my head and he was just being polite?

"You from around here?" Hot tub guy asked and I was once again stuck as I floundered to figure out how to respond.

Apparently I didn't need to worry.

Paxton responded for me.

His voice was a quiet growl, the normally friendly candor he used when he spoke to me entirely missing as he said, "We came here on vacation with our kids."

The guy blinked.

I blinked.

Paxton glared. He straightened to the full extent of his height. Water rippled between his pecs, his nipples hard, the curls that danced across his chest flickering in the aqua light that emanated from the hot tub.

He glared the other man down, the muscle in his jaw flickering with tension—like he was an animal ready to fight to protect his territory.

I stared at him, my flush only climbing higher as my brain processed what he'd done. Maybe to an outsider, it wouldn't mean much but… fuck. Anyone who heard "we came here on vacation with our kids" would assume one thing and one thing only.

He'd basically claimed me as his fucking husband.

"Oh." Hot tub guy smiled at us both, his eyes assessing before he seemed to figure out what Paxton was implying. "Have a nice night, you two."

He rose from the water and I watched him go, unable to help the way I admired the droplets that dripped down the back of his legs. I wondered what Paxton would look like when he got out of the water. Delicious as fuck I was sure.

I'd have to make him get out first so I could watch his thighs flex.

When the guy was out of ear shot I turned back to Paxton, more than a little aware of his hot gaze on my face.

"He wanted you," Paxton said, his voice dark, his eyes darker.

I swallowed.

My cock gave a needy twitch.

I liked him growly. I liked him mean—my big teddy bear turned feral.

"Why?" It didn't make sense.

It wasn't like I was in my twenties anymore. Sure, I worked out. I took care of my body but…I wasn't…the kind of guy people lusted after on first sight. I was an acquired taste.

"What do you mean, *why?*" Paxton asked, some of the darkness in his gaze fading away as he shifted his foot off my lap. Soon enough he crossed to my side of the hot tub, the steam rising around him as he slipped beside me till our thighs were pressed flush together under the water.

I could feel his leg hair where it brushed against mine and I shuddered, distracted by his presence alone. He loomed over me. Delicious. I watched a water drop trickle down his throat and I fought the desire to lean over and lick it off.

The heat was helping my sore back already so the only thing on my mind at that moment was what I would have to do to convince Paxton to slip his cock inside me again.

Being fucked once wasn't enough.

I needed more.

We had a lot of lost time to make up for.

"Baxter," Paxton grumbled, clearly not happy that I'd dodged his question.

"I mean…" I chewed on my lip. *What had he asked me?* Right. "Why would he want me? I'm just…"

"Just what?"

"Just…me."

Before I could blink I was yoinked through the water. Bubbles fanned in my wake and a startled laugh burst from my lips as Paxton deposited me across his lap, my belly settled against his thick thighs, my cock twitching where it almost brushed against him. I had to keep my weight on my hands for fear of sinking too far in the water, though the feeling of surprise didn't leave as I tilted my head to look back at him.

"Why—"

His hand came down on one of my ass cheeks, a gentle smack that would've hurt had we not been floating inside a hot tub. Instead it just served as a reminder that in his eyes I'd been naughty enough to be spanked.

"You're perfect." Paxton growled, not bothering to smack me again. He just shifted his grip, fanning his fingers along my ass and pressed his thumb inside my crease so he could rub at my covered hole.

I was still a bit sore from earlier but it was the good kind of sore.

The kind that made my skin buzz and my hole twitch.

"You're perfect, so of course he's looking," Paxton hummed. He probably meant for his voice to sound thoughtful but all I heard was the possessive bite of his jealousy. "Let him look," he seemed to decide after a moment. "Let him look because we both know who's going to be the person that takes you up those stairs and fucks that little ass of yours." Paxton's eyes were dark with lust and I whined, thrusting forward so that my hard cock could grind up against his thighs. He gave my hole another eager rub and I humped him, my toes curling. "You're *my* honey bee. He can find his own fucking hive."

And with that he proceeded bend me over the lip of the hot tub, yank my shorts down, and finger fuck me till I was a needy, sobbing, desperate mess. Later, after we'd rinsed off and hurried our way up to the room, Paxton sunk inside me for the second time that day.

He felt somehow even larger than before.

Thick.

Delicious.

Fucking wonderful.

I clung to him, my hole fluttering as I arched my back and let him take me.

I buried my whimpers into the covers as he tangled our fingers together and his pelvis slapped against the meat of my ass. He smelled like sweat and sex and the hint of wilderness, and I found heaven each time he ground against me. I couldn't help the way I greedily took his cock, clenching at it each time he pulled out.

The slick squelch of our coupling was loud in the silence.

Our moans were quiet.

Both of us were aware of the kids that slept in the adjoining rooms, but were unable to help our carnal desire as Paxton sank inside me and I saw stars dance behind my eyelids. The way the fat head of his cock ground against my prostate had my toes curling and my hard cock leaking eagerly against the bed covers.

When I came Paxton caught my pleasure in his palm, saving the sheets. I didn't have the heart to tell him that I'd already made a mess of them. When he came I squeezed him tight enough I heard his breath catch and felt his rhythm stutter. We curled together, snuggled like two puzzle pieces. I watched the snow through the window as it came down in a flurry and I wondered, not for the first time, how the hell I'd gotten so lucky.

It felt too good to be true.

Paxton snuffled against me, rubbing his nose along my sweaty throat as he curled his heated body around mine, smashing me into the mattress.

"Stop overthinking," he murmured softly. "We're safe. We're happy. The kids are happy."

I nodded, smoothing a gentle kiss across the top of his fluffy head.

He still smelled like chlorine.

I traced over his tattoos, my fingers dancing as I tried to force my wandering mind to become still. I couldn't do it though. That was the problem. It would be easy enough to hold it all in, hide away as I'd done for all my life but…after several tense seconds of silence I spoke. I was trying to be better, in more ways than one, and I realized that keeping my worries to myself for all these years had never stopped people from worrying about me.

It was the braver thing to do to voice them.

Maybe then…maybe then I could move on?

"I'm worried about the bakery," I said softly, well aware that I had never really talked to Paxton about this. He made a grunty little noise and fanned a kiss against my collar. At first I thought he might be asleep but then he spoke, his voice rumbling against me.

"What are you worried about?"

"I…" I didn't know how to explain my feelings. Everyone else always made this part look easy. How could I put words to the dark mess of tangled yarn that was my heart? "I'm scared." I swallowed. I tried again. "What if…what if I can't get it running? I can't go on like this. Like I've been doing since July. It's too much."

That was the crux of it all.

The guilt came too because when I'd first started my business I'd run it from home and I'd done that for years with no issue. I wasn't sure why it felt different now—why it was harder.

"If I can't be a baker I don't know what I could do," I told him honestly. "I put all my eggs in one basket. I don't have any other skills."

"Sugar," Paxton murmured softly, shifting around till he was on top of me, leaning on his elbows so I could see the flicker of warmth in his beautiful amber gaze.

He called me honey bee.

But he was the one with honey for eyes.

"Nothing is gonna happen to your bakery." Paxton said, his voice soft. "I know you're in the thick of it now, but things always have a way of working themselves out."

"What if they don't?" I asked, because the thought had been plaguing me. As much as I liked to think all I needed was some expensive equipment to get the business running again, I knew that was naive. When I'd bought it I knew it was basically run into the ground—and here we were, over ten years later and I had never had the means or time to fix the things I'd sworn I'd fix. "What if it's just…dead?"

Paxton stared at me. The nervous part of me worried he'd brush me off, or that he'd find my feelings annoying and I'd watch the warmth in his eyes bleed away as he realized—finally—that I was too much to handle after all.

Paxton weighed his next words before he spoke.

When he did, his voice was whiskey and smoke, curling around me, sweet as syrup.

"I'll take care of you," he promised softly. "Whatever happens is going to happen. You can't control the future." He blinked those gorgeous dark lashes at me as he shifted so he could cup my face in one large scratchy palm. His thumb ran reverently over my bottom lip, tracing it like he was cataloging my features, so he would never forget them. "I can't promise everything will go right. That's not in my power. But I can promise you— whatever happens—I'm gonna be right by your side."

My eyes burned and I fanned a kiss against the tip of his thumb, my lips wobbling into a broken smile as my heart gave an unsteady *thump* in my chest.

"I know we haven't known each other long," Paxton said softly. "But I'm the kinda guy who doesn't give up when he finds something he wants." I kissed his thumb again. "I want you, Baxter. I want you when you're sad, when you're happy, when you're worried, when you're old and gray and covered in wrinkles."

I snorted, though my eyes were wet, so really, it was more of a sob.

"I want to believe you," I whispered. But it hadn't been long since we'd started this, whatever it was. His devotion seemed too good to be true. "I really do but…"

"Let me show you then," Paxton said softly. "Let me show you."

I didn't know what that meant but I said yes anyway.

I fell asleep with his heartbeat against mine and snowflakes for company, and for once in my life I was content to let sleeping dogs lie.

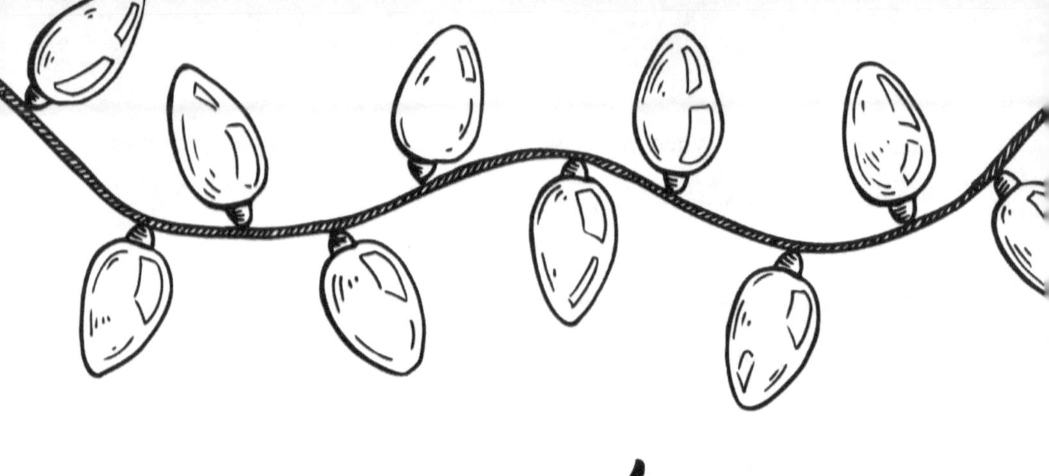

twenty

PAXTON

WITH ONLY A WEEK TILL Christmas the surprise crew and I were working overtime. With the ski lodge behind us and the magic of that weekend tingling at the tips of my fingers I was even more determined than before to finish Baxter's bakery.

I could see the way it weighed on him, and I wasn't the only person that had noticed the tabs he kept leaving up on his computer for new equipment to replace the mixers that had decided to fuck off to hell some time last summer. I couldn't get his worried face out of my mind. That conversation we'd had blanketed by snow and silence had haunted my memory.

Becca found me the Friday before Christmas, her hands covered in protective work gloves, a pair of goggles tucked over her face in a way that made her look suspiciously like one of those yellow…blobby guys. *Minions?* Or something like that.

"Mr. Montgomery?" She asked quietly, latching onto my elbow and gently steering me away from the crowd of men I had working on painting the back room. Trent had shown up with Ben in tow. It hadn't taken long for Nathan to take charge of them and begin directing their effort where we needed the most help.

There was no way we'd finish in time for the Hullabaloo but…I had another idea up my sleeve I was sure would be even better.

It was time for the world to give back to Baxter after it had done nothing but take.

I followed after Becca obediently, trying not to be charmed by how serious she was about everything. Man. Wouldn't be surprised if that kid was the first soufflé to run for president. I had to hide my smile against my shoulder as the thought made me laugh.

She led me all the way outside to the back of the bakery.

Despite it being overcast, the sun still caressed the glare of snow tucked behind the building atop the dumpsters and nearly empty parking lot. It was peaceful, though chilly. I glanced at Becca, waiting patiently even though I was fucking cold and she had to be even colder than I was.

She didn't have my muscle mass.

"Um…" She started, then stopped, chewing on her lip. Her little bobbly bun flopped around and I had to force myself not to reach out and flick it. That would probably be rude. I'd never had a daughter though, so what did I know?

And that was the crux of it all honestly.

Becca was…well.

If her father and I stayed the way we were then Becca was mine as much as Nathan was.

That meant I really needed to listen to her now, especially with her eyes a little wet and her lips twisted into a grim wobble.

"What's up, kiddo?" I asked softly, surprised by how gentle my voice came out.

Becca wilted, the tension leaving her shoulders as she crossed her arms tight around her chest like she was trying to hold herself together.

"Um. So…" She swallowed. "Ever since the beginning of the year I've been working jobs?"

I nodded.

"But the reason I've been doing that is because I wanna help my dad."

My heart lurched.

"He's been so stressed out. And I looked up how much one of those mixer things he keeps looking at costs and they're like—*two thousand dollars*. And I've been saving up and saving up but I still don't…I don't quite have enough."

I thought about the pile of cash we had stashed safely inside a cabinet in the bakery and my throat grew suddenly dry. It was so much more than she needed and yet…she hadn't said anything. Hadn't tried to touch it, even though her goal was the same as all the people that had donated.

She wanted…what?

To do this on her own?

Or…

"The money inside is for a freezer, which he super needs," Becca told me, clearly a mind reader. "And I have…Um." She fiddled around in her pocket, shimmying to grab her phone out of her stupidly tight pants— kids were so dumb these days, was it not cool to have proper circulation? She took her glove off one hand and swiped around the screen for a tense couple seconds before she held it out for me to take.

I stared down at her bank account, my heart thudding, my palms slick.

"I'm five hundred short," Becca told me quietly. Her phone screen was cracked to hell and back and I realized suddenly why I'd seen Baxter shopping for phones when he'd been tucked into my bed this past week. He was going to buy one for her, even though it would mean months more of the madness without his bakery.

Jesus, these two were sweet.

Fucking idiots.

Sweet idiots, though.

"Do you think…" Becca swallowed and I handed her phone back, suddenly aware I'd been waiting too long. "Do you think I could take a loan out from you? And maybe…I could keep working for you after the bakery is done? I'm good for it, I swear. I just…"

Her lip wobbled and my eyes stung as emotion was brought to the surface I didn't even know I had.

This sweet baby.

Jesus.

"I'm going to hug you now," I warned her. Her eyes widened, though she held her arms out immediately, a smile teetering across her face as I wrapped my arms around her. I lifted her from the ground, squeezed, and gave her a shake.

Christ on a cracker.

She weighed about as much as a tom cat.

"'Course I'll fucking help you." I gave her a gentle shake, amused when she started laughing and I felt her toes bump up against my shins. She smelled like her dad. Something else too—deodorant?

Anyway.

I set her back down only to realize I must've done something right because she wouldn't let me go. Her tiny little arms squeezed me tight. We hugged for long enough my nose grew cold and my ears began to sting. I wasn't really…an affectionate person. At least—I hadn't been. But apparently when it came to family I had no boundaries.

"Can we pick a cute one?" She asked, sniffling against my neck. "His favorite color is yellow."

"Of course it fucking is."

Becca laughed.

My heart soared.

"I'm so glad my dad has you now," Becca said quietly, her eyes wet as she stared up at me. "Thank you for being there for him."

It wasn't clear whether or not she knew about us from her words alone, but…when I looked into her eyes it was easy enough to guess.

We picked out the brightest, most obnoxious, yellow mixer in the history of the universe. And that sweet little girl beamed at me like I'd hung the fucking moon. I realized then that it didn't matter that I'd just met her. Didn't matter at all. She was mine.

I rustled her hair till she cackled and shoved me off the same way Nathan always did. When I caught his gaze across the room he was watching us with a smile so wide and bright I couldn't help but return it.

I had the feeling his crush for Becca was…well.

Not very crush-like anymore.

He came over with a hop in his step, paint smudged across his cheek, and his two uncles cat-calling for him to come back. I just hugged him with my other arm, slinging my two kids together till we were smooshed up in a sweaty, warm hug. They shoved me off at the same time and I rolled my eyes, for once in my life the Christmas spirit tingling at my fingers.

I couldn't wait to surprise Baxter.

We went tree shopping at the Montgomery tree farm the next day. Trent was more chatty than usual—probably because the fucker was horrible at keeping secrets and kept almost slipping up whenever he looked at Baxter too long. It was an anxiety-ridden mess of a few hours as I kept deflecting his well-meaning hints and distracting Baxter as much as I could while I flipped Trent off behind my back, trying to keep the secret from falling apart.

Becca was clearly enjoying my turmoil because she joined in on the hint dropping. I couldn't help but glare at her as she and my shithead brother grinned my way like twin gremlins whenever Baxter wasn't looking.

Nathan, my angel, spent all his time admiring the trees until he decided with complete certainty which one was the absolute best.

We already had a tree up at home so this beauty was going to be set up in Baxter's living room. When he'd told me he'd never had anything but plastic I'd had to remedy that immediately.

You could take the boy out of the tree farm but you couldn't take the tree farm out of the boy, or however that saying went.

As Trent cut the tree down and made the kids help him get it into our truck, I shoved Baxter behind a thick line of trunks and snuck my hand down the front of his pants. I played with his leaking cock till he was a shuddery, red-faced mess, enjoying the way he clung to my chest. His back pressed tight to a tree, his green eyes wide with fear and excitement as he peeked over my shoulder on the lookout for passersby.

I felt like a teenager again, sneaking kisses—and more—from my boyfriend when no one was looking.

When it was clear that a little groping wasn't enough for either of us I shoved him toward the farm house, fully intending on taking advantage of him in the bathroom.

The way he giggled all the way there made my heart soar.

When I got him inside and the lock clicked into place Baxter surprised me, a wicked twist to his lovely lips as he dropped to his knees and immediately went for my belt. His mouth was slick and hot—eager as fuck—as he sucked on my crown and I had to force myself not to grip his hair and force him to take it all. He choked a few times, and the way his eyes watered made my cock twitch and my balls draw up tight.

Unfortunately, Trent found us before we could finish what we'd started.

He pounded on the door, a grin in his voice. "Truck's packed you lil' horn dogs!" He teased, rapping at the door again, this time in an even more annoying manner.

Apparently we weren't subtle.

Or sneaky.

Baxter whimpered, pulling off my dick with a slick little noise that made my eyes roll back and my hips twitch. I grabbed his face, squeezing his cheeks as I gave into my desires and pressed the tip of my cock into his mouth one last time. Obediently, he sucked.

"C'mon!" Trent banged again and I groaned, pulling my cock out with a frustrated grunt. I helped Baxter to his feet, well aware of the fact we both suffered from creaky-knee syndrome. He smiled gratefully at me, his cheeks bright red with embarrassment as he wiped a hand over his mouth and glanced at the closed door with a furrow in his brow.

"He doesn't care," I said softly, leaning down to kiss his salty-sweet lips. Fuck, he tasted good. Like him and me, a cocktail of pleasure. I licked inside so I could chase my own flavor as I felt Baxter's long dexterous fingers begin tucking me back inside my jeans. "I've caught him with more boys than I can count when we shared a room."

Baxter's fingers brushed the head of my cock as he finished and it jerked against the scrape of my jeans.

If they felt restrictive before, they felt doubly so now.

My dick leaked, flexing eagerly as Baxter gave it an apology rub through denim before he finished buttoning me up.

"Give us a minute," I called to Trent reaching for Baxter's face again. I curled my fingers around his cheek then shifted so I could tangle them in his hair. His stubble scratched against my palm and I groaned, leaning in for one last slick kiss before I was forced to pull back and make sure we were both presentable.

Apparently Trent hadn't done as instructed because when we left the bathroom he was waiting across the hall, his arms crossed, a wicked grin on his face.

"Unfair," he hummed, shaking his head. "Share with the rest of us."

I growled at him and he cackled.

I knew he was just playing, but that didn't stop me from tucking Baxter protectively against my side, hiding him in the folds of my coat to cover both our still semi-erect cocks.

We managed to get into the car without any casualties. I could feel the pent-up energy buzzing between us as Baxter folded his hands over his lap and I watched the way his cheeks faded from ruddy-red embarrassment to chilled-pink. I wanted to give his thigh a gentle squeeze but…

Nathan was behind us.

I wasn't ashamed of my sexuality. I'd known I was bisexual since high school, but…I hadn't gotten around to telling him yet. I didn't think he'd care. He was a good kid. Sweet. But I couldn't shake my own anxiety over the encounter. Nathan was my everything. The most important person in my life. He deserved more than a quick, "Dad is dating your crushes' dad" talk. Especially because I had no idea how that would affect his feelings for Becca. It was complicated. Messy.

I wanted it to mean something when I told him, especially because Baxter wasn't just some fling.

Hell.

I'd never connected with someone the way I did with him.

He was…fuck.

He was sugar cookies, hot cocoa, and Christmas mornings.

Sunbeams, summer days, and laughter.

Everything I'd ever wanted—and I wasn't about to fuck it up.

That was why I decided that I'd have to tell him after Christmas— before my other plans all came together.

It was only fair.

We dropped the kids off by Baxter's car and watched them pile inside it. They were showing *It's a Wonderful Life* at the movie theater and Becca had insisted they go. The sky was overcast, foggy sunlight filtering through the clouds to decorate the half-melted snow. It looked like a storm was brewing, though I knew there wasn't one because I'd watched Baxter check the weather three times before agreeing to let the kids go alone.

I was proud of him. I could see how it worried him, and yet…he didn't let that anxiety stop him from doing what needed to be done. He was choosing to work through his own feelings in what seemed to be a more healthy manner and I couldn't help but be warmed by the sight.

We pulled into the driveway as soon as the kids had peeled away and I shut the car off, my pulse thrumming as I glanced Baxter's way and saw a mirrored hunger reflected back in his evergreen gaze.

We were on the same page.

I herded him through the front door, down the hallway, and to the kitchen.

Pogo gave us the stink eye as we passed him and I laughed as I watched his furry little body make its way up the stairs as far away from us as possible.

Baxter had been icing cookies before we left to the tree farm and there were ideas brewing inside me as I picked him up, and gently tossed him onto the kitchen counter. He giggled the whole way, his belly twitching with laughter as I shoved his sweater up so I could lean down and nuzzle the softness there with my beard. That only made him laugh harder and I couldn't hide my own grin as I shoved his sweater the rest of the way up and off, and tossed it to the side.

Baxter shuddered when the cool granite met his feverish skin. His nipples pebbled and I licked my lips, admiring the flushed buds, like little roses winking at me from his creamy freckle covered skin. I wanted to bite his freckles, taste each one till I had them memorized.

I watched the way he trembled, saw the vulnerability in the twitch of his lovely body and the swell of his broad shoulders.

"Look at you, sweetheart." I hummed, stroking a hand over his trembling stomach, toying with his belly button, before sliding my fingers up between his pecs. He tensed, but it was a good kind of tension as another shiver wracked through his body.

I watched in real time as the flush that spread across his sweet cheeks traveled to his ears, down his throat, and ended splotchy between his rosy nipples.

There was a bowl of icing to my left, covered with plastic wrap and a wicked idea began to take place.

"Are you done with this?" I asked softly, cocking my head toward the bowl. Baxter blinked, shaking the fucked-out fog from his eyes as he tipped his head to the side to see what I was talking about.

He caught sight of the bowl and I watched as a sexy little grin spread across his lips.

I wanted to kiss him, so I did.

I kissed him till his smile faded, and his body was wriggling up against mine, eager-as-fuck and ready for the pleasure I was more than happy to bestow. The only thing that would make this better was if I had him decorated in nothing but red ribbon. A gift for me to unwrap. My own fucking Christmas present.

The one I'd been waiting for all my life.

It didn't take long to get us both naked. We were eager, hurried, excited as we shucked our clothing across the room and I double-checked that the front door was locked in the off-chance someone decided to pop by unexpectedly. We had at least three hours till Becca and Nathan were back and I had every intention of taking advantage.

With Baxter spread out before me, all long limbs, muscle, and sex-fogged eyes, I stood back for a moment to admire him. I traced his knees, rubbing along his flexed thighs as his body tensed and his dick jerked against his abs.

He was so hard for me already.

His sweet little cock was leaking, red and eager, its pleasure dripping onto the thatch of golden curls at its base. Every time I looked at him there I wanted to suck him down, listen to him whine, and bury my face in his musky sweetness till I didn't know what it felt like to be anything but connected to him.

"Up," I urged, latching onto the backs of his thighs and giving him a gentle nudge so he could scoot up the counter. The cool slippery surface clung to his sweaty skin and he whined as he had to wiggle to get himself moving.

Watching him struggle made my dick twitch and I couldn't help myself as I reached down to give the base a tight squeeze. I wanted this to last as long as I could make it.

We'd had the talk earlier about condoms and fuck…

The idea of watching my come drip out of his well-fucked hole made my head spin and my balls ache to empty inside him.

It wasn't lost on me how excited I was to cream-pie my baker.

I reached for the icing, well aware of Baxter's gaze as he admired the heave of my chest, the flutter of my breath, the way I couldn't help but shudder at the thought of sinking inside him.

"Legs up, honey bee," I murmured, watching as he complied obediently. I pulled the plastic wrap from the bowl and dipped my fingers inside the soft warm icing. It was softer than it would've been fresh out of the fridge. I was glad for that because even though watching Baxter jump from the cold was entertaining, I wanted him to be entirely focused on me—and not uncomfortable.

With a wicked grin I grabbed a dollop of buttercream and raised it up so he could see it.

"Yes, or no?" I asked softly, waiting for his response.

His green eyes were flooded black with arousal, his lips bitten red as his tongue flickered out to wet them. Fuck. I remembered what it felt like to be inside that mouth—sinking into his heat—enjoying the way he sucked on me like I was a treat he couldn't wait to taste. He choked so prettily, eager little slut.

My cock gave an impatient twitch and I groaned, using my free hand to reach down and give the base another punishing squeeze.

God, he turned me on.

He was my fucking catnip.

I dragged my gaze across his body, tracing over his freckles, his straining nipples, the way his cock lay fat and eager, the smear of precum on his belly even thicker than it had been moments ago.

My little baker liked the idea of being played with.

The icing grew even warmer as it sat at my fingertips, melting a little before my gaze caught on his balls, pulled tight, and pink with tension. I bet he wanted to come—no, *needed* to come. With the way his legs spread open like that there was no denying how badly he desired this.

I could feel the feral quality to my smile, though I couldn't see it, as I reached down with my icing decorated fingers and gently spread the sweet treat in a stripe from the base of his balls all the way up the long curve of his lovely dick. It was bigger than you'd expect for his size— long. Lovely. Sexy as fuck. I rubbed icing under his crown and listened to the way his breath hitched. He was sensitive there—but not as sensitive as he was at his tip.

"Paxton—" Baxter whimpered, his slit dripping away as I reached into the icing bowl for more, then without preamble, decorated the tip of his cock in a smear of sugar.

I pulled back to admire my work, the hand on my dick squeezing tight so I wouldn't come immediately at the sight.

He looked like a treat.

Jesus.

So fucking pretty.

The icing was obscene as it began to melt, slipping down the red skin in buttery bliss. I leaned down, unable to help myself as I gave the vein that ran up the underside of his cock an eager suck. Sugar exploded on my tongue, the perfect accompaniment to the salty sweet taste of his skin.

I couldn't get enough.

The way Baxter whined was music to my ears as I gave the inside of his thigh a sticky squeeze and trailed my lips teasingly up and down his long, hard length. He jerked a little, a needy sound escaping that had me all sorts of bothered as I gave my own dick another squeeze and forced myself not to fuck my fist.

I wanted to save it.

I wanted to really make it last when I sunk inside him. I wanted it so sensitive that I felt every dip and ridge of his body with the utmost clarity. He felt like a vice, hot and wet. I wanted to enjoy it. Drag it out. Listen to the way his breath hitched and watch the way his eyes grew sex-stupid.

My honey bee was a slut for my cock and he made no move to hide that.

We didn't play games like that.

Baxter reached for me, his fingers tangling in my hair as I gave the crown of his cock another eager suck. He was trembling and my ego buzzed as I shoved his thigh up higher and slipped my mouth down to the sensitive sweaty skin just behind his balls.

I released his thigh and reached for the icing again, scooping up a liberal amount before my fingers trailed across his skin, smudging it along his thighs till I reached where my mouth was currently sucking. I pulled off and Baxter whined, reacting to the loss so beautifully it made my head spin.

I shushed him, a soft growl as I rubbed the rest of the icing along his taint, pressing hard at the spot between his hole and balls that I knew would make his prostate sing. He was so sensitive there—all long-limbed debauchery as he spread his legs wide and shoved his needy ass toward my fingers.

"You're so sexy," I hummed, my dick flexing as I listened to the high-pitched whine that left Baxter's lips. "Show me that little hole, I wanna see where you want me."

Baxter complied immediately.

He lifted his hips, relaxed his thighs, and exposed himself to me. His ass cheeks spread enough I could see his sweet pink entrance, winking eagerly. God. I wanted to stick the head of my cock against it and shove till he opened up for me—but no.

Prep.

I needed to prep him.

I'd never hurt him.

He wouldn't need much, not when we had been fucking like bunnies at every opportunity but…still. The idea of hurting Baxter was a major turn-off.

I grabbed more icing, more than a little eager as I gave his cock an apology suck and began to rub the buttercream up and down, up and down his crack. Every time I got close to his hole he'd wiggle to try to force me inside but I didn't comply.

I teased him.

The more I teased, the louder he got.

His dick was leaking steadily against my tongue, the taste of sugar and salt mixing in a way that made me harder than steel. I couldn't wait to pound his ass, to take him till he cried, till I got to see his eyes blur with tears and he spilled his pleasure onto his creamy, freckle-dotted belly.

God, I didn't think I'd ever been harder.

My balls ached as I gave up my teasing, too eager to be inside him to be able to handle it anymore.

"Thank you—" Baxter whimpered, his voice barely more than a breath as I snuck my slicked fingers down toward his hole and finally—finally— pushed home. He was hot inside. Eager. Tight. He sucked at my fingers as I twisted them gently, searching, searching, searching for the spot that I knew would make him sing.

I couldn't help the way I panted, catching my breath before sucking his cock down again. Two fingers became three. I swallowed as Baxter bucked against my face, his cock hitting the back of my throat and making me gag a little. I wasn't deterred.

When I looked up I caught a glimpse of his face. He was bright red, tears slick down the sides of his cheeks, his eyes scrunched tightly shut as he caught his bottom lip in a tortured dance between pearly white teeth.

Jesus.

I hummed around his dick to get his attention and Baxter looked down at me. His reaction was instantaneous. His pupils were blown wide and black as he squeezed around my fingers, eager and delicious. His eyes glazed over with need, and his mouth dropped open in awe as he watched me suck and fuck him at the same time.

It was too much.

Fuck.

I slipped away from his cock with a soft *pop*. He whimpered unhappily at me—the brat—but I ignored him as I gave his balls a few eager wet kisses before sliding my way down his sugary skin to where my fingers were currently disappearing inside his body.

I licked along his rim, sucking at the icing that was pushed out every time I twisted.

The noise Baxter made was barely human.

His hole was so relaxed I knew all it would take was a tiny flex and I could sink my entire cock inside him in one go.

I pulled my fingers out, ignored his whimper, and shoved my tongue inside him, desperate to taste.

The musky sweet flavor was only amplified by the taste of the icing. I sucked at him, licking, rubbing, fucking as I chased the sugar till I wrung every last drop out of his slutty little hole. By the time I pulled back Baxter was a mess. I'd never seen him leak so much, his belly smeared, his eyes foggy.

At some point he'd stopped grabbing at me and just dropped his hands to his sides, spread his legs, and surrendered to me completely.

Fuck.

My cock jerked and I groaned, biting my lip to stave off my own orgasm at the sight.

"So fucking perfect," I growled, watching the way his sweaty chest rose and fell as he panted. "I need lube, baby."

Baxter nodded, but it seemed words were no longer possible for him. He was too far gone.

I returned as quickly as I could from his bedroom, the lube already smeared over my cock and fingers as I hurriedly pressed them inside him. With my free hand I scrubbed over his body, warming him up, making sure he was still mentally present as I finally—blissfully—pressed the crown of my cock against his gaping hole.

He was so loose I was sure I would be able to sink straight inside.

"Yes?" I urged softly, unable to help the way my hips flexed and my cock sunk the barest of centimeters inside him.

"Yes," Baxter agreed, breathless and wanton with lust. He arched his back a little, wiggling his hole against my cock and forcing me another centimeter inside.

I groaned, scrambling to reach the root of my cock so I could give it a tight squeeze so I wouldn't come.

Fuck.

He was so fucking hot.

I wanted to fuck him so bad I couldn't breathe.

My cock sunk inside him, the hot clutch of his hole sucking me deeper. My eyes rolled back and I groaned, low and deep. The noise vibrated through my body as I disappeared inside Baxter's slick, wet heat. It felt like coming home. My dick twitched and he twitched back, squeezing around me tight enough that for just a moment my eyes fluttered shut.

I wanted to wait.

To drag it out.

But I couldn't.

I couldn't help myself as I grabbed the back of his thighs and slid the rest of the way home. He clung to the counter and I watched the way his arms drew back and his fingers wrapped around the lip behind his head. His whole face was scrunched up aside from his sweet little mouth. It hung open, panting, his pink tongue winking at me.

I fucked into him again, watching the way his tongue curled as his cock jerked.

"You're so hard for me, baby," I purred, my hips grinding deep. "Look at that needy little cock. So pink. So sweet." His cock bobbed and I grinned, moving in a slow circle as I drew out then fucked back in again.

The squelch of the lube made a noise so obscene I couldn't help but groan.

Fuck yes.

Fuck.

No more holding back.

I fucked him.

God, did I fuck him. I'd never chased someone else's heat as exuberantly as I did then, thrusting forward in a relentless grind that had Baxter whimpering and whining, his sweet brow scrunched. It felt so fucking good I couldn't hold back. He squeezed around me, slutty as ever as my movements grew more brutal and my thighs flexed with the need to get deeper, fuck harder, breed his sweet little hole with my cum.

When I finished, I growled, hips snapping, my nipples drawn tight with pleasure. I could see where I was disappearing inside him. Admire the pink suck of his body as my cock split him open. I jerked forward, emptying inside his body, fucking my cum into him with a primal need to stake my claim.

When I pulled out I let the head of my cock stay inside him for just a moment, admiring the way his body twitched around me. He wanted to suck me back inside. I could see the way he was chasing it, and even though my dick was softening I gave him one last deliberate thrust before withdrawing completely.

Watching my come leak out of his hole was enough to make my already spent cock tremble with the need to spill again.

Without preamble I sunk down low, my lips wrapping around his hole as I gave it an eager suck. I could taste my cum as it leaked onto my tongue mixed with the flavor of icing. God, he was sweet. I'd once wondered if I licked him if he'd taste like sugar and here I was—proving that very fact.

When I'd chased every last drop of my pleasure from his sweet little hole I dragged my lips up his taint, sucked at his balls, and reached for the lube again.

Baxter was a sobbing, needy mess as he tangled his fingers in my hair and I sunk my fingers inside him at the same time I sucked his cock all the way down into the velvety vice of my throat.

He came moments later—too overstimulated to do much but buck into my throat and squeeze around my fingers. I rubbed his prostate, toying with him as I flicked my tongue into his slit, catching every stray bit of his cum as he came down from his high and eventually the hands in my hair that had pulled me closer pushed me gently away.

"Too much," Baxter whimpered, oversensitive and fucking adorable.

He was flushed from head to toe, sticky as fuck. Beautiful.

I watched his chest heave and leaned down to give his pink nipples one last teasing suck each.

"Paxton—" Baxter complained and I growled, glaring up at him from where I was worrying his chest with my teeth. He quieted down with a little grin that told me the fucker didn't actually want me to stop. He just liked to complain.

Naught, naughty.

I gave his prostate another rub before withdrawing both my fingers and lips at the same time.

Fuck, he was gorgeous.

Flushed from head to toe, his green eyes hazy, his freckles dancing.

He was also wrecked.

I'd need to take care of him—take care of the kitchen—before the kids came home.

I helped him down from the counter, gentle as I could, careful of his sore back and no doubt sore ass. I carried him up the stairs in a mirror of the position we'd used all those weeks ago when I'd brought him to bed.

With my hands supporting his ass and his legs wrapped around my waist I couldn't stop my questing fingers from seeking out his hole once again. He sucked me inside him and I grunted against the side of his neck, worrying my teeth against the skin as I felt him clench around me after each step I took.

I ran a bath. Baxter settled, clearly less out of it as he curled up in the hot water and watched me with curiosity as I pulled on a pair of his boxer briefs—way too fucking tight—and moved toward the doorway to head back downstairs again.

"Aren't you going to join me?" He asked softly, his skin flushed from the heat of the steam rising from the water. He looked lovely like that, all soft and sweet. *Well-fucked,* my brain supplied helpfully.

"Gotta clean up the kitchen first. Don't want the kiddos to touch anything."

He nodded, relaxing a little. Clearly grateful.

I leaned down and gave him a long lingering kiss before I forced myself away to take care of business.

Pogo followed after me dutifully, hopping down the stairs and padding into the kitchen, clearly ready for treats.

As I cleaned the counter and rinsed out the icing bowl I couldn't help but grin to myself.

Fuck.

This was going to be the best Christmas ever.

twenty-one

PAXTON

THIS WAS GOING TO BE the worst Christmas ever.

I stared blankly at my kitchen table, my heart in my throat as I listened to the crunch of tires on the driveway and thought—not for the first time—that I should've fucking said no. Said no to the phone call the night before Christmas fucking Eve when Tracy had decided to remember for the first time in months that she had another fucking kid.

Nathan…

God.

The sweetheart forgave her the moment she called to ask for him to visit.

I'd helped him pack his bag, hid my heartbreak, and sent him off in my truck. Hell, I wouldn't be needing it. I didn't have the stomach to face my family alone, to see the pitying looks. To watch the way my parents grimaced between each other when they thought I wasn't looking.

I just—

I couldn't.

I didn't know what to do.

It was eleven in the morning, I'd finished all my work in preparation for Christmas, and it wasn't like I had anyone to entertain, so I just wilted my way into the living room, cracked open a bottle of beer and drowned my sorrows in *Charlie Brown* reruns.

I knew I should call Baxter. Hell, I wanted to. Of course I fucking did.

He'd turn this whole thing around, somehow twist the shitty holiday into something beautiful and full of magic—that was just his way. I'd known this about him even before I'd started dating him. In fact, before we'd gotten close it was one of the things I hated about him.

Maybe because I'd been jealous.

I didn't have his magic touch, despite the way he always fucking called me Magic-hands Montgomery—the dork.

I finished my second beer and plopped the glass onto the coffee table, my morose mood only growing darker by the minute.

How was this fair?

I'd had plans, dammit.

None of them included spending the holiday alone with my kid driving two fucking hours to his mom's wonderful little suburb with her wonderful little husband, and her wonderful new job. I wasn't bitter about her life in the way that I missed her. Fuck, if I never saw or heard from her again in my entire life it would be too soon.

But she had what I wanted, and it was…fucking unfair.

The family, the warmth—the stability.

I craved that.

That's why I did my best to always give it to Nathan. Except at the end of the day, where did that leave me? Fuck. Maybe I *was* just a bratty little kid.

I could still go to my parents' place.

It was on the edge of town, barely ten minutes away. But somehow that distance felt unsurpassable. I could call up my brother. I knew Trent would pick me up—but I didn't want him. I didn't want anyone except…

I wanted Baxter.

I wanted him to curl up under the blankets and watch this shitty show with me.

I wanted to smell the sugar in his hair, to nuzzle into his warm skin and forget my sorrows in the crook of his neck.

I didn't want to be selfish though.

Christmas Eve was the busiest day of the year for his bakery. He'd been prepping for it all week—Becca as well. I knew for a fact they'd been running deliveries across town today since nearly five in the morning, and it wasn't bound to stop until seven. That's what he'd told me anyway when we'd talked on the phone the previous night.

So, yeah.

Miserable, grouchy, scrooge-y Paxton it was.

Fuck *Charlie Brown.*

Fuck everybody.

I stared at my Christmas tree and the gifts that sat wrapped beneath it and tried not to feel like an absolute douche-nozzle. I should be happy for Nathan. *Why wasn't I happy for him?* I *wanted* his mom to treat him better.

But selfishly I just wanted my fucking kid on Christmas Eve.

I'd had the whole day planned, down to the diner that was open in the mornings, the sled I had packed into the truck bed so we could head down to Knoll Park and blast our way down the massive hill till he was frozen cold, and I could treat him with a big jug of homemade cocoa.

Our tradition.

Didn't feel like much of a tradition now.

Evening came around, though it took a fucking million years to arrive. Baxter had texted me at some point, asking if I was home and I'd…lied. I didn't want to admit to him that I hadn't gone to my parents' place. Didn't want to talk about the fact that Nathan was gone.

That was why I was pretty fucking surprised when I heard the rustle of a key in my front door and the quiet chatter of voices.

What the fuck?

I pulled my blanket up higher around myself where I sat like a slug on the couch, beer bottles scattered in a pile of shame atop the coffee table in front of me. I hadn't bothered turning on the lights—even though it was late enough into the winter that the sun went down at fucking four.

Fuck everything.

There was more rustling.

More laughter.

And then the front door burst open and a flurry of snowflakes blasted into my front hallway. Maybe I should've been weirded out—but I knew the only person who had a key to my house, and he was the only person I *wanted* to see right now, even though I was ashamed of how low I'd been brought.

"Go! Quick!" Baxter's voice echoed down the hallway. "I'll grab the goods."

Becca's laughter squealed as I listened to her thunder into the kitchen. She passed right by me—didn't even notice where I sat. I supposed that made sense, hell I hadn't even turned the Christmas tree on. It was dark as fuck.

What were they up to?

Baxter came back.

I heard the door shut and I could taste the burst of winter in the air. Baxter's footsteps were just as rushed as his daughter as he began…what? *What was he doing?*

Moving very slowly, because I didn't really want to be noticed, I turned to watch from behind the back of the couch.

What I saw made my heart race and my eyes burn.

He was…fuck.

He was hanging stockings on my stairwell. They looked hand painted, like they'd spent all night making them. Nathan's was covered in flames and skateboards and mine…fuck. I'd told Baxter once about how much I missed playing football with my brothers. It'd been our thing growing up—and I'd played all the way through high school and then college.

That dream had evolved however when I found out Tracy was pregnant and Nathan had taken over my future. I'd never regretted how things had played out, but…

The little footballs that were decorated around my stocking made my head spin and my hands sweaty. The burning sensation in my eyes only grew worse as I covered my mouth with my hand and tried not to openly sob.

He'd remembered.

Jesus.

It was a small thing.

But the fact that he paid attention to me, that he was here—surprising me. Solid and sure. Reliable. Affectionate, considerate.

I couldn't—

Wait.

Oh god.

Baxter was dressed as an elf.

An elf.

I hadn't noticed at first but laughter bubbled up inside me, desperate to escape. He had striped stockings on, tiny little green shorts, and a jolly jingly hat that dinged every time he shifted. I watched as he finished tying up the stockings and began winding fake green…tree stuff? Up the railing. I didn't know what to fucking call it.

After that, he bent over, rustled around in the frankly massive black trash bag at his feet, then popped back up with his arms full of little tiny gifts. He filled our stockings and I was almost too floored by the sweet gesture to look at his ass. Almost.

God.

Santa sure was lucky if he had that view all day.

I could see light bleeding down the hallway from the kitchen where Becca was still rattling around.

"They don't have a can opener!" She yelled, clearly irked.

I snorted.

It was true.

We didn't.

I usually just used the pocket knife I kept in the kitchen drawer.

"Look for Paxton's pocket knife!" Baxter called, once again flooring me because…fuck. He *really* paid attention to me. Almost like I was… important?

"You want me to…*knife* the can?"

"Stab it, yeah." Baxter's little hips swiveled as he finished packing the last of Nathan's stocking and moved on to mine. His broad shoulders flexed. "Then twist."

"Yeah, I'm not doing that."

"Becca."

"Dad. I'm not a caveman."

"You cannnn do it!" he called, cracking up at his own joke with a jolly little jingle.

"Ughhhhh." Becca's answering groan was loud but…soft. As much as she pretended not to like her dad's shenanigans I knew she was softer for him than anyone else. As I admired Baxter wiggling around, I noticed—with a jolt—that he was wearing—ohmyfuckinggod. He was wearing his New Balance tennis shoes! With his elf outfit.

If I didn't love him before I fell in love right then.

"When are they coming home?" Becca asked after her whining stopped. I wasn't sure what she was up to but I figured it had to have something to do with…cooking? Maybe I should put a stop to all of this? There wasn't anyone to cook for after all.

"Paxton said yesterday he's usually there till nine or ten."

"'Usually' doesn't help."

"I can call him," Baxter called, and horror immediately overwhelmed me. No.

No, no, no.

Baxter already had his phone out. He still hadn't noticed me and fuck—there was no getting around this. My phone sat on the coffee table, the screen black. The second it started buzzing he would look over and see me here and I—

The sadness overwhelmed me again as I looked down at myself—really looked. I was a mess. Sweaty, exhausted, bundled up like a hiker in a winter storm. The beer bottles spread across the table were more telling than they should be. I didn't make a habit of drinking, I just…fuck. At least they'd been spread out throughout the day—it wasn't like I was still drunk, but…

Embarrassment made my throat close up and my eyes burn as I watched my cellphone on the table and waited for it to betray me.

The screen lit up and it buzzed.

Loud as fuck.

I heard Baxter jump, a startled little noise escaping him as humiliation tore through my body. I felt catatonic as I pulled my blanket up high and hid beneath it. The buzzing stopped. Everything stopped. A beat passed and then I heard the quiet pad of footsteps approaching.

I pulled the blanket over my head, my throat tight, the burning in my eyes forcing me to blink away wetness.

"Paxton?" Baxter said softly, his voice gentle, sweet.

I shook my head, and he made a quiet, crooning little sound.

"Why are you home alone in the dark, baby?" He asked. His voice was as warm as summer days, apple cider, and sugar cookies. I could feel his presence in front of me, squatting between my thighs, his hands hovering like he wanted to touch but he didn't know if it was allowed.

I shook my head again.

I didn't have the words.

"Can I take your blanket off?" Baxter asked, and I nodded, even though I didn't want him to see me like this. I wanted to be strong—I *liked* being strong. That was my thing. But this…fuck. I felt like a crumpled up paper bag.

The blanket was gently extracted but I couldn't look at him as inch by inch it peeled away and my stare bore a hole into my unlit Christmas tree. For a moment Baxter just looked at me. Then he moved. His fingers fanned along my cheeks, stroking over my sideburns, his sweet lips pressing a sugary kiss against my furrowed brow.

"You precious thing," he murmured softly, curling fingers gently in my hair before he began carding it out of my face. I always got sweaty when I was upset. It was a curse. But Baxter didn't seem to mind as he gently pushed my bangs away, and stroked his thumbs under my eyelids.

I let my eyes fall shut, still unable to look at him though I soaked up his warmth desperately. Inside I felt ice cold, like my heart had frozen over.

"Where's Nathan, sweetheart?" He asked softly, continuing to scratch at my scalp as my eyes burned beneath my lids and a few wayward tears escaped. I wanted to force them back inside. I hated this. I hated *feeling* like this. Hated that I couldn't just turn it all off. It wasn't fucking fair.

"His mom's house," I said softly, though the words came out a weak, quiet croak.

"Oh, baby." Baxter sighed, his fingers stilling for just a moment before he swiped away my tears and I felt his lips brush up against my temple. "I'm sorry."

That was…fuck.

That was all I wanted.

I didn't want pity—or rationalization.

I didn't want to hear how lucky I was that I'd had him for the holiday season at all.

All I wanted…was to be held, and for someone to understand. To let me just…feel my sadness, so I could push past it.

My heart caved in and I grabbed onto Baxter with desperation. He made a startled noise as I plucked him into my lap, craving his closeness—craving the scent of his cologne—craving his touch, his warm weight. When he settled across my thighs he didn't protest, he just continued to pet my hair as he pulled my face against his chest and let me cry.

I listened to his heartbeat as my sorrow leaked heat down my cheeks.

"You're coming home with me," Baxter whispered, lacing sugary-sweet kisses onto my sweaty head.

I just nodded, because there was nothing else I could say.

I went home with him.

twenty-two

BAXTER

IT WAS CLEAR TO ME that Paxton was embarrassed by his own emotions. Luckily for him though, I was well versed by now in emotional outbursts. So I used that knowledge to support him in all the ways he'd taught me how.

Becca, because she was an angel, didn't say a single thing as we piled into the car.

I left the stockings on the stairs and she left the Christmas cake we'd baked on the table for later consumption. The uneaten dinner was left behind in the fridge. I blasted Christmas music, made sure Paxton buckled himself in, and then fought off my own anxiety as we began the arduous trek home through the snow.

When Paxton offered to drive I gently refused him.

I'd at least had the forethought to pack a few of Paxton's things before we left, so when we got to the house I set them up in my bedroom and steered him toward the bathroom.

Just like he'd done for me earlier that week I ran him a bath. He watched me, so startled by the care and kindness it made my heart wobble in my chest. His big honey-colored eyes were wet as he watched the hot water trickle into the tub and I reached out to gently begin plucking open the buttons on his flannel.

"Gingerbread or apple cider?" I asked softly as I got down to the last button. Paxton's eyes were red-rimmed and wet as he turned his head to look at me. He was still so quiet, so still. Like his sadness had filled his limbs with ice. When I reached for his hands they were cold so I rubbed them between my own till he startled to life again and shook his head. "Apple cider it is."

I dumped a bath bomb into the water, watched it fizzle, then helped Paxton out of the rest of his clothes and into its heat. He didn't react, though I saw the way the tension in his shoulders softened as he curled his arms tight around his massive chest and glared at the faucet.

"You should be with Becca," he said quietly, his voice a weak rumble. "It's Christmas Eve."

"Becca is busy," I told him gently, wanting to nip that thread of conversation before it began to unravel. "She's surprising me with a Christmas dinner I'm not supposed to know about."

He blinked. His brow furrowed and he turned to look at me through narrowed eyes. "If you're not supposed to know about it, then how do you know?"

"She's not exactly sneaky," I laughed softly. "She used my credit card."

"Right." A little smile crossed his lips and I crowed my triumph internally as I reached for his now damp skin and began to liberally rub the stress out of his neck and shoulders. He rarely let me touch him like this. Paxton liked to be big and strong all the time—he liked being the one that other people relied on. His vulnerability was an honor he rarely bestowed on anyone else.

I treated him gently as I took care of the gift he'd given me, because that's what this was.

A gift.

By the time I'd washed his hair and gotten him bundled up in a fresh hoodie and jeans he looked like he was feeling quite a bit better.

"You think she's done yet?" I asked, peeking out my bedroom door and cocking my head to see if I could hear Becca rattling around in the kitchen.

Pogo sighed dramatically from somewhere down the hallway—probably on the stairs, since they were his favorite—but other than that, all I heard was silence.

"I reckon so," Paxton hummed, his voice a quiet familiar rumble. I glanced up at him with a little smile, my heart giving a nervous flutter as I watched the way his eyes warmed and his chest rose with each steady breath.

"Let's go see!"

Dinner was surprisingly delicious. Becca preened under the attention, and her eyes kept flickering over Paxton as if to check if he was put together once again. I figured it had probably freaked her out to see him so broken—but…hell.

Maybe it was good.

She needed to understand that sometimes even men with their shit together, like Paxton, had moments where they needed someone else to hold them up.

Bless her heart, she didn't ask about Nathan.

I figured I'd explain later, but was glad she had enough tact not to mention his absence.

After watching *Elf* again, because it was my favorite—obviously—we piled onto the couch and I passed out a single gift to both of them.

Paxton eyed his distrustfully, clearly not sure what was going on.

"Open it," I urged, grinning.

Becca was grinning too and I beamed at her, leaning down to smoosh a kiss against her fluffy head. She didn't shove me off, which was a major Christmas miracle.

Paxton was clearly confused as he gently peeled each individual piece of tape away.

"Oh my god," Becca floundered, flapping her arms. "Just rip it! Jesus."

"It's nice paper," Paxton replied.

I hid my laughter against her neck and felt the way a giggle vibrated inside her.

Paxton continued to painstakingly open the package and by the time he finished, Becca's fingers were twitching like she wanted to reach over and tear it open herself.

"I hope they fit," I hummed, pulling back to watch the wonder unfold on Paxton's handsome face. He spread his big hands across the flannel fabric, lips parted, his cheeks flushed.

"Are these?"

"Pajamas?" I hummed. "Yes. It's tradition."

"Dad always gets us matching pajamas each year," Becca explained with importance. "Nathan has some too, they're under the tree."

I grimaced a little, unsure what Paxton's reaction would be, but he just smiled, the expression unfolding like sunshine on a winter day. His eyes twinkled and he bunched his fingers in the fabric before tipping his chin up to meet my gaze.

"Thank you," he rumbled. I couldn't help myself. I leaned down and smooshed a kiss against his cheek. I probably should've asked him first— hell, I probably should've asked him how he wanted to go about telling people about us…or not telling people about us.

Maybe I'd fucked up?

But I didn't think I had, because he just grabbed the front of my sweater and pulled me down so he could smash a kiss of his own against my cheek.

I sent Becca to bed a few hours later and she staggered her way sleepily up the stairs with a yawn. Her hair had half fallen from its bun and it draped itself in a wild mess of golden curls along her back as she trudged steadily onward.

My little Christmas soldier.

Paxton turned to me then, a nervous twitch to his fingers as I snuggled up against his side again on the couch and twined our legs together.

"I can sleep down here," Paxton murmured softly.

I'd made it clear he was spending the night.

The Christmas tree's lights sparkled at us, the presents glowing beneath its lovely branches. The scent of pine and cocoa was thick in the air as I traced over one of Paxton's tattoos and looped my fingers through the sleeve of his matching pajama set.

"Come to bed, baby," I murmured softly, playing with his arm hair as I nuzzled into the relaxed muscle of his pec and tipped my chin up to catch his gaze.

"But…Becca—"

This was a bigger issue than just sharing a bed, I knew that.

I could hear the uncertainty in his voice.

I could taste that same vulnerability in the air that he'd shown me earlier that day.

This was it.

I'd made my choice and it was clear he hadn't realized.

"I already told Becca about us," I said softly, my belly flipping with nerves. I hoped I hadn't messed up—hoped I'd done the right thing.

It was apparent I had because Paxton sagged in relief. He pulled me close, tucking me up under his chin and nuzzling into my hair as I listened to the steady *thump, thump* of his heartbeat echoing through his supple chest.

"She's happy for us," I said softly, gently. "Said she figured it was only time. After that day we went to the movies and were just…"

"Just what?"

"In tune."

"You'd call *that* in tune?" He snorted, but gave me a squeeze to soften the sting of his words.

"We were just out of sync. Playing the same song at different intervals."

Paxton made a contemplative sound, nuzzled into my hair again, and laced a kiss against my forehead. I hadn't ever had affection like this. I hadn't ever had someone who made me feel whole the way that Paxton did.

It was as terrifying as it was, wonderful.

There were so many things that could go wrong.

But I was trying not to focus on that anymore.

Waiting for the other shoe to fall wouldn't prepare me for when it did. It was better to remain present, to find magic in the things that were happening to me and not focus too much on what could happen to ruin them.

Therapy was helping, and I was glad, more than anything, that I'd gotten to a point in my life where I felt open to taking in that information.

"Bedtime?" I urged softly, because even though I wanted to stay up, I was getting old, and the early deliveries that morning had taken a lot out of me.

"Bedtime," Paxton agreed.

I slung his arm over my shoulders and supported him all the way up the stairs. I couldn't carry him—not in the way that he could carry me, but I did my best.

As we sank into the covers, I tangled our legs together again, admiring the way our matching pajamas clung to our thighs. Paxton's feet were larger than mine, his legs too. But at that moment, he was small as I tucked him into bed and nestled up against his chest. "Goodnight," I murmured, though the words felt wrong because there was another phrase I'd wanted to say to him, more than anything, but hadn't.

I love you, hung like a promise in the air.

Maybe soon I'd have the courage to say it.

Maybe.

Waking up to discover Nathan passed out on my couch nearly gave me a heart attack. I slipped down the last few steps, landing with a *thunk* and a wheeze as my hand slapped over my still beating heart, and Nathan's fluffy head popped up over the back of the couch.

"Hi, Mr. B!" he yelled. Jesus. It was seven in the morning. Why was he yelling?

Also…

How the hell was he here?

Wasn't he supposed to be at his mom's house?

How did he get into our house?

"You know, it's really unsafe to hide your spare key inside a rock that says 'There's no key in here, nice try!'" He blinked at me, then a big sunny grin burst across his face. My heart was still pounding as a startled laugh left my lips.

"I thought it was funny?"

"Only funny till you get robbed," Nathan told me, very wisely.

I laughed again, and rose to my feet. Pogo padded over, woofed at me, and made his way to the kitchen in a clear demand for food. I followed after him with a snort and wiggled my finger at Nathan to get him to follow.

"What about your mom's?" I asked curiously as he began helping me set the table. I'd made a casserole the night before in preparation for an early morning. Becca wouldn't be up till eight at least and after the night we'd had, Paxton wouldn't be either.

I grinned to myself.

"Yeah…" Nathan sighed, the plates clinking as they thunked onto the table. "She's great and all—and I love her—I really, really do. But I just…" He shrugged. "She's not my dad?"

I nodded, my cheeks hurting as I turned to beam at him.

Maybe I was biased.

Maybe that made me a shitty person, but I couldn't help but be glad he was here.

"Sorry we stole him away."

Nathan shook his head. "I'm so happy he has you, Mr. B." He bit his lip. This new Mr. B thing was…weirdly cute? He'd never called me that before. It felt a little too formal though.

"You can call me Baxter," I said softly, distracted for a moment as I filled up Pogo's bowl and watched the way he immediately began to chow down.

Nathan made a noise and I looked at him, my stomach flipping as I realized the glowy smile on his face had wavered.

"Can we…you know…table that discussion for later?" He asked softly.

I wasn't sure what he meant so I just nodded. "Sure thing."

Paxton's face when he saw Nathan was priceless. No words were exchanged between them. It was silent as he crossed the kitchen, wrapped his arms tight around his son, and pulled him into his chest. They stood there for what felt like eons and I beamed at them both as they pulled apart and the oven dinged.

Becca wandered in not long after, her hair an absolute rats nest, her mascara smudged as she flopped into her seat and sleepily plunged her fork into her food. She didn't even open her eyes as she ate, just wilted slowly forward, exhausted.

When I joined them, Paxton scooted his chair close, our thighs brushing, his heat bleeding into me as I dug into my own food and peeked at my family with barely concealed glee.

I couldn't remember the last time I'd been this happy.

My heart soared.

There was still the elephant in the room though. Becca knew about us but Nathan…well. Paxton had admitted to me that he hadn't told him. Hadn't told him anything really—and I was content to wait till the time was right. That didn't mean it wasn't hard though, forcing myself not to kiss the big bearded man every time he grunted his approval after each eager bite.

The fact that he survived most of his life off of pizza and TV dinners did not escape me.

Maybe one day…they could move in with us. We could have dinners, breakfasts, lunches—together. I'd cook for them all, watch them like I was doing now and just…

Bask in the family we'd created.

Even when I'd lived with my parents it had never been like this.

I wondered if somewhere beyond the grave Rebecca was smiling down on us.

I hoped so.

The rest of the day was a blur of presents, hot chocolate, and snowy adventures. I ignored the way my heart lurched every time I thought of my missing sister. I ignored the way the anxiety of the bakery's inevitable closure loomed over me.

Like my therapist had instructed, I tried to be present, and for once it worked.

My demons remained on the horizon, but I didn't let their talons sink inside me yet.

That would be a problem for another time.

twenty-three

PAXTON

THERE WERE SIX DAYS UNTIL the Hullabaloo and I had everything ready. Well, except one incredibly important thing. Something I'd been putting off for years. My heart was in my throat as I waited patiently inside my truck for Nathan to finish up inside the grocery store.

He'd wanted a few things—claimed he was going to cook dinner from a recipe that Baxter had given him.

Apparently he'd even written down instructions for the kid.

Jesus.

With every day we spent together, it became more and more clear that this thing between Baxter and I was here to stay. It was timeless. Gentle. Patient.

All things I'd never realized I could be.

Nathan hopped his way over to the car, giving me his brightest smile right before he stumbled over a crack in the sidewalk. I cocked my head in concern, only for him to pop up a second later, his grocery bags held high in triumph. His smile returned and he continued on his way to the car—more carefully this time.

"Black ice," he lied with a shudder as he pulled his door open and slipped into the passenger seat. Lazy shit just carried the groceries across his lap. Clearly it was too much effort to put them in the back.

"Sneaky bastard," I agreed, nodding my head toward the crack he'd tripped on. It had snowed the night before, and the night before that too, and the entire town of Belleville was cast in Christmas wonder. The lights that decorated Main Street twinkled as we drove by, crunching our way through the still unplowed roads.

The plows were run by citizen volunteers for the most part, and as much as they tried, they never seemed able to keep up with the storm.

After dinner I could feel my window of opportunity slipping away.

My courage was waning, my palms slick as I set my fork down and gave Nathan my full attention.

"Dinner was great, bud," I lied. Dinner had been terrifying. Too salty. Too hard—and not at all like the meatloaf Baxter had promised Nathan had no way of messing up. Still, though. He'd done his best, and he deserved points for that.

"Thanks, Dad." Nathan perked right up, bobbing his head like a cockatiel as he shoved his last bite into his mouth, cheeks puffing up as he chewed.

I stared at him for a while and he let me.

He was getting bigger every day.

Taller, wider, wiser.

If I turned I'd be able to see the notches on the doorframe that had marked this journey from childhood to adulthood inch by inch—year by year. But I didn't.

"I have something I need to tell you," I said quietly, even though my heart was in my throat.

I rarely felt nervous like this.

Never.

I refused to put myself into these kinds of situations—and yet here I was, willingly stepping out of my comfort zone. Somehow I couldn't be angry about it though. Even though technically it was Baxter's fault I was here—it wasn't really. He hadn't forced me to do this. Hadn't done anything but support me actually.

I had no doubt he would've kept quiet the rest of our lives rather than make me uncomfortable or force me into a decision.

That was why I was so sure this was the right call.

I swallowed the lump in my throat as I caught Nathan's big brown eyes. He still had that little chip in his front tooth from when he'd slammed his head on his skateboard going down the stairs when he'd been thirteen. I'd told him to make up a story about it so the kids at school would think he was cool, and every time he'd told someone I'd added on details so they'd believe him.

He was my little buddy, through and through.

My partner in crime.

I didn't know what I'd do if I lost him, especially over my own happiness.

I swallowed the lump in my throat again, though the choked feeling remained.

"Dad?" Nathan asked softly, setting his own fork down, his hands held expectantly in his lap.

I was freaking him out.

This wasn't like me.

Stop it, I urged myself, squaring my shoulders and popping my neck to release some of the tension before I replied.

"I'm bi," I said, no preamble. Then realized maybe he wouldn't know what that was. "Bisexual," I tacked on.

Nathan blinked.

He blinked again.

I watched his face move, my heart lurching, my palms slick with nervous sweat. And then…he smiled.

It was a soft sort of thing, tentative, sweet. His lips curled upward, his dimples flashing as he rose from his seat and made his way around the table. I rose to my feet to meet him, unsure what was happening. Was he…happy?

Nathan's eyes were wet as he reached out with both arms and enveloped me in one of his signature hugs.

"You're not…mad?" I asked, completely fucking baffled.

I thought at least he'd be pissed I hadn't told him, even if the fact itself didn't bother him.

"Of course I'm not mad." Nathan gave me a squeeze and I felt my bones creak. I squeezed him back, relief melting through my body as I sucked in a shuddery breath and inhaled the scent of his deodorant. Jesus. The kid smelled like an Axe Body Spray can had shat all over him.

I didn't care though.

"You don't seem surprised," I hedged, a little nervous as Nathan pulled back enough that he could look me in the eye again. He was nearly as tall as me and the thought made my heart hurt. It felt like just yesterday he'd been my little kiddo. Four feet tall. Chubby as fuck. Covered in bandaids as he ran into walls and cried when the kids at recess didn't want to play the games he wanted to.

That stubborn lump in my throat came back with a vengeance.

I'd never been the kind of man to get emotional but I couldn't help myself as I gave him a gentle squeeze and waited patiently for him to piece his words together. When he did they came out a little choked, soft, gentle.

"I've been waiting for you to tell me," Nathan said softly, blinking up at me. My heart lurched as confusion filled my body.

"What…do you mean?"

"I mean…" He shook his head. "I've known since I was like fifteen? And I overheard the guy at the drugstore talking about how you…" His cheeks started to turn a bright ruddy red and horror struck me as I realized what he was implying.

The one fucking hookup I'd had in fifteen years and he'd—

Jesus Christ.

"Umm…the *guy*? That you…yeah. He's cousins with one of the cashiers and he was…"

"Blabbing like a shithead about it." Shocked, I shook off the emotion as I forced myself to process what that meant. "So you…"

"Knew? Yeah."

"Then why…" Our earlier conversation about Baxter came immediately to mind. It had only been a few weeks ago that Nathan had asked me if the reason I disliked Baxter was because he was gay. "Did you ask me that about Baxter?"

"I didn't know if you were like…one of those guys who hates from inside the club."

Jesus, what a way to put that.

I shook my head, processing what he'd said though I refused to let him go as I gave him another deliberate squeeze. "I'm happy with who I am," I finally said.

"Why didn't you tell me, then?" Nathan asked, clearly confused. "I wouldn't have cared—I mean. I don't care, that is."

"I never really thought that was something you needed to know about me."

"Of course it is."

"Why?" I released him, though my hands remained on his shoulders.

Nathan blinked, clearly floored by the question. His face twisted up for a moment and then a laugh burst from his chest.

"You know what? I think you're right this time. I'm not sure why I wanted to know."

"Figured my sex life was kinda…private. Didn't really want my kid to know that shit about me."

"So why did it change?" He already knew the answer, the shithead. I could see the twinkle in his eyes.

"Baxter," I grunted, brutally and completely honest.

"So you're telling me because…" He just wanted me to say it.

My cheeks burned.

My throat grew dry again.

I thought of evergreen eyes, a freckled nose, and laugh lines. I thought of days spent snuggled in bed avoiding work, of laughter, of warmth and care. I thought about coming home to fuzzy sweaters, matching pajamas, and cocoa-filled thermoses.

I thought of Baxter.

"I love him." The words popped out of my mouth with surety. I hadn't even admitted that to myself and yet here I was. "I want him in our lives. I want…" I swallowed. "I want you to love him. I want him to be a part of our family."

Nathan nodded.

"I know this complicates things with Becca, but I—"

"Dad." Nathan interrupted me with a shake of his floppy head. I could feel the way his breath *wooshed* from his body, his shoulders relaxing as he popped a lopsided smile in my direction. "I don't like Becca anymore."

Relief tasted citrus bright on my tongue as I dropped my head and sighed.

"We kissed at the movie theater and—" Nathan gave a whole body shudder. "We both mutually decided it was…" I looked up at him and watched the way his face twisted in disgust. "Ugh. It was like kissing my sister. Pretty sure I'll have nightmares for life."

There were worse things to dream about than kissing girls, but I didn't say that.

"So you…" I swallowed. "You don't mind then?"

"Mind?" Nathan blinked. Then he pulled "a Becca" and rolled his eyes heavenward. "Jeez, Dad. All I've ever wanted was to see you happy. You have my blessing, honestly. Just don't…" His nose scrunched up again. "Don't give me any details."

"Deal." I slipped my hand from his shoulder and held it out, grinning when he slipped his palm inside mine and we shook on it.

"So we're adopting them then," Nathan hummed a moment later with glee.

"The Bakers?" I asked, my lips twisting into a smile. He nodded. "Yeah, bud." I grinned. "We're adopting them."

twenty-four

PAXTON

IT WAS SURPRISINGLY EASY TO get Baxter out of the house without him suspecting anything. His green eyes had lit up when I asked him out for the day—determined to spend New Years together now that both our kids were aware of what we were. Becca feigned a party, and Nathan feigned sickness, though all three of us were bouncing off the walls with the surprise we had planned.

Baxter was honestly adorable in every fucking way as I helped him hop up into my truck—he didn't need the help, I just liked touching him—and we pulled our way out toward Main Street.

Baker's Bakery was just around the corner, but even if he glanced at it there was no way to see what we'd done with the interior.

I had plans for the day.

While I kept Baxter occupied, pretty much everyone in the entire town was getting the Hullabaloo prepared. I didn't mind that the celebration's planning had fallen almost entirely on Becca's shoulders. It wasn't my thing. Parties. Planning. People.

I preferred what I'd already done. Commanding a working crew was different. It wasn't the same feeling I got when I attended big social events. Baxter though, he thrived on them. As much as I knew this was bound to drain me, I couldn't wait to see the look on his face when he stepped into the crowd of people and saw what we'd all banded together to do for him.

He was wearing his heated coat again, and the cream sweater I'd given him. I'd donned the pink houndstooth scarf he bought me for Christmas. I actually liked the color, which surprised me. He claimed it brought out the creme brûlée in my eyes. Whatever the fuck that meant.

Honestly if he'd given me a puke-green scarf covered in cow shit I still would've worn it.

So maybe I was biased.

Baxter was more than a little giddy when I took him to the movies.

He held my hand the entire time, chattering away about little tidbits he'd Googled in preparation for the film. Apparently they'd filmed it only two hours away from here? Which was kind of cool, admittedly.

"Where to next?" Baxter asked when it finished, with barely concealed glee. He'd admitted to me earlier that this was his first real date since high school and he was more than a little nervous. I got the feeling the one in high school hadn't been exactly memorable.

"Hot chocolate?" I offered, tugging him across the parking lot toward the coffee shop we'd both admired that day we'd attempted to set our kids up for the first time.

It was laughable actually, how much had changed since then.

"Did you know Nathan and Becca kissed?" I asked, more than a little curious as we waited in line and I—purposefully—slung my arm over Baxter's shoulder and snuggled him against my side. The girl working the counter winked at us and my cheeks flushed a little. I normally wasn't touchy-feely like this in public. It wasn't my thing but…

Baxter melted into me and his warm muscled heat against my side was enough to make the rest of the world fade away.

I couldn't help the way I pulled him close or the way I craved his touch.

"Becca told me they both hated it," Baxter laughed softly. "I was actually just about to tell you!"

I snorted and leaned down to lace a kiss across his fluffy blond head. Jesus, his laugh was cute. He was wearing the snow boots I'd gifted him for Christmas, and I couldn't help but admire the supple swell of his thighs where they lay encased in tight dark denim.

When I slipped my hand into his back pocket and gave his ass a lingering squeeze, Baxter just flushed bright red and giggled quietly to himself.

Keeping Baxter occupied took no effort at all. In fact, he was so fucking cute for most of the day I forgot I was supposed to be distracting him at all. It was only when we'd exited the local hat shop with matching beanies on our heads that I remembered to check my phone.

Becca: Um. Where are you? It's almost Tim

Becca: *Time

I checked the time stamp and snorted when I realized the messages had only been sent five minutes previously.

There was a text from Trent there too.

Trent: So I spilled a bunch of hot cocoa in the kitchen but I cleaned it up. No biggie. Becca's freaking out though. You coming soon? I think my new niece is about ready to bite my head off. Help.

I snorted down at my phone. It was easy enough to picture Becca—with her yellow, bouncy head telling all 250 pounds of Trent where he could stick his hot chocolate if he messed up her event.

The nerves came back, fluttering at my fingertips as I shoved my phone back into my pocket and Baxter latched onto my gloved fingers with a content little hum.

"Where to next?" He asked, peeking up at me, his blond hair sticking out of the edges of his beanie. It was red. With a frankly ridiculous pom pom. I couldn't believe he'd convinced me to not only buy a matching one, but wear it too.

God he was sweet.

I reached down to pinch his cheek, giving it a little wiggle that had his freckled nose scrunching up and his eyes twinkling.

"One more stop, baby," I murmured, my heart in my throat, on my sleeve—everywhere.

This meant more than words could ever explain.

One look at what I'd done and he'd see everything.

He'd see my feelings for him grouted between checkered tile, caulked between hand-cut trim—painted on the walls in strokes of sunny yellow.

There was no hiding it.

I realized, in that moment, with snowflakes decorating his cold pink nose as he sniffled and shuffled closer that there was nothing I wanted more in this world than to make him smile every day for the rest of my life.

I'd never been the kind of person who loved fast or fell hard.

But Baxter was an avalanche I was gladly walking toward.

I wanted him to smile for me.

Not the fake ones, the ones he'd worn for years to hide the cracks beneath his surface—but the ones he shared with me in the safety of our bedroom. When he lay blanketed by my embrace, protected from the cruel realities of the outside world with his nose against my neck and his heartbeat fluttering against mine.

I wanted to be his home, just like he was swiftly becoming mine.

The walk toward the bakery was excruciating.

We crunched through the snow and Baxter chatted away—fully believing the lie that we were about to go to the bookshop just across the street from the bakery. I'd seen the nerves on his face and it didn't take a genius to realize that he had mixed feelings about seeing the bakery again, but I figured the pain would be worth it when he saw what we'd done.

As we rounded the corner, my breath puffed out in a chilly fog as I caught the flicker of confusion on Baxter's face.

The bakery was lit up from the inside.

He cocked his head, more than a little confused as we picked up the pace and I watched in real time as his chest began to burst with rapid breaths and his lips twisted into a confused little frown.

"What...?"

Ten feet, five feet, two.

He stopped in front of the doorway, his whole body shaking.

I let him go first.

As the door pushed open, a heated breeze burst toward us. It caressed the tips of his golden hair and Baxter released a wounded, hurt little sound as the howl of "*Surprise!*" filled the air and he saw inside the bakery for the very first time.

twenty-five

BAXTER

THERE WAS EXCITEMENT BUZZING UNDER my skin as I took a step through the door and was immediately accosted with an explosion of delicious scents and the chatter of excited exhalations. Everyone I knew was gathered into the small space, crowded against the walls—sitting at booths and tables that had never been there before.

There was a long counter—new—that bisected the open area and across it lay what looked like hundreds of crock pots, platters, and plates loaded to the brim with delicious delicacies.

The bakery looked nothing like I remembered it.

The ugly wallpaper was gone, replaced by a pale yellow decorated with muffins and suns. Pastries flickered in a mural of cartoon grins as I stared in slack-jawed awe before my gaze snapped to the freshly tiled floor and my heart started to thunder.

My palms began to sweat and my eyes blurred with tears.

The bakery was…

It was…

I turned around, catching Paxton's gaze. He stood behind me, quiet in the doorway, his big shoulders hunched uncomfortably. It was clear this wasn't his scene. He'd never been a party goer—never even attended one of my Hullabaloo's before but in that moment it was more than clear who had orchestrated this whole thing.

"You…" My words wobbled on the way out and I had to take another stuttered breath before I could speak again. "You fixed the bakery?"

Paxton nodded. It was a slight nod, almost embarrassed. Like he didn't know what to do with the emotion that bled across my face. I couldn't hide how overwhelmed I was, how grateful.

I heard the chatter behind me but the words blended together as I took a hesitant step toward my…my *what*? My lover? My boyfriend? None of those words seemed to fit what we were to each other.

He was my constant.

The moon that rose every night.

The crisp taste of snow in the air before the storm ever hit.

He was warm hugs, hot cocoa, and wood shavings.

"I don't know what to say," I admitted, the words choked as our knees brushed and I tipped my head to look up at him. My eyes were burning. I didn't know what to do. I wanted to kiss him. I wanted to hug him, to thank him, to—to *something*. But I didn't know where we stood in a room surrounded by the people we both interacted with on a constant basis.

I watched Paxton's eyes flood with heat and wonder.

Confusion too.

Like he wasn't sure why I wasn't crossing that last distance between us.

He glanced around, and my cheeks flushed. Then…an expression crossed his face that I'd never seen before. He looked nervous. His dark brow lowered, his eyes flickering with want and fear as he curled an arm around me and tucked me in tight against him.

Facing the crowd again I counted their smiling faces.

There was Ernie, the pest control expert.

Charlie, the locksmith.

Jason, the grocery clerk.

Barbara, from the Boutique.

Every friendly face I'd memorized since we'd moved to Belleville all those years ago. Warmth flooded my chest along with my own confused indecision. I had so many feelings—relief, gratitude, love—that I didn't know how to sift through them.

I didn't want to make Paxton uncomfortable, but my gratitude was too big for platonic feelings.

I swallowed the lump in my throat and gave his side a squeeze. He was warm, despite the chill on his coat. His scarf—the one I'd bought him—tickled my cheek as he cleared his throat. I watched his cheeks turn a dark red, embarrassment coloring him in a way that at first made me eager to pull away. I didn't want to upset him.

Coming out to our kids was different.

The entire town?

Fuck.

I never would expect him to do that.

Paxton cleared his throat again, more loudly this time. The crowd began to quiet. The warmth inside the bakery was making my insides twist up, or maybe that was the way that Paxton's grip on my hip grew possessive and not at all friendly anymore.

Becca popped her head out of the doorway that led to the kitchen and surprise and relief sagged inside me.

Then it dawned on me who the little mastermind behind the decorations was. She knew me better than anyone—it made sense that she would've stepped in to help but…how? When would she have had the time?

With sickening clarity I realized what she'd been doing all this time instead of attending cheer practice.

My eyes burned.

Had she really…for *me*?

Becca waved at me, her sunny grin splitting her adorably flushed face. I could tell she'd been yelling. She always got red when she yelled.

I wondered who was the subject of her ire, then almost laughed when I watched a grumbly Trent enter the room after her, along with a whole set of men that looked like they could be Paxton's twins but just squashed or stretched to fit their own individual canvases.

The Montgomery brothers.

All of them.

It seemed like the entire town was there and my heart hurt all over again as I wondered…no. Yes? Was this all for me?

It was silent. Only the quiet crooning of the radio could be heard filtering through the crowded space as I felt Paxton tense up, his body rising to its full massive height.

He was nervous. I could feel the way his hand shook.

I had no idea what he was about to do but I was wise enough to let it play out.

"I'm not a person who gives speeches." Paxton's voice was rough and low but it traveled easily through the small space, bouncing off the walls and echoing between booths.

Speeches? Because he'd fixed the bakery up?

Oh.

"But I figure this deserves at least an effort." Paxton swallowed, and my heart began to race. "Thank you to everyone who came together this past month to make this all possible." His hand was shaking and I reached down to give it a gentle squeeze. I wished we weren't wearing gloves so I could feel his skin. But alas.

My heart was pounding as I listened to his sharp intake of breath.

"You all probably know me as the grouch who lives on the south side of town." There was a rumble of laughter through the air and I felt it bubble up inside me in answer. "But I'm more than that, apparently." Everyone silenced again.

It was clear no one knew what was happening—aside from Becca. Her shit-eating grin was so bright it could've blinded an entire country.

"I'm a father," Paxton swallowed again and I watched his throat bob, enthralled. "I'm a craftsman." Another swallow. It was clear he didn't like this, the talking to people bit, the attention. He was like one of those flowers that only bloomed when you left it alone. Why was he doing this?

"I'm a lover."

The crowd erupted in excited chatter and I watched Becca's hands slap over her mouth. I was numb with shock as I stared at Paxton's face, my heart beating erratically in my chest. A lover? What was he...

Surely he wasn't.

In front of the entire town?

"Fuck." More laughter. "This shit sucks." Paxton scrubbed his hand over his face, burning bright red, clearly uncomfortable as his words sped up. "I guess what I'm tryin' to say is that I'm in love with Baxter Baker."

I'm in love with Baxter Baker.

I'm in love with Baxter Baker.

I'm in love with Baxter Baker.

"And I'm keepin' him. If that's alright with him. My asshole-ry aside." Paxton glanced down at me, his lips wobbling. "Not that it's any of your business—aside from Baxter's of course. But I figured you all have the right to know that I'm gonna be takin' care of him from now on."

His quiet rumble trickled over my body and I shuddered, still in shock as I tipped my chin up so I could stare into the fathomless honey of his sweet gaze. The crowd erupted in excited conversation, but I ignored them as Paxton stole every ounce of my attention.

His eyes said, *let me love you.*

They said, *I'm sorry I'm not better.*

They said, *I'm proud to call you mine.*

They said, *give me a chance to show you.*

"I have something to say too—" The words burst from my lips before I could reign them in. The crowd's celebration paused again as they stared at me. I'd always been the man full of smiles but at that moment my eyes were wet and I could do nothing but reveal my cracks to the crowd of people who had been nothing but family to me since the day we'd met.

"I'm actually pretty good at speeches," I joked softly. Laughter. Paxton squeezed me tight. "But um. Right now if it's okay, I'd like to just be honest?"

I watched a few heads nod, my gaze snapping to Becca. Nathan had joined her while I'd looked away and they stood side by side, their arms tucked together. I swallowed the lump in my throat.

"I have a lot of problems," I announced to the room. "I know you've all been worried about me for a long time but I just wanted to say that I've decided to go to therapy. Started therapy I mean—"

"Not that it's anyone's business," Paxton grumbled, but I shushed him.

"I'm taking care of myself now. I really…I appreciate you…all of you. The way you took care of me when I had no one. The way you loved me, supported me. The way you held me up when I couldn't do it myself." My words were choked. "But if it's alright—I think it's time for me to stop pretending I'm happy when I'm really not." I could feel the hot slip of tears as they burned down my cheeks. "When I moved here you all stepped up. You became the family I never had. We raised my baby together and every time I fell you picked me back up again."

My heart throbbed.

"Thank you for everything you've done—I don't know what I would've done without you." My throat felt tight and clogged. "Paxton is amazing—and I know he says he's gonna take care of me but I just wanted you all to know that I'm gonna try to take care of myself first. It may take a while for me to learn how to do it, but every step forward is…a step in the right direction."

I blinked, realizing I'd missed something very important.

With a wet smile, I tipped my face up to meet Paxton's once again.

When he met my gaze the rest of the world melted away.

"Oh, and I love you too." I said softly.

When he kissed me he tasted like Christmas, laughter, and stability. His beard tickled my cheeks, his fingers bunching possessively around my hip as hoots and hollers echoed through the room behind us.

Paxton grinned.

I kissed him again.

He tasted like home.

twenty-six

PAXTON

THE HULLABALOO WAS A RIOT. Coming from me, that was a wildly positive statement. After the initial awkward speeches we got to chow down on food. Baxter cried when he saw the freezer and the mixer in the kitchen that Becca had painstakingly picked out for him. When he'd hugged her it had lasted for ages, long enough that I left and guarded the door to the backroom so they could have privacy.

They talked for a long time.

Now though, I got to enjoy the way he chattered away at everyone. His smiles weren't brittle, his green eyes bright, like admitting what he'd been struggling with had lifted a weight from his shoulders.

Leanne, the bookstore owner sidled up to me, a massive plate loaded with goodies in hand as she cocked her head toward Baxter. "He looks better, doesn't he?" she hummed.

She was an older woman. Old enough she'd been around back when old man McMillan had started up the first bakery, or so she said. Her eyes were kind, crinkled at the corners, her lips smudged with red lipstick that was slightly smeared as she dabbed at it with her New Years themed napkin.

The whole party was decked out in platinum and bronze—Becca's idea. She'd brought a TV from home and the countdown for the new year was going to play in just a few short minutes.

Baxter had made his way through half the room now, thanking everyone for coming, practically glowing from the positive attention.

Watching him smile made me smile.

"He looks great," I murmured in agreement, not sure what she was getting at.

Leanne gave my arm a gentle squeeze and I arched a brow at her, tearing my gaze away from Baxter for a moment as she tipped her chin up and gave me a nudge. "For years we've watched that boy wither away," she said softly. "Doing our best to give him the support he needed but…"

At the end of the day Baxter had needed to make that step for himself.

It warmed my heart to realize he'd come far enough that he was now able to take care of himself.

Every step forward was a step in the right direction.

I swallowed the lump in my throat. Leanne gave me another pat and then walked away. I remained on the outskirts of the party where I liked to be as my thoughts whirred.

How long had I hated Baxter?

How long had I resented his easy laughter, his smiles, his happiness?

Had I really been so blind?

The answer was right in front of me. Apparently I was the only person in all of Belleville that hadn't seen his cracks. My heart throbbed as I realized how stupid I'd been all this time. Even Nathan had seen how much Baxter was hurting and yet I'd…

Fuck.

I downed the rest of my cup of apple cider, my skin prickling all over. A gentle grip on my arm made me flinch before I glanced over and realized Baxter had found his way back to me. "Hi," he beamed, all gleaming white teeth and scrunched up freckles.

I tweaked the pom pom on his hat.

"Can I kiss you now?" he asked softly, shuffling up against me. I couldn't help but think about the crowd of people around us, but figured after my speech earlier we could indulge in as much public indecency as we wanted. I leaned down and Baxter flexed onto his toes, reached up and curled one long-fingered hand around the hinge of my jaw to pull me closer.

He tasted like champagne and I licked the flavor from his soft lips.

The kiss lingered, far longer than was probably appropriate, but I couldn't bring myself to care.

When Baxter pulled back he didn't go far. His thumb ran gentle soothing circles along my cheekbone as he met my gaze and our bodies melted together the way that felt second nature to us both.

"Thank you for all of this," Baxter said softly. The awe and wonder in his voice was so genuine I couldn't help but react. My throat grew dry all over again and my eyes burned. I glanced around the room, seeing it through his eyes, the act of love had become more apparent than ever. "You're the sweetest man I've ever met."

I'd never been called sweet before.

Hadn't realized it was something I craved.

I ducked my head, the burning in my eyes growing stronger as I shifted us up against the wall till Baxter was crowded against it and I was blocking him from view of the rest of the room. He smiled at me, sensing my need for silence as I dropped down till our foreheads pressed together and our breath mingled.

"I love you," I promised softly, the words throbbing their way through my heart.

"I love you," he returned, stroking over my cheekbone in a way that made me weak-kneed and breathless.

"I'm going to take care of you," I swore, my voice wobbling.

"I know you will, Paxton." Baxter laced a gentle kiss against my lips that had my pulse fluttering and a hot tear slipping down my cheek. "I'm going to take care of you too."

My heart shuddered and I pulled him tighter against me so I could absorb his warmth inside my soul and let the sweetness of his words seep inside my own cracks. Maybe it would take us both a long time to heal. Maybe we never would. But in that moment, all I felt was sunshine as we clung together, and the shadows in our hearts grew light.

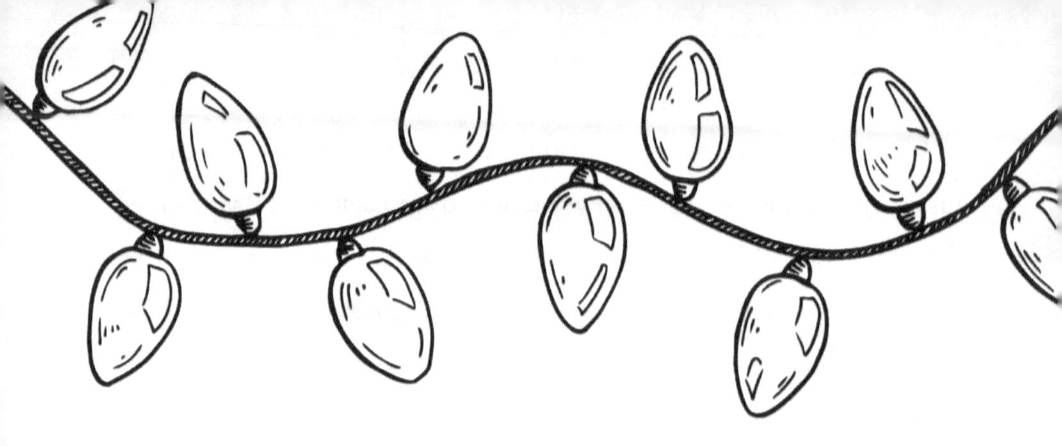

epilogue

BAXTER

One Year Later, Christmas Day

"OH MY GOD," BECCA WHINED as I handed her the last of the boxes. "There's more?"

"Yes." I laughed, bumping our hips together before gently nudging her toward the bakery door.

"I thought we finished setting up last night."

"Apparently not."

It was time for the Christmas Hullabaloo again. The official one. The bakery had been running smoothly all year and with the addition of the coffee bar that Paxton had set up, business had been booming. I'd never had so many customers or so much free time on my hands.

Apparently Nathan loved to bake because he'd started apprenticing under me that January and I'd spent months training him until he felt confident enough he could both open and close the shop on his own.

About six months into dating his dad, Nathan had tentatively pulled me aside to ask me if he could call me something other than Baxter. So apparently my name was now Blond Dad and/or Small Dad.

Becca was another story. As much as she loved the bakery—because she'd grown up living and breathing it—she much preferred Paxton's line of work to my own. She'd decided to go to trade school right out of high school, and I couldn't be prouder of her.

She'd also packed on quite a bit of muscle and was clearly proud of it because I caught her flexing in the mirror with curiosity at least three times a day.

"Everyone but Paxton is arriving at six," I told her, my plans whirring inside the back of my head. Paxton would arrive first—he'd be all confused the place was empty. He'd ask me where everyone else was, and I'd reach into my pocket, pretend to grab my phone and say… "Let me give them a *ring?*"

Then I'd produce the simple black engagement band I'd had made for him over the summer.

It would be *perfect*.

Literally nothing could ruin it.

A burst of hot air swam toward us as we made our way toward the kitchen. There was a hop in my step and Becca rolled her eyes at me as I set the last of the boxes full of decorations down on my beautiful—custom—bread table and tried to swallow my own excitement down enough that I could get the shop all prettied up.

Nothing could ruin this.

Nothing.

Well.

Except that.

When I wandered my way into the front portion of the shop my jaw dropped to the floor and Becca's laughter cackled away behind me.

The little shit had known about this and not warned me.

Rose petals decorated the floor, candles bleeding wax onto the granite counter. I hadn't noticed before, but now that I was in the center of the room I couldn't help but catch the scent of hot cocoa in the air.

Paxton knelt on one knee, surrounded by what looked like a hundred or more roses, his massive body shaking with nerves as he stared at me, cheeks ruddy.

"No," I gasped softly, realizing with horror what was about to happen.

He looked taken aback.

The black velvet ring box trembled in his grip. It was so tiny in his hands it looked like a toy, and I couldn't help but flounder, trying to backtrack as best as I could as I saw the flicker of hurt and uncertainty glint in his eyes.

"Fuck! No. I mean…" I wobbled forward, hopping over the roses as my own hands shook and I scrambled into my back pocket.

"No?" He looked hurt.

"I mean! *Yes!*" I quickly blurted as my fingers met the smooth wood of my own ring box. I pulled it out, a laughter bubbling up inside me as I shoved the box toward him. The hurt in his eyes melted away and his brow lowered, a quiet little grunt leaving his lips as he cocked his head and inspected it.

"You…" he started, then stopped.

"I had a pun planned and everything."

Paxton snorted, the sound devolving into a throaty chuckle as he shook his head and I took what felt like a million years to get down onto my own knees. "You ruined my plans," I complained softly, though I was only joking as I shuffled through the petals till our bodies pressed together and our chests bumped.

Paxton's breath fanned along my cheek as he dropped his head down to lace a gentle kiss against it.

"Is that a yes, then?" he rumbled, already reaching for my hand.

"Of course," I laughed, more than a little delighted. Giddy, as what was happening finally caught up to me, and I let him maneuver my hand. As the little silver band slipped onto my finger I twisted to stare at it, my breath stuttering in my chest, my eyes burning.

"Will you marry me, Baxter Baker?" Paxton asked, formally.

I swallowed the lump in my throat.

I thought back on the last year together.

Paxton supported me, loved me, and made me laugh. He was quick to anger but even quicker to soothe—his ire rarely ever pointed in my direction. Despite his gruff exterior he was excellent at communicating and every day he got better about telling me his feelings, just as I got better at telling him mine.

After a year in therapy I knew a lot of my issues stemmed from the fear that nothing would be permanent—people died, life moved on, things changed…but Paxton.

Paxton was this immovable force.

Solid, sure, true.

And even with all my fears I never once doubted his love for me.

I loved everything about him. I loved how grouchy he was in the mornings. I loved the way he fretted over Nathan. I loved his laughter, his anger, the way he thought I was the cleverest man on Earth for showing him the ways of heated coats.

Most of all, I loved the fact he'd chosen to lean on me, to trust me. To let me into his heart. To let me love and protect him the way he did me.

"I was worried you wouldn't want to say 'I dough.'" Paxton murmured, a shy little smile on his lips.

I laughed. "Did you Google pastry puns?"

"I did."

Then I kissed him, sure and sweet, my fingers tangling in the back of his hair as my own ring fell to the floor with a soft little thud. He groaned into the kiss, pulling me in close, his body hot where he pressed along mine.

He shoved me back till my shoulder blades met the cold floor. As he pressed between my thighs his tongue slipped between my lips. I groaned around him, my heels digging into his hamstrings as I felt him fumble for the discarded ring beside us.

We broke the kiss only long enough for me to slip the matching band on his finger.

His tongue was hot and slick where it slipped along mine and I whined, wiggling closer, desperate to taste him.

"Ew!" Becca's voice echoed behind us and we broke apart, laughter shattering the tension in the room as my heart soared. I tipped my head back to get a look at Becca and her now familiar shit-eating grin.

"Get a room." She tossed her hair over her shoulder. She'd graduated to a ponytail now. Her buns, abandoned. Maybe she thought it made her look older? Nothing would change the fact that she was a little cherub though. "You two are like teenagers."

I'd often thought that myself but hearing it from my daughter only made it funnier.

I snorted, Paxton's answering laughter rumbling through my chest. I watched the way he grinned, young and uninhibited and I realized... maybe she was right.

Paxton made me feel young again, like all the years I'd spent in limbo had coalesced into the flutter of my butterfly wings as I escaped my cocoon.

Somehow along the way he'd taught me how to be Dad, business owner, and Baxter.

Balanced in a way I didn't know was possible.

Ignoring Becca's protests, I curled my left hand around the back of Paxton's neck and pulled him down into another greedy kiss, audience be damned. The weight of the ring on my finger tingled as a promise settled in the air between us.

Forever would never be long enough, but it was a good start.

The End

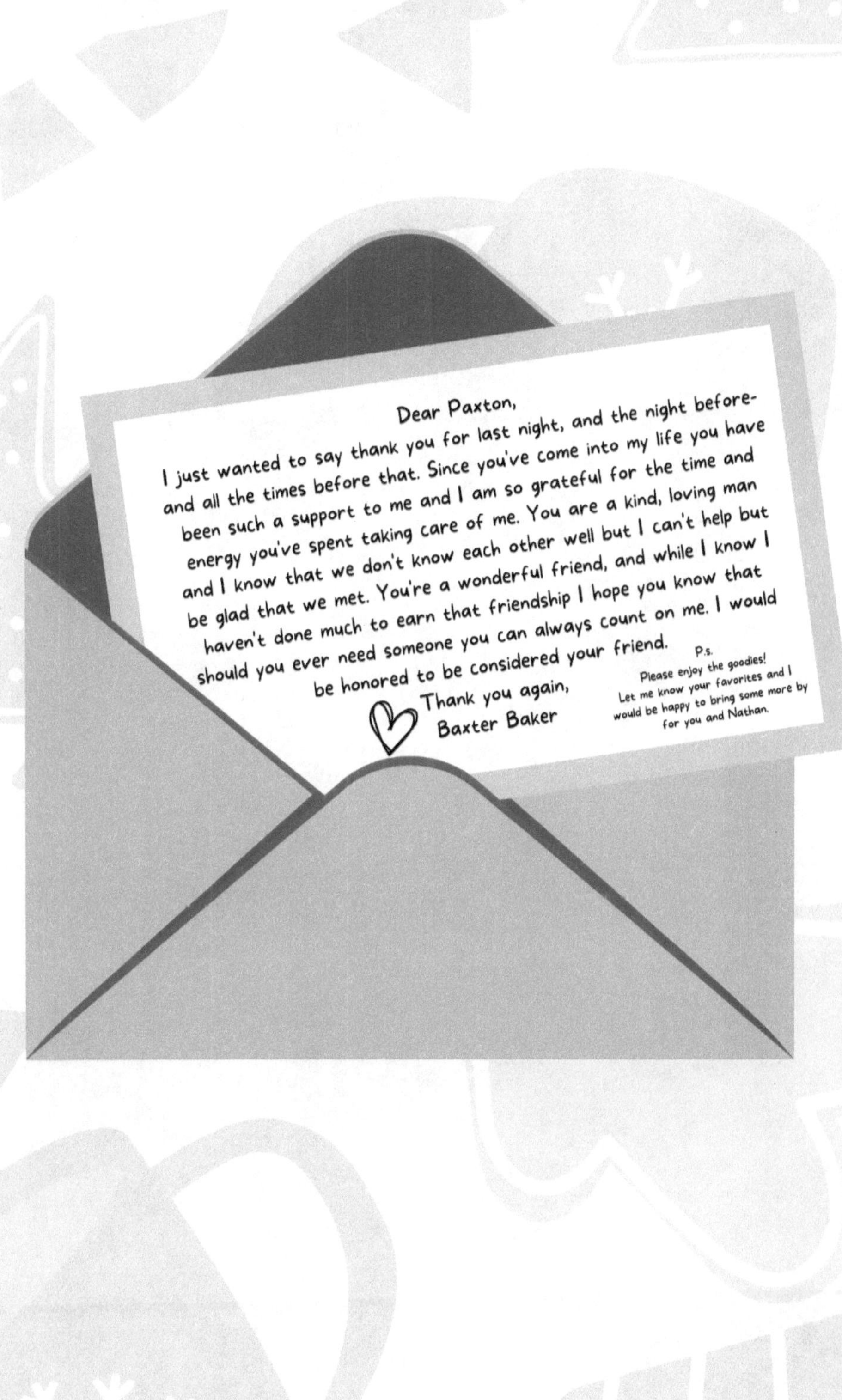

Dear Paxton,
I just wanted to say thank you for last night, and the night before-
and all the times before that. Since you've come into my life you have
been such a support to me and I am so grateful for the time and
energy you've spent taking care of me. You are a kind, loving man
and I know that we don't know each other well but I can't help but
be glad that we met. You're a wonderful friend, and while I know I
haven't done much to earn that friendship I hope you know that
should you ever need someone you can always count on me. I would
be honored to be considered your friend.
Thank you again,
Baxter Baker

P.s.
Please enjoy the goodies!
Let me know your favorites and I
would be happy to bring some more by
for you and Nathan.

thank you!

THANK YOU SO MUCH to everyone who has made this year magical. I wanted to create a story to spread some love this holiday season to all of you. 2022 has been a wonderful year full of adventure, surprise, new friendships, and a whole lot of writing! I can't wait to take you on more journeys next year with all my new projects. Thank you so much for your kindness, your enthusiasm, and your support, you mean the world to me. Happy Holidays! I'll see you in 2023.

If you'd like to keep in touch with me and receive free content including a free ebook of *There's a Monster in the Woods* and exclusive chapters of my serial *Cloudy with a Chance of Dildos*, you can sign up at **faelovesart.com/newsletter**. Or join my Facebook group, **Fae's Faves**! You can also find me on Instagram **@fae.loves.art**.

I love you all so much! I can't wait to spook with you once again!

All shares, comments, reviews, and discussion of *Let Your Hearts Be Light* are encouraged and appreciated!

about fae

FAE is obsessed with anything romance. From a young age she realized she had a passion for falling in love over and over again. She loves to tell stories through both her art and writing. With a passion for classical monsters, meet-cutes, and contemporary romance you can often find her with her nose stuck in a book and her pet corgi Champa on her lap.

She currently resides in Utah with her amazing husband and her collection of squishmallows. When you read one of her books you can expect to find love stories between humans, monsters, and loveable assholes that will make you laugh (and cry) as you get lost in their worlds for just a little. Every story comes with a happy ever after guarantee.

Find her online at:
WWW.FAELOVESART.COM

www.ingramcontent.com/pod-product-compliance
Lightning Source LLC
Chambersburg PA
CBHW021138310726
48971CB00002B/378